DESI GIRLS

DESI GIRLS

Stories by Indian Women Writers Abroad

Edited by Divya Mathur

hoperoad : London

HopeRoad Publishing Ltd
P O Box 55544
Exhibition Road
London SW7 2DB

www.hoperoadpublishing.com
First published in Great Britain by HopeRoad Publishing 2015

ISBN 978-1-908446-44-2

eISBN 978-1-908446-43-5

Contents

'Where women are honoured, there the gods dwell.'

Verse from *Manu Smriti*

'As a woman, I have no country. As a woman,
I want no country. As a woman, my country is the
whole world.'

Virginia Woolf, *Three Guineas*

Foreword

Writing is one way in which women can express themselves freely and open a window onto their secret worlds.

These twenty-two stories by Indian women writers deal with issues of loss of identity, migration, betrayal, cross-cultural marriage, and growing old in an unfamiliar environment. Another theme, that of domestic violence, is portrayed in Shail Agrawal's unforgettable story *Good Morning, Mrs Singh*.

The Table by Ila Prasad is the gentle account of an old wooden stool that belonged in an Indian village home, but then found itself in Texas, misplaced and unwanted. Would the stool ever find a new purpose? Perhaps the stool was a metaphor for its owners, since all migrants are like square pegs in round holes until they finally settle into the new country and become 'just like them'. I myself moved to London at the age of twenty-one, to study art, and thought in my naivety that London would be like an extension of Delhi. After all, I had spent my life in convent schools with Irish nuns, my parents spoke English, and Agatha Christie was virtually an aunt! How wrong I was.

Achala Sharma's character in *Things Are Not Always What They Seem* comes from Pakistan, keeps his head below the parapet as an illegal 'overstayer' in the UK, and has not seen his wife and children for more than a decade. But then life takes an unexpected twist . . .

Marriage remains a perennial theme of life, and of literature. A great scholar I knew once compared marriage to a bitter fruit that everyone wants to taste, regardless! Usha Raje's tale *But Salina Had Only Wanted To Get Married* – about a poor woman's dream to be married in a white dress that she cannot afford – makes for grim reading. Divya Mathur's own story *My Better Half* explores the insecurities in a cross-cultural marriage. It's bad enough having to swiftly adopt alien cultural norms, but an overbearing mother-in-law can be the final nail in the coffin. Indian marriages are too often broken up by other family members – a possessive ma-in-law, greedy sisters, devilish step-children *et al.*

Death, like marriage, is another great theme to be explored and explained. In Susham Bedi's *Remains*, Kamla, who was once young and active, is now a resident in an old people's home in New York. Possessions lovingly collected by her are not valued by her children or grandchildren – so what should she do with them? The young people do not want her silk saris, her knick-knacks and paintings – not even her 'old-fashioned' jewellery. Each jar, every stick of furniture is a repository of happy memories of her late husband – but now, at the end of her life, she must discard them.

In our lifetime, traditional societies have broken up, travel is cheap and easy, people move round the world, chasing jobs or chasing girlfriends, and there is a great deal of personal freedom for many. In such circumstances, we are compelled to re-invent ourselves, perhaps even to truly become the individuals we are meant to be. This applies even more to women. The old roles imposed by culture, religion, patriarchal societies and economic dependence have to be revised. Women must find a new way to be comfortable in their own skins while at the same time being as successful as men.

Sharing stories is a powerful way of inspiring others to become part of the dialogue of growth. Books are like the magic flying carpets of India, transporting us to the limitless layers of our own consciousness. A collection such as *Desi Girls* brings us solace, broadens our horizons, shows us different points of view, and helps to universalise our consciousness.

The Japanese Buddhist monk Ryokan wrote: *Life is like a dewdrop trembling on a blade of grass.*

Our thanks go to Divya Mathur, who has brought us this admirable collection – so let us read on and enjoy it before the dew dries up.

Mohini Kent
lilyfoundation.org.uk **(against human-trafficking)**

Editor's Note

My aim with this collection is to publish the finest work being produced by Indian women writers living abroad. These stories are the expressions of women who have chosen to live away from their native land and who have evolved in the countries where they now live. Through their characters and the unique structure of the short story – with its classic sting in the tail – they offer us a viewpoint and a commentary on the countries they have adopted.

The title, *Desi Girls*, appealed to us all. In spite of their higher education, and their extraordinary achievements in varied fields, the Indian women in these tales are often expected to remain 'Desi' – in other words, to follow Indian traditions, be pure and unblemished, to always give and ask nothing in return . . .

I am often asked why my anthologies include solely stories by women. One reason is that women's achievements are never purely personal. Also, we continue to work phenomenally harder than men to qualify for equal recognition in many walks of life. In this day and age, women are still subjected to prejudice, violence, poorer resources and lower wages. The workplace can still feel like a man's world. Like all big social movements, feminism has run into problems, yet the campaign for the rights of women must go on.

The twenty-two writers included in this anthology – now settled in Canada, Denmark, Norway, the UAE, the UK and the USA – were all born in different parts of India. They come from varied backgrounds, and have widely varying qualifications and professions. Between them, however, they have woven a colourful and original tapestry of human experience. The diaspora can be a challenging place!

As well as contributions from award-winning and seasoned authors, I have also included stories by new and upcoming writers. May I take this opportunity to thank all the contributors for their work, and for the trust they have placed in me. If you turn to the back of the anthology, you will find a short biography of each writer.

The Vatayan: Poetry on the South Bank project is delighted to be associated with HopeRoad Publishing, and partly supported by The Big Lottery Fund, in bringing these wonderful stories to you.

Divya Mathur
London, 2015

Jagruti, Beware!

Vayu Naidu

Canterbury, Kent, UK, 2002

Jagruti stood with her back to the door. A stainless-steel spatula was clutched in her left hand and a meat cleaver in her right, and she was staring intently ahead. She stood poised like a Hindu goddess, armed with domestic weapons and practising martial arts. Her arms were raised, ready to slice: it was best to keep out of her reach. But it wasn't a late-summer wasp that had caught Jagruti's attention.

She was staring at the Tamil chart of tropical fruit that was lying on the wide oak kitchen table. She studied the fruit shapes and imagined their flavours as a map of her life. Green pickling mango for who she was, gooseberries and lychees for who she would be, and a cluster of yellow speckled sweet mountain plantains for who she would become. The fruits had nothing to do with her perception of body shape. In fact she was well aware of her attractiveness, and felt more desirable giving herself in small, long-awaited doses.

1

Jagruti, whose name meant 'awareness, awakening', wondered what stage she was in now. The lilies of her womanhood had bloomed after dangerous journeys of self-discovery. She had been curiously Eurocentric when she was in India, where she had been born and had studied and worked. That had driven her to come to England for 'further studies', as the folks back home would say. Were the further studies a move towards self-exile, or more to do with playing for time? She had decided not to marry the chosen one from what she called the cattle market. How she would shriek with laughter when she told the story of the men she had nicknamed 'a Fine Proposal'.

Her favourite story from among the many Fine Proposals she had received was that of the balding man, who could have been attractive if only he hadn't been scripted by his Business Management course.

It was 1980. He came to Jagruti's family house in Madras, as Chennai was known then. It was a humid day in December. Although the sea breeze would kick in at 3.30 in the afternoon, that year Madras had had a gas leak from the Manali oil refinery. So the air was scented with the sweet smell of the lethal chemical. It seemed like an omen for Jagruti. Her parents were in the study and prayer rooms respectively; her father was writing a letter in English to the Corporation Bank, and her mother was singing in Telegu to the pantheon of Hindu gods.

Jagruti was sulking in her bedroom, dressed tastefully yet casually in a block-printed, vegetable-dyed, indigo silk sari. Then the Proposal arrived, escorted by some of his relatives and some well-meaning older cousins. The Proposal met Jagruti's father and said he wanted to see the 'girl' as soon as possible as he had three other appointments after this one.

Jagruti was furious. '"Girl" indeed,' she fumed to herself. 'This is the late twentieth century, we have Indira Gandhi as Prime Minister – and he's coming to see the "girl"? Is he in a time-warp? Did he time-travel here on a bullock cart? Other appointments, indeed!' Was he telling Father there were other 'girls' from his matrimonial shopping list that he had to see? It felt like prostitution. Bad start.

She walked coolly into the living room – where everyone was seated, as though waiting for a drama to unfold – with the silver tea tray, the fine china and the hot milk. The Proposal watched her walk. She moved like an Air India hostess, the sari palla firmly pinned on her shoulder and sliding its peacock tail onto the coffee table. She looked straight at his bald head.

'Sugar?' she asked politely, continuing to look at his head.

'Yes,' he said. There was a moustache of perspiration clinging to his upper lip, and a mossy undergrowth of stubble was emerging from his round cheeks and cleft chin.

'How much?' she asked, arching the brows on her cool, high forehead.

'Er . . . one and er . . . OK, just two,' he replied, his breathing getting shorter.

Jagruti stirred two heaps of the thick granulated sugar from the ration shop into his teacup. He couldn't take his eyes off her, and she couldn't take her eyes off his bald head.

By the time she re-entered with the next tray of sweet Mysore pak, chocolate cake and savoury rice moorkus, the Proposal had indicated that he wanted to 'interview the girl separately'. He was led to the room with the TV and Jagruti's paintings from art class hanging on the walls.

Then he began. 'As you know, I'm a gold medallist from Hyderabad and now I'm Director of the chemicals division of Sandoz in California. Just answer me three questions. First . . .' he proceeded to count on his fingers '. . . are you very religious? Second, are you in good health? And third, have you ever gone out in the evening with a man, alone?'

The letters J – E – S – U – S! were exploding all across Jagruti's mind. Was this guy for real? Was she supposed to be living in a monastery?

'Yes,' she replied calmly, even though she wanted to pick him up by his armpits and chuck him onto the malaria-infested dung heap by the side of the road.

She loved her parents, she began reasoning, and had talked herself into this meeting. She was willing to accept that they did this in her best interests, but why the hell were they so naïve about guys like this, who felt that being accepted by North America meant that they could run back to India and lasso an Indian girl into marriage so that she could cook and breed for them in the land of the Green Card? Had Mum and Dad not gained a deeper understanding all those years ago during Partition? Weren't these meetings all part of that outdated system? Hadn't they shared the vision of an independent India? Surely they had fallen in love? After all those years of liberal thinking, why were they making her walk into the fire with Egghead over here?

'OK. At least you're honest.' The Proposal shook Jagruti out of her self-absorption. 'I will ask your father if we can have dinner tomorrow. But I've got to go now – it's getting late for my next appointment.' Saying that, he leaped up, unaware of his bulk, and almost skipped into the other room where everyone else was chatting and looking jolly.

Jagruti was still sitting in the TV room gripping the armchair, her knuckles white. *Is this guy a masochist? Has he even thought for a moment about what he's getting himself into?* she thought, gritting her teeth.

'Yes,' he came back beaming. 'Uncle has agreed. I'll be here at 7.30 sharp tomorrow evening. Be ready, OK?'

'My father is not your uncle,' she nearly spat at him. But she decided that silence was the best form of rage.

At 7 p.m. the next evening, when her fate was to be decided, she dressed in beige chiffon. He came and took her to the Golden Dragon restaurant. As she bit into the chilli-dusted Kung Po tiger prawn, he said, 'What do you think of American TV?'

Before she could reply, he went on, 'I really don't like all that kissing and nudity they have on late at night.'

'I'm sure there's a choice of fifty other channels in the US,' she said, dabbing the side of her red lips, pouting a little so the pristine white napkin wouldn't get stained. Looking at him with her smouldering brown eyes, lined with kohl, her eyebrows trembling and her diamond nose-stud flashing, she said softly: 'I thought you said yesterday you were worried I'd be too religious?'

He watched her; the glass of water he was lifting halted in mid-air and the fine line of perspiration forming over his forehead turned to cold sweat.

'N-n-no, no – what I'm saying is that anything extreme is bad. If someone is too religious, then having children would be difficult,' he tried to joke.

'I see,' said Jagruti, placing the two gleaming candle-holders between them wider apart.

'Do you go swimming?' he dared to ask, desperate to move on to something else, now that the joy of the expensive Chinese meal had vanished.

'Have you read M.K. Gandhi's *My Experiment with Truth*?'

'I must look out for it for my book club,' he said nervously, almost willing to admit to anything, even religiously erotic literature, if she accused him of reading it.

'It's been around in India for more than thirty years,' she said. 'It is a cornerstone of Independent India. Pity you haven't heard about it.'

When he dropped her back, her father was waiting up. She went inside after wishing the Proposal good luck. Once indoors, she could hear him telling her father: 'She's too aloof. Your daughter is cold. She probably reads too much. That won't make her a good wife or mother.' A few days later her father received a letter from the Proposal's oldest brother:

We felt very privileged to meet your family. However, Manmohan feels that he needs to choose a bride and secure her acceptance by the 3rd January 1981.

That means there are barely fifteen days left. We would like to resolve this urgently so that he will be eligible for a marriage allowance before the next financial year. We found the girl very well brought-up, and from a good family. However, Manmohan

*feels she is too tall for the match to be appropriate,
and she also does not seem to be willing.
    We wish you all God's grace and our good wishes.*

*Yours sincerely,
Dorai*

All Jagruti's father said to this was: 'Too tall? No wonder – he's an absolute shrimp! What does he think marriage is, a cattle market?'

She was relieved and wanted to hug her father, as he did her. They had both forgotten, for one brief shining moment, that they had declared war on the subject of middle-class manipulation, as Jagruti felt that to be forced into marriage was a breach of her human rights.

Jagruti's father wanted to stick to the Hindu Ashramas, or stages in life. He was at the stage when he wished to fulfil his responsibility as a father and see his daughter married – 'well settled' – and was unfortunately oblivious to the unhappiness it was causing her. Jagruti, of course, was at that stage in her life where education meant independence – and in her case an added dose of rebellion.

Her parents had known it would be a bumpy ride with Jagruti from their first glimpse of the firm chin of her toothless baby smile and her wide forehead. That was why they had named her Jagruti – a fiercer kind of being. So Jagruti had inherited that force with her name.

She had no choice.

Meharchand's Prayer

Achala Sharma

North London, UK, 2010

'Your luck is about to change, Meharchand,' Navin Bhai announced, looking up from the newspaper he had been reading.

At that moment, Meharchand, formerly known as Mehar-e-Alam, was concentrating on cutting Hari Bhai's hair.

The good thing about Navin Bhai's Hair & DVD Salon was that one could always find the day's newspaper there. Unfortunately, the newspaper was useless as far as Mehar-e-Alam was concerned, since his boss Navin Bhai only read the *Gujarat Samachar*. So Mehar-e-Alam would try to take a peek at the headlines in the *Daily Jang* and read about Pakistan in Urdu whenever he got the chance to go to the local Halal butcher.

'My luck? How is that, Navin Bhai?' he asked, then paused, thinking it was wiser to stop talking and concentrate when doing the delicate job of cutting Hari's hair. The latter would complain and threaten to stop allowing Mehar-e-Alam to touch his hair *ever again* if even a centimetre of it was left uneven. In that event, Mehar-e-Alam would lose his tip of one or two pounds, which Hari Bhai always generously but surreptitiously dropped in his pocket before paying the seven pounds at the counter, as if Hari didn't want Navin to see him giving a tip. Mehar-e-Alam himself was confident that Navin Bhai wouldn't mind because it was he who had given Mehar-e-Alam this job, along with his new name – Meharchand.

'The problem is that most of my clients are staunch Hindus who are strict vegetarians,' he had explained. 'So, you will be called Meharchand if you wish to work here.' In this way, Navin Bhai had plainly set out the terms of employment.

At first, Mehar-e-Alam didn't like the idea. He would have preferred to have been asked to change his name to an English one like Mike or Matt: it didn't feel right to adopt a Hindu name. What would his family and friends say if the shameful news ever reached Pakistan? They would refuse to see him again. But after a long and painful consideration, he decided that names were not so important after all. He would not lose his faith just because he had to earn a living for the sake of his family. Condition accepted.

Another change in his life was his routine. Before working at Navin Bhai's salon, Mehar-e-Alam used to say his prayers five times a day, but now he was kept so busy all day long that he had to find an alternative. He read the *Fajar Namaz* before leaving for work and *Kaza* at night, which clubbed the rest of the prayers – *Johar, Asr, Maghrib* and *Isha* – together. He was confident that he fulfilled his duties as a Muslim. The rest was in the hands of Allah. Navin Bhai was a good man; he allowed him leave to go for Friday prayers. And if a regular client enquired about him during his absence, Navin Bhai was always ready with a good excuse.

Even though two other men, Ramesh and Vinod, worked at his salon, Navin Bhai trusted Mehar-e-Alam more than either of them. So much so that he often sent him to the bank to make cash deposits. Therefore, if Navin Bhai said that his luck was about to change, then it must be true.

'OK, Hari Bhai. It is done.' Mehar-e-Alam held a mirror up for Hari to see the back of his head.

'This is not the style I asked for,' the man grumbled.

'Hari Bhai, that would only be possible if you let me use the clippers, which you have forbidden,' Mehar-e-Alam tried to explain. What he really wanted to say was that the fellow hadn't got enough hair left on his head to create any kind of style.

'Why don't you give me a head massage today?' Hari went on.

Mehar-e-Alam wished he could wriggle out of it. He wanted to talk to Navin Bhai, to ask what he had meant about his luck changing. He wondered if Navin Bhai too was waiting for Hari to leave before saying anything further. But Mehar-e-Alam had no wish to offend a good client like Hari. Had it been anyone else, he would have found some excuse. But with no other clients waiting, he had no valid reason, and he was the only one available as Ramesh and Vinod were out at lunch.

'Which oil would you prefer?' he asked politely.

'Olive oil.'

'You know, Hari Bhai, almond oil is better for hair because it is lighter than other oils and therefore quickly absorbed.'

'Very well, if you say so, but the massage should be really good.'

The little hair that Hari was left with was mainly at the back of his head. But he still made a point of coming in for a haircut every fortnight. While massaging his head, Mehar-e-Alam occasionally glanced at Navin Bhai; his boss was still sitting behind the counter with his eyes glued to the newspaper. Perhaps Navin Bhai had completely forgotten what he had said earlier about Mehar-e-Alam's future. He wondered if he would get a chance to talk to him after Hari left. But if somebody else came in for a haircut after Hari left – then what?

He looked out of the window. It was a Saturday, and there were more people around and more traffic on the road than on weekdays. People from surrounding areas came to buy fruit and vegetables here. There were three big greengrocers not far from each other, and all of them were crowded.

'It seems there is more profit in selling fruit and vegetables, Navin Bhai,' he had said one day, expressing his thoughts out loud.

'Meharchand, I believe that one can only earn profit when one does the work one knows best,' Navin Bhai had replied wisely.

How true! In the beginning, Shakeel had fixed him up with a job at the Halal butcher. But Mehar-e-Alam had no aptitude for it. All his life he had been a barber. He and his brother had owned a hairdressers in Lahore. Unfortunately, the partnership hadn't lasted very long because of a family dispute, and Mehar-e-Alam had lost everything. A distant cousin, Mushtaq, who lived in London, suggested that if he joined him there, all would be well again. But London seemed so far away! After the sale of the shop, his share came to 250,000 rupees. Mushtaq gave him the name of the agent who could help him with visas, etc. He met the agent, who told him that the cost of getting a tourist visa for six months would be around 150,000 rupees.

'And what will happen after six months?' he had asked.

'You could just disappear, like many others do,' the agent advised.

By the time he got the visa, the total cost came to 200,000 rupees. He still had to buy some new clothes and a ticket. When he left Lahore he had only 10,000 rupees, which he gave to his wife, saying that he would soon send money when he got a job in London. But no jobs were waiting for Mehar-e-Alam. How hard he had had to work to earn every pound since then! Only he knew the truth of that – and, of course, Allah.

'Is it enough?' he asked Hari Bhai, who seemed to be enjoying the head massage.

Hari slipped two pounds into his tunic pocket and went to the counter to make the payment.

'You are charging a lot more than you used to, Navin Bhai,' he said sternly. 'You know, when I had more hair on my head, you charged me five pounds; now, with less hair, I am supposed to pay seven.'

'Blame it on the recession, Hari Bhai. What can I do? But I can assure you, my salon is still the cheapest. If you go to any other barber they would charge you no less than fifteen to twenty pounds,' Navin Bhai said as he returned the change to him.

'Let us hope things get better after the election.'

'Nothing will change, Hari Bhai. All parties are aware of the fact that whoever comes to power, economic conditions will only get worse. What an irony! A country ruled by a queen is beginning to look like a country with a begging bowl.'

It was quite difficult to get rid of Hari Bhai, who always lingered as if he wanted to get as much for his seven pounds as he could. Apart from his haircut, he would engage Navin Bhai in debates about world affairs. When he grew tired of speaking in Hindi, he switched to Gujarati. Gujarati was beyond Mehar-e-Alam, though having worked with Navin Bhai, he had learnt a few words: 'come', 'how are you' and 'what is the news'. But beyond that his tongue got stuck.

'OK.' An indication that Hari Bhai was about to leave. Thank God! Mehar-e-Alam was very grateful to Allah when Hari left.

He moved closer to Navin Bhai and asked, 'What were you saying, Navin Bhai, about my luck . . .?'

'What was I saying?' This was Navin Bhai's way of remembering things he had forgotten. 'Oh yes. The Liberal Democrats are telling us that if they win this election, they will give amnesty to all those illegal immigrants who have been in the country for over ten years.'

'What does that mean, Navin Bhai?'

'It means that people like you will get a legal status. In the beginning you will get a two-year work permit, and after that a permanent visa. That would allow you to travel to Pakistan and still live here legally. Later on, you may also get a British passport. And yes, they also assure us that these illegal immigrants will be allowed to invite one of their family members to this country.'

Mehar-e-Alam's heart started to pound, as if he had worked out in the gym for an hour. 'Really, Navin Bhai?'

'That is what they claim. My advice for you is that you should learn English. I have told you time and again that it would be helpful if you learnt a bit of the language.'

Mehar-e-Alam had started to go to classes a few years ago, but gave up after a short time. Navin Bhai was absolutely right. He must learn English. He simply could not afford to postpone it any longer. He would register for a course next week.

'Are the Liberal Democrats likely to win?' he wanted to know.

'I think the Tories will win this election,' Navin Bhai said after a moment of deliberation. 'But whichever of the two major parties, Tory or Labour, gets more seats, neither of them will be able to form a government without the help of the Liberal Democrats. And once the Liberal Democrats come into power, they will insist on their own policies being implemented. So keep on praying.'

'Inshallah! I will pray for them, Navin Bhai, and when they come to power, I will say a special *Namaz* to thank Allah.'

When Mehar-e-Alam left work that evening, he was still confused. He could not understand how the Liberal Democrats could be part of the government if they did not win the most seats. He decided that he would call on Fareed Bhai on his way back home. He might be able to throw more light on the subject. May Allah bless Fareed Bhai, who had helped Mehar-e-Alam when he had been working at the Halal butcher. Fareed Bhai had been a regular customer. One day he had complained to the shop owner, Aslam.

'The last time I bought a chicken from your shop some novice must have prepared it. It was not cleanly chopped – it had quite a few small bones.'

'I am so sorry. I can assure you, it will never happen again. This new chap Mehar-e-Alam is still learning. The poor fellow needs some work, that's why I have employed him. But please don't worry, from now on I will personally chop it for you,' Aslam had apologised.

'The fact is, butchery is not a skill one can learn, but an art,' Fareed Bhai had remarked jokingly.

Mehar-e-Alam would never forget that day. Without a clue as to what Aslam and Fareed Bhai were discussing, he had made his entry exactly at that point and asked Aslam, 'Where shall I start cutting? The back of the shop would be nice because the weather is good.'

Fareed Bhai misunderstood the situation. He cautioned, 'Be careful, Aslam, you are not permitted to tether the lamb in the shop. If somebody finds out, you'll be in trouble.'

'He is not talking about the lamb, Fareed sahib,' Aslam chuckled, 'he wants to give me a haircut. He is in fact a barber by profession. That is what he did in Lahore. These days, we all are his clients.'

'Oh I see.' Fareed Bhai had laughed heartily. 'I was really alarmed. That reminds me, I need a haircut too.'

'Shall I do it now?' Mehar-e-Alam asked eagerly.

'Not here. Why don't you come to my place in the afternoon? I live quite close by.' He had given him the directions and left.

That was Mehar-e-Alam's first visit to Fareed Bhai's house, equipped with his one and only old pair of scissors. Fareed Bhai took one look at them and warned him that no gentleman would ever let him cut his hair with those scissors. When Mehar-e-Alam told him his life story, and how he had lost everything in Lahore but had somehow managed to come here and was still struggling to earn money to buy new tools, Fareed Bhai gave him a bag for the tools and twenty pounds to buy the necessary things. He told him that he might also get him some clients.

Fareed Bhai seemed to be a well-educated man, unlike Aslam, who was only good for Halal meat. Later, Mehar-e-Alam learnt that Fareed Bhai came from India, but that he always showed a keen interest in the happenings in Pakistan. Since that first day, Mehar-e-Alam had visited his house many times. Fareed Bhai was a very friendly man and he treated Mehar-e-Alam as an equal. One day he said, 'You know, to have a haircut at home is a real luxury in London. This reminds me of my childhood.'

His wife was a bit more reserved with Mehar-e-Alam. On one occasion he gave her a haircut as well, but she said, 'Your hands smell of raw meat. I don't want you to cut my hair in future.'

It was only natural that his hands should smell of meat. At that time, he worked in the Halal butcher for six days a week, and on Sundays gave haircuts to four or five clients. Though he used to wear plastic gloves in the shop while handling raw meat, and would wash his hands with soap every so often, the smell seemed to penetrate through to the pores of his skin. It was sheer good fortune that one day he met Navin Bhai, who offered him a job at his Hair & DVD Salon. Since then, Fareed Bhai came into the salon whenever he needed a haircut.

When his tourist visa expired, it was Fareed Bhai who showed him the way forward, advising him to see a solicitor and apply for political asylum. So he met one solicitor, who said that unless Mehar-e-Alam claimed

16

that his life would be in danger if he returned to Pakistan, his case would not be strong enough. What could he say? The truth was that if he returned, the biggest danger would be that his wife and children could die of hunger. He had never been interested in politics. Somehow, the solicitor filed an application for asylum based on a half truth, which was rejected. So were subsequent appeals. He grew tired of going to the solicitor's. The money he wasted in the process was another concern. Once, somebody suggested that he should get married to a woman with a British passport. Of course, it would cost him. No girl would be ready to marry him without getting paid. He toyed with the idea for a long time. One day he discussed it with Fareed Bhai.

'Don't be stupid,' came the rejoinder. 'The Home Office is well aware that many immigrants take this route in order to get permanent residence. This might complicate your case further.'

His existence now was that of an illegal immigrant who lives in Britain but does not exist. One of the benefits of this situation was that whatever he earned, he did not have to pay any tax at all. But he constantly lived in fear that somebody would report him, and that he would be deported to Pakistan. He tried to look after his health so that he would never have to go to a hospital, which would expose his real status. He avoided arguments or conflicts. Just minded his own business. So far, this strategy had worked. By the grace of Allah, nobody had lodged any complaints against him. And why would they? He was not the only one in this situation.

It was now eleven years since he had come to this country. He hadn't seen his family since. He had left his wife and four kids behind in the hope that once he settled in the UK, they would also join him here. But that had proved impossible. He could neither invite them nor travel to Pakistan himself, because if he went, he would not be able to return. He sent money every month, and thanks to Allah his family were managing fine. However, there were times when he felt anxious about them. Last month his wife Saqina told him on the phone that his elder son Pappu, who was now nearly seventeen, was keeping bad company and had been arrested for theft. The boy was later released, but Mehar-e-Alam regularly prayed to Allah after saying his *Namaz*:

'O Almighty Allah, please guide Pappu in the right direction. He should become an honest man, he should stay away from bad company, he should focus on his studies, respect his elders and make the family proud of him. *Aameen*. May Allah fulfil my wishes.'

If there was any truth in what Navin Bhai had said, that the Liberal Democratic Party would come into power, and that he would be allowed to invite one family member to the UK, then he would definitely make sure Pappu came here. Then Pappu too could have a good life like him. True, Mehar-e-Alam had been nothing but a small-time barber before he came here. He could just about read a bit of Urdu and that was it. Now, he could at least understand a few words of English as well. People treated him with respect. He had already learnt to drive when he was in Pakistan but to get a UK driving licence was a whole different ball game. He had to take lessons, paying £10 a time. He had passed the theory test in Urdu and had passed the driving test the very first time whereas Ramesh, his co-worker, failed three times before he got through.

Mehar-e-Alam was proud to have a UK driving licence. Whenever he was free, he drove for Junaid's minicab company. It was good to have some extra income. But of course, it was hard work. Not that he hadn't worked hard when he was in Pakistan, he certainly did. But whatever he earned, there was never enough. And on top of that, he never got a moment's respite, and he, too, has some needs. True, he had to work doubly hard here, but he couldn't complain that he didn't get a good return. How he had changed in the last eleven years!

In the early days he had shared a two-room flat with four men. It was so overcrowded that he felt suffocated, and it was impossible to find a clean corner to say his *Namaz* prayers. The rest of them lived in filth. Quite often in the morning he would find bones from the chicken they had eaten the night before scattered around on plastic plates. He hated that place. How could he possibly be living in such conditions in the UK? Perhaps one of the reasons why he felt this way was because he had seen Fareed Bhai's beautiful and clean house. Anyway, he lived in that flat for five years. Had he opted to rent a place on his own, it would have cost him a lot more than what he paid there.

When his financial situation improved he started to look for a room of his own. He found out about one flat which was above a shop close to the local Indian sweet shop. He took Navin Bhai to see it. The flat consisted of a small living room, two small bedrooms, a kitchen and a bathroom. It was not in great condition, but it felt like heaven compared to where he had been living. But the rent was four hundred pounds a month, which was too much for him. He loved the flat, but he worried that if he paid four hundred pounds for rent, what would he eat or send home?

Navin Bhai made a sensible suggestion. 'You won't get such a cheap flat again. Why don't you look for a tenant? You only need one bedroom for yourself. The other can be rented out.'

Mehar-e-Alam liked the idea, but there was one concern. What if the tenant did not keep the place clean? But a much greater concern was how he would get a tenant in the first place. Navin Bhai told him, 'Why don't you put an advert in my shop window or in the newsagents? Write your phone number on it so that whoever wants the room can contact you.'

By that time Mehar-e-Alam had bought a second-hand mobile. Days went by but he didn't get a single call. He had already paid a month's rent in advance for the flat. Suddenly, one Friday, when he was returning from the mosque after saying his Friday *Namaz*, the mobile rang. It was a woman's voice, probably speaking Gujarati. Mehar-e-Alam, in his broken English, tried to explain that he didn't understand.

'No Gujarati,' he said.

She switched to English. Mehar-e-Alam was even more confused. He could understand a few words, but comprehending full sentences of English was unthinkable. He became frustrated, interrupting her with: 'Talk Urdu!'

That worked. In short, she needed a room. She was going through a bad patch. Her husband, with whom she had come to the UK, had left her. Her in-laws, too, had disowned her. She had nowhere to go. Mehar-e-Alam was worried about two things. Firstly, how she would pay the rent, and secondly, that she was a woman.

She assured him that she worked in a shop nearby in Wembley and would pay the rent regularly.

Mehar-e-Alam was still uncertain. All this time he hadn't even thought about women. All his energy was focused on one thing – he had to make something of his life so that his family in Lahore could exist comfortably. To live under the same roof as a woman might cause some trouble. He didn't know anything about her. God alone knew what she might be involved in! And to make matters worse, she was a Hindu. Navin Bhai was a Hindu, but he was different. Mehar-e-Alam was aware of how Hindus think. He had often heard Hindus abusing the Muslim community and Pakistan at Navin Bhai's salon. His blood boiled when he listened to such comments, but he restrained himself.

He recalled how explosive some of the conversations became after the London bombings of 7 July 2005. He could sense the venom in their words.

One day, Ramesh and Vinod both sided with Chetan Patel when he said, 'In my opinion, all Muslims should be banished from this country, starting with the Pakistanis. Have you ever heard of a Hindu involved in a bombing? Muslims are such thankless people, they bite the hand that feeds them.'

Ramesh responded, 'You are absolutely correct, Chetan Bhai. Poor Hindus are hardworking people. The majority of the good-for-nothing asylum seekers are Muslims who simply enjoy the state benefits.'

And Vinod, glancing at Mehar-e-Alam, added salt to the wound by saying, 'I'd never trust a Muslim even if he'd changed his appearance to look like a Hindu.'

Mehar-e-Alam was itching to say something to counter their belief that Muslims were all either terrorists or seeking state benefits. When he had applied for political asylum, he was probably among the very few who declined the free food coupons even though he was entitled to them. The reason being that he considered earning his living through hard work to be the true way of Islam. Mehar-e-Alam wanted them to know this, but before he could utter a word, Navin Bhai appeared. Vinod and Ramesh were well aware of the fact that Navin Bhai did not tolerate such talk. Navin Bhai had told them about Mehar-e-Alam, but had also sternly warned them: 'Do not ever reveal his identity in front of a client.'

Navin Bhai often took him to Hindu homes for children's haircutting ceremonies, where Mehar-e-Alam earnt good money on top of his salary. On one occasion he asked Mehar-e-Alam to accompany him to Swami Narayan Temple and said, 'Hindu Pundits need a haircut.'

Mehar-e-Alam was apprehensive. 'But Navin Bhai, if somebody comes to know who I am, there could be trouble.'

'Nobody will know. Your name is Meharchand. Just don't say anything.'

How many Muslims have visited the Swami Narayan Temple? Mehar-e-Alam felt proud. It was all because of Navin Bhai.

And it was Navin Bhai who now convinced him that the poor girl seemed to be in trouble and that offering her a room to stay in could be a noble thing to do. True, Mehar-e-Alam thought, he owed his life in this country to the blessings and noble deeds of others. Now it was his turn to help someone else.

The day Nandini came to his flat as a lodger, Mehar-e-Alam felt his status rise to that of a landlord. One thing he liked about her was that she too was keen on keeping the flat clean. In the initial months, the two of them hardly exchanged any words, but gradually a kind of friendship developed. And now it was a different story.

He called her Nain. Somehow, he found it difficult to pronounce her full name, Nandini. He began to stammer whenever he tried. One day she explained that 'nain' means 'eyes'. This pleased him. What an apt name he had given her – for he found her eyes to be the best feature on her face.

The access to his flat was via a staircase at the rear of the shops, where there was a car park as well. But what irritated him most was that the narrow gully was generally littered with empty cardboard boxes and tins which belonged to the adjacent shops. He had to struggle to clear a pathway to get to the staircase. As he climbed up the first step this evening, he thought of buying Indian sweets for Nain. She loved Jalebi. The good news must be given along with sweets.

He headed back to the shops and found that the Indian sweet shop was as busy as it always was at the weekends. The shopkeeper made special Jalebi and people from far and wide came to buy them and Gujarati Dhokla.

Mehar-e-Alam bought 250 grams of Jalebi and took the opportunity to remind the shopkeeper, who happened to be his landlord as well, about the kitchen tap that had been leaking for over a week now.

'Yes, yes. I remember,' Mr Patel said hurriedly. 'Shall I pack some Dhokla as well? It is freshly made.'

'No, Jalebi is fine.'

In fact Mehar-e-Alam had had no clue what Dhokla was before he had met Nain. The first time that she made it at home and offered it to him, he hesitated. When she urged him to at least taste it, he took a bite. It wasn't bad, but certainly not one of his favourite foods. In the beginning, when Nain had first moved into his flat, he had cooked for himself or would eat kebabs on the way home. But one day Nain insisted: 'Why don't you eat at home? I cook for myself and am happy to cook for you too. Of course I can't make non-vegetarian food, but if you feel like it, occasionally you can cook meat yourself. I have no problem with that.'

Mehar-e-Alam agreed. He suspected that he would get tired of eating vegetarian food regularly. But to his surprise, Nain was a good cook and offered a wide variety of dishes. He relished her food so much that he hardly thought of cooking meat or fish. What if he forgot the taste of non-vegetarian food? He found the thought quite amusing. Just to reassure himself he sometimes went to the kebab house and occasionally cooked at home as well. Not often though, out of consideration for Nain.

The couple settled into a routine, and had their dinner together. Sometimes they watched a Hindi movie on a DVD after dinner. Nain loved Hindi movies and he could always get the latest ones from Navin Bhai's shop. Mehar-e-Alam had hardly ever watched Hindi movies when he was in Pakistan, though they were freely available. And now he rarely missed a new movie. After the film, Nain would go to her bedroom and he to his room.

Mehar-e-Alam would never forget that one night, four years ago, when Nain had come to his room. She had stood in the doorway for a few seconds.

'What's wrong? Can't you sleep?' he had asked.

'Can I sleep with you tonight?' she whispered.

Mehar-e-Alam was shocked. He could clearly hear his heart thudding in his chest. What kind of challenge did Allah want him to face? It wasn't that he didn't like her or didn't feel sexually attracted to her, but at that moment he simply couldn't utter a single word. He moved to one side to make space for her and she quietly came to lie down beside him. After so many years he felt the warmth of a woman's body next to him. He was quite surprised when she took the next step and undressed herself as well as Mehar-e-Alam.

What followed seemed natural and destined.

When he woke up for the early morning *Namaz,* she was not there. Maybe it had all been just a dream. But it was not a dream. When they met for breakfast she said, 'I hope you will not see me as a fallen woman.'

Mehar-e-Alam gently took her in his arms. It was perhaps the first time in his life that he had taken a woman in his arms. In Lahore, his relationship with his wife had been merely a sexual one, which had resulted in the birth of their four children. It was a completely new feeling for Mehar-e-Alam – how an embrace alone could be so satisfying.

Since that night, Nain often came to his bedroom, but she always left before dawn. Mehar-e-Alam wondered why, but was never able to ask her. Nor did he have the courage to take the initiative. He feared that if he did either of these two things, the magic of those nights would be lost. He simply waited for her to make the first move.

Tonight when he opened the door to his flat, there were quite a few papers and pamphlets from various political parties scattered on the floor. He picked them up, wondering if Nain was back from work or not. If she were, surely she would have picked these up herself. But noises from the kitchen reassured him. She was definitely back and preparing the dinner.

'The food is not ready yet. You can have a shower in the meantime,' she called out.

Mehar-e-Alam always took a shower when he returned from work. It felt necessary after cutting people's hair all day long. He looked at his beer belly in the shower and felt ashamed. Lately he had been drinking a lot of beer, or sometimes having a glass of red wine instead. Somebody had told him that red wine was good for the heart. Last year, he had gone to the gym regularly – four times a week, in fact. Nain had suggested it, saying he had developed a paunch. He paid an annual membership for the local fitness centre and within a month became much fitter. Nain had smiled and said, 'Look at you. You look so young.'

'Young?' he had laughed. 'I am forty-five years old.'

What an unusual relationship we have, he thought now. It was five years since she had moved in. She paid her rent on time each month, though Mehar-e-Alam found it embarrassing to take rent from her now. Once he protested, but she responded by saying, 'Well, you do the grocery shopping each month. Think of it as my contribution towards running the household in partnership.'

He mused. It was true, of course. They were indeed running this household as partners. Or as friends! But was it just friendship? he wondered.

When he stepped out of the shower she said, 'Dinner will be ready in another ten minutes. I am sorry, I was running late today.'

'Can I help?' Mehar-e-Alam asked even though he knew that his role in the evenings was to do the washing up after dinner.

'No, it's fine. Why don't you say your *Namaz* while I finish. I will call you when it is ready.'

'I have brought Jalebis for you.'

'Yes, I have already seen.' She smiled.

Mehar-e-Alam read the *Maghrib Namaz* and returned to the living room. He took a bottle of red wine and poured some into a large glass. If Nain could see this she would object, saying, 'This is a beer glass. Not meant for wine.'

But for some reason, Mehar-e-Alam did not enjoy drinking wine in a small glass. What was the point of sinning and not fully enjoying it? He took a long sip and tried Fareed Bhai's telephone number once again. He heard it ring several times. The landlord had hardly supplied him with any furniture except for a broken chair. When Fareed Bhai bought a new sofa, he gave Mehar-e-Alam his old one. The room looked decent enough now. He remembered how on Nain's suggestion, he had bought paints and brushes, and how together they had painted the whole flat. It all looked so much better. He loved to return to this flat after a day's work.

He loved to return to Nain.

'Let us eat,' she said, interrupting his train of thought, and he went into the kitchen. She had served dinner on the small dining table, which he had bought from a second-hand furniture shop.

Mehar-e-Alam took a spoonful and complimented Nain. He knew that she expected him to say something about the food; she liked to hear his feedback whether it was good or bad. But how could Mehar-e-Alam ever criticise her cooking?

'Navin Bhai says that people like us will soon get legal status.' He gave her the information while eating.

'Really? How come?'

'That is what the Liberal Democrats are promising.'

'But only if they come to power, isn't that right?'

'They will certainly come to power. I have prayed to Allah for their victory.'

'Then nothing will stop them from winning,' she said. Then: 'OK, tell me, what is the first thing you will do after becoming a legal?' She looked at him with her big curious eyes.

'I will visit my country. It has been eleven years since I saw my family.'

'And after that?'

'I will call my eldest son Pappu here.'

'And then?'

'I haven't really thought about it. What about you?'

She did not respond but just looked at him.

'What is this? When it is your turn to answer, you hide behind silence,' Mehar-e-Alam challenged, with a hint of pique in his voice.

'I have never really thought about it,' she said quietly, and then maintained silence.

Mehar-e-Alam saw that she was deep in thought. But what was she thinking about? How little he knew of her life, while his own life was like an open book, of which she had read every word.

'I am going for a bath. I had no time in the morning,' Nain said, and left the room.

He did the washing up and after cleaning the kitchen returned to his bedroom. He lay down, waiting for Nain

28

to come. Would she come tonight? Or wouldn't she? He tried to find an answer to this question and his thoughts drifted to the future. By the grace of Almighty Allah, if he became a legal, and if he got a permanent visa to stay here, his life would be so much better. He would bring Pappu here and ask him to do some training, make him learn English, and then, when he got a British passport, he would bring the whole family here.

He dozed off while sketching out his future plans, and was awoken when an alarm went off on his mobile. It was time to say his prayers. He got up and went to the bathroom. It was empty, but the scent of Nain's soap lingered. He did the *Wuzoo* and returned to his room, where he rolled out the *Janamaz* on the floor and sat for prayers. After the *Namaz* he prayed to Allah:

O Allah, please look after the whole world
O Allah, look after the Islamic world
O my Lord, smooth my path, ridden with difficulties
O great Almighty Allah, please forgive my sins
O my Lord, I am a sinful man, shower your blessings
on me
Help me my Allah and solve my problems
O Allah, let the Liberal Democrats win and form a
government
Ameen. May Allah fulfil my wishes.

When he got up after saying his prayers, he saw Nain standing in the doorway wearing a nightdress made of flimsy material. The dim light in the background shone through it and he could see the lines and curves of her body. Mehar-e-Alam could not take his eyes off her. She moved slowly and lay down on the bed, with one hand under her head. Her eyes searched his eyes questioningly, as if asking, 'What did you wish for?' But for the first time Mehar-e-Alam's eyes had read an answer in the lines and curves of her body. He had only felt her body in darkness before this.

The door was still half open and the dim light coming from the corridor looked like a milky path leading up to his bed. That night, as he walked with Nain on this path, he felt that Allah had been so pleased with one of his noble deeds that he had rewarded him with a special tip.

When he woke for the *Fajr Namaz* in the early hours, he saw Nain still sleeping in his bed. That meant she had not gone to her room last night. One of her arms was still around his neck and a lock of her hair was lazily spread on her forehead. He gazed at her face. She looked so innocent in the early morning light. This was his first experience of waking up with her in the same bed. He felt contented, at peace.

Suddenly, a thought hit him. If Pappu came here, all this would disappear. His life would not be the same. And at this moment he did not want it to change even a little bit. He didn't even want to move, fearing that if he did so, this moment would be lost, like a reflection in the water.

Without getting up, he raised his hands in a prayer and said, 'O Allah, I do not care whether the Liberal Democrats win or lose, whether they form a government or not, whether I get a legal status or not, I am happy the way I am with your blessings. O my Allah, please shower your blessings upon this sinful man as you always do. Ameen. May Allah fulfil my wishes!'

A Diwali Night

Anil Prabha Kumar

New Jersey, USA, 2005

Lattu stopped the car in the driveway, opened the
door and climbed out. With slow and heavy steps, his
father Mayadas followed him towards the house, then
stopped in front of it. Quite often, he would admire his
own house as if it were someone else's – a large white
building, covered in small white tiles. Above the big
front door, a huge crystal chandelier could be seen in
the first-floor window.

It looks like the Taj Mahal, Mayadas thought. His lips
moved, giving thanks to God. Then his heart twisted
and he wished that the house was in India, so that his
neighbours and friends could see how magnificent it
was.

There was no one around on the street. It was a
November night, still quite mild, but there were signs
that the cold weather was on its way. The leaves were
telling a tale of the season, their colour changing as thcy
fell flat on the ground. Everything outside was starting

to look the same . . . A car passed by and the headlights startled him, absorbed as he was in looking at his house. There in his neighbourhood, looking at his house, he became distressed. It was Diwali, and not even a hint of light showed in the houses on his street. Only the branches of the trees were filtering some faint, fading light from the sky.

Lattu grabbed the last plastic bag and marched briskly towards the house. 'Papa,' he said, 'come inside. It is getting cold.'

With tired steps, Mayadas entered the house from the garage door. With his hands folded together, he passed the small temple to the left. Then he went over to the right, placed the bags he was carrying onto the table there, put his coat on a chair and sat down. He felt as if he had been sitting alone in the silence of this twilight for years on end. This was the moment of homecoming, the moment which was neither completely day nor completely dark. It troubled him. He remained, sitting still in the vacuum of darkness, nothingness sinking within him as in a well.

Nobody was waiting for anybody.

He began to feel as if he was in a still-life picture in black and white. In this picture there were many things: dirty dishes stacked in the sink; on the counter someone had hurriedly opened a packet of biscuits; an old pizza box lay next to a half-drunk bottle of soda. On the stove stood a wok, and on the other side a pressure cooker. In the corner were a mixer and toaster – but their lines were indistinct. If someone else could see him, sitting on the chair, he thought, they would probably consider him part of this still-life as well.

He gazed around at the family room. The still-life was now not only still, but weighted down. There was a thick carpet, and a big sofa with cushions on it whose colours he could only guess at in this dim light. Everything was motionless, as in his own inner life. He inhaled deeply, as if trying to breathe some life into this halted existence.

He sensed some movement among the cushions and guessed that his wife Lakshmi had fallen asleep there. He could smell cooking in the house, so perhaps this picture had some liveliness to it after all. For a long time Lakshmi hadn't cooked much. The poor woman had done enough cooking over the years. She was over seventy years of age and her heavy body had been grabbed by many diseases.

Lakshmi got up slowly. When she started walking, her body swayed from side to side. She switched the lamp on. In the light everything looked clear.

'When did you come in?' she said. 'I did not know that you were here.'

Mayadas stayed silent.

Lakshmi came close and asked him affectionately, 'Will you take some water?'

He replied, 'No, I am fine. Now we will have dinner. Are the children not home yet?' He asked this question out of habit – and then noticed the hollow note in his voice when he said the word 'children'. Their eldest son Kuber was forty-five, Monika (Mani) was forty-two and Lattu was thirty-six. At these ages, their children should have had their own kids. How much he wanted Mani to get married! She had been engaged to a doctor, but it turned out that he had only wanted to get married in order to obtain a Green Card. So the engagement was broken off and Mani never trusted another man ever again.

Kuber had also postponed his marriage for a long time. They all knew that as a doctor, he would make an attractive groom. But Lakshmi was concerned that if the older brother got married first, then his wife might not want him to spend any money on his younger sister Mani's wedding.

Lakshmi herself had three brothers. Her older sister-in-law had once told her wisely, 'Sister, everything has its price tag, and moving to America also has its price.'

Listening to this, it felt as though someone had touched a raw wound. Her children were old enough and yet not married – it gave people opportunities to taunt them. *'If you were in India, your children would already be married.'*

Now the couple also felt doubtful. Had their children swapped their youth for a fat chequebook? If the years of their lives were given to them in coins, they would realise what price they had paid – and what had they gained?

Lakshmi had insisted that it was time for Kuber to get married. She was ready to let him go. Shree was perfect as far as Mayadas was concerned – she fulfilled all the criteria for a suitable daughter-in-law. She too was a doctor, who had studied in India. Right now she was doing her second-year residency in Chicago. There had been no danger of her failing her medical exams before she could come to America. Mayadas had got what he wanted, but soon learned that he had lost at the bigger game. Shree had become a doctor, but never the kind of daughter-in-law that he had hoped for.

While Shree was based in Chicago, Kuber was practising in New Jersey. There was a kind of uneasiness in the family regarding Mani. They were not sure how Shree would react to her but that uneasiness was somewhat dispelled as Shree rarely visited them and when she did, she was more like a guest than a member of the family. On completing her residency, Shree had to go back to India for two years according to the agreement. After returning from India she again joined the fellowship programme in New York. Everybody was hoping that she and Kuber would start their family. Maybe Shree would like to become a mother now that she had finished her education. But she was unable to find a job in her specific field in New Jersey, and began to look for opportunities in other states. At this point Kuber lost his patience.

'After studying so hard you don't expect me to stay home, do you?' Shree had demanded.

Kuber was speechless at her answer. He was beginning to understand the meaning of 'compromise' in reference to domestic life.

This year they celebrated Diwali without Shree, the Goddess of Wealth.

Lakshmi got a little irritated by the shopping bags, scattered all around. Then she remembered something – and swallowed her annoyance. Since Mani's engagement had been broken off, her shopping habit had crossed the limit. She bought things non-stop. Things to decorate the house, personal things, things for her brothers, her mother, her father – things of necessity, but mostly items that were unnecessary.

'Where has all this clutter come from?' Lakshmi used to say crossly. But Mani kept on piling up the house with things, as though the house had a vacancy that could never be filled. Now, Lakshmi no longer said anything to her.

'Please call Mani down from upstairs,' she said instead to her husband.

At her command, the young woman came running downstairs.

'Is Lattu up there too?' Mayadas added. 'What is he doing?'

'He is sitting on the computer, probably looking at girls on the internet,' Mani said snidely.

'Don't be silly.' Mayadas lovingly took his son's side. 'Go and fetch him too.'

'Papa, he is planning to play with the firecrackers which Shree brought for him from South Carolina.'

'No, no, no,' Mayadas said immediately. 'Don't ever let him do that. Fireworks are illegal here in our state.' He was always concerned about his youngest son's lack of common sense.

'How can firecrackers be illegal at Diwali?' Mani frowned.

Mayadas kept quiet, for what answer could he give? To change the subject he said gently, 'Mani, today is Diwali – at least prepare for the ceremony.'

Mani replied that she had just got home from work and was very tired. She turned on all the lights in the house. With a feeling of faint hope she looked around at her father, but could not see any exciting-looking shopping bags with presents in them. Disheartened, she fell silent. She thought about how things had improved for them, only a few years after their arrival in this country. Kuber's medical practice was flourishing. Even Papa had won the second innings in his life through hard work. He had established his business as a clothing wholesaler, and had then handed over the reins to Lattu and taken a back seat. But Mani was the first one who had started working in that house. She had begun in a clerical position and was now a manager. Now four salaries were coming into their household. Since Kuber's practice had joined with Shree's, everybody was talking about buying an even bigger house.

At the first Diwali after Kuber's wedding, the women in Mayadas's house received gold jewellery. There were also sweets in abundance that year. They had Christmas lights in the windows for two months. But Shree was in Chicago for her residency and Diwali happened without her. Then the gifts slowly started to stop. It seemed that this year there would be none at all for the family.

'So, what is for dinner tonight?' Mayadas asked.

'I have only cooked the legumes this afternoon,' Lakshmi said helplessly. Nowadays she couldn't stand for long in the kitchen.

'Don't worry. I have picked up naan and matar paneer along with sweets from the Edison. Isn't today a Diwali day?' Somehow he wanted to feel and to make other people feel that today was a special day.

Lakshmi sat down and started to cut up an apple. When they had first come to this house three years ago, she had been full of enthusiasm. On that first Diwali, her three brothers and their families had been invited. Just two days later it was Bhaiya-Duj, so she asked them to stay until then. Back then, she would dance around with happiness.

She used to feel overwhelmed at the thought of owning such a big house. Sometimes she could even spot deer in the backyard, and would give them leftover food. She was astonished by the land they owned. She would look at the cars parked at their driveway and wonder, 'Do these cars really belong to us?'

That day, Lakshmi's eldest brother asked her, 'Lakshmi, do you like America?'

'Yes, I like it a lot. It is very clean. There is no dirt or dust, and we always have running water and electricity.'

'Everything here has its price though, sister,' her eldest sister-in-law commented, as usual.

Lakshmi was irritated. 'Why? We aren't short of anything.'

'In India all of your children would have been married by now.'

This remark branded Lakshmi like a hot iron. Both she and Mayadas were left with a bitter taste in their mouths.

Mayadas said with an arrogant air, 'Whoever marries Kuber will roll in money.'

Money was a trump card for them; they thought it could solve any problem in life.

*

The garage door opened and closed. Kuber entered the house. While removing his tie from his neck he called out, 'I am starving, Mani! Please serve the food.'

His sister quickly microwaved some food to warm it up and put paper plates and plastic spoons in front of everybody.

They all began to eat quietly, except for Mani herself. Her voice was like a broken record, plaintively repeating in the background, 'It is Diwali, and no one else in the house has any interest in doing anything.

38

How much can I do by myself?' But her words remained unheard.

'Mani,' Lakshmi said eventually, 'go inside the home temple and start getting things ready for the pooja. We all will be coming soon. After all, we have to perform pooja at Diwali.'

Everyone went and sat in the temple room. On the big silver tray stood seven silver diyas (lamps), glittering. There were some special marble statues from Jaipur, and for the family, there were brocade clothes, gold-plated jewellery and a red carpet which was only used for poojas. Mayadas was overwhelmed. Kuber and Lattu sat down against the wall, both silent and exhausted.

Lakshmi had difficulty sitting on the floor. Her left knee was bothering her and it was painful when she tried to bend it.

She asked her husband, 'Please bathe these coins of Ganesha and Lakshmi in the milk and then honour them with saffron and rice tilak.' She opened the box of sweets in front of the deities, closed her eyes and started saying a prayer. The light was dim in the room. The flames from the diyas were trembling.

Mani sat at the back of the room next to the big holy basil plant. In the past, every Diwali, one little hope used to quiver in her heart. Maybe the next Diwali would be in someone else's home and she herself would be the lady of that house. She would wear a deep red sari adorned with gold jewellery, and she would glance at somebody lovingly and say, 'Could you please place a little tikka on the foreheads of Ganesh and Lakshmi?'

She closed her eyes. Today there was not even a glimpse of that thought flashing through her mind. How many more Diwalis would pass in this house, just like this? From the hollow of her chest came a moaning sigh, which dissolved in the darkness.

Lattu's gaze was fixed on the diyas; he held an answering fire in his eyes. Earlier that day, Papa had said in the car, 'Lattu, you are thirty-six years old, but it does not matter. We can still get a young and beautiful bride of twenty-four or five for you from India. People marry off their young and beautiful girls to the boys who have money. No problem.'

Lattu smiled contentedly to himself. His hair had started thinning and he had recently acquired a crew-cut hairstyle. He stroked his bald head and turned his neck to pose like a movie star. Suddenly he remembered that he'd been waiting for Melissa's phone call – so he left the room and ran upstairs.

Kuber was thinking about Shree – she was never home for Diwali. Actually she was hardly home at all. She just came hurriedly twice or thrice a month on her days off – and then rushed back to work in the same frenzy, leaving behind complete disorder. If she had been here today, his mother would probably have asked her to perform pooja. How would Mani have felt then? Mani was two years older than Shree. He gazed at the statues of the deities, touched a little prasad to his lips and got up.

'I'm going to sleep,' he told them. 'Tomorrow I have to wake up early.'

'Who will eat all these sweets?' Lakshmi asked, and right away wished she hadn't. Mayadas and Lakshmi's eyes met and settled on the picture of Krishna as a child. He was holding a butter ball in his hand.

Both husband and wife stayed, sitting quietly in the lamplight. Nobody noticed or missed Mani when she slipped away. Mayadas was listening to the exploding of firecrackers in the distance. Tonight was the night of the new moon, and the desires of light were rising in his head.

'Next Diwali we will celebrate in India,' he announced. 'All of us will go. It only requires money.'

The wax flames crackled. His own voice had a stranger's hollow ring to it, which made him nervous. Lakshmi kept on staring at him, her face without expression.

Upstairs, Kuber was moving towards the bed when he nearly tripped on something. In the darkness he reached down and picked it up. It was Shree's sari, which she had thrown carelessly onto the chair. He was about to put it back, then stopped himself. Lifting it slowly and carefully, he placed it near his pillow, where Shree used to put her head.

A Breakable Bridge

Anshu Johri

California, 2006

I am lounging aimlessly on this white couch which sits in the living room of my one-bedroom apartment in San Jose. And she must be in one of the rooms of her house, which stands quietly on the slope of a hill, overlooking a lake. She is probably in her dining room, where the poor dining table is pinned down by six chairs – until they are pulled out by someone with a desire to sit on them. She must have pulled out one of those chairs, giving the table some room to breathe, and then have stood there for a moment looking out before sitting down. The entrance to her house is clearly visible from her dining room.

The golden hands of that black oval clock on the cream walls of her dining room will be busy measuring the periphery of their confinement, and the clock will be ticking as usual. It always seemed to me that the clock's hands were waiting for the batteries to drain, so that they could have a break from their never-ending circular sojourn. My thoughts return to her: she must from time to time throw glances at that clock and its golden hands.

The doors of her house will be open, except for that screen door, which has always remained closed. The screen door has many advantages: it allows fresh air to fill the inside of her house while keeping mosquitoes and other creepy-crawlies away, and she can always see through it while remaining indoors.

The screen door must be rattling in the wind as it always did – as if it had a heartfelt desire to stay closed. But then it could never fight the force of the wind, and ended up being battered against the door-frame, time and time again!

Her sleep was very often disturbed by this clumsy rattling. Many a time, she told me, she would be woken by the noise in the middle of the night, confuse it with a knock and get up to check if somebody was at the door. Then she would go back to bed and lie awake for hours, making fruitless attempts to get back to sleep. One of her favourite ways was to gaze at her children while they slept. She would look at their curly brown hair, framing their fair foreheads; their closed eyelids under which their eyes dreamed on carelessly – and her own weary eyes would well up with tears.

I could never work out how hot tears could soothe those burning eyes of hers, and help her to get some sleep. 'But you see,' she explained, 'when my tears flow, they somehow embark on the banks of sleep.'

When she woke up the next morning, her eyelids would be glued together. She told me that when you sleep with tears in your eyes they become trapped, so they glue the eyelids together to stay trapped. She would smile after saying that. Her smile was enigmatic like the *Mona Lisa* of Da Vinci! It was sad, happy, contented, discontented, detached, affectionate, incomplete, perfect . . . I could never decide which emotion was dominant. They were all there, each one – equally present and equally absent.

*

On that first day, I saw her waiting at the bus stop with her two young daughters, and I pulled up in my car to ask if they needed a lift back home. I had just met her in a conference and it was this formal goodwill gesture which took me to her home for the first time. She smiled, thanked me, and then hopped into my car. 'Can we collect the young one's car seat from reception?' she asked, and I nodded in affirmation.

By the time we reached home her daughters had fallen asleep. In a second goodwill gesture, I offered to carry one of the girls inside. She hesitated for a moment, but then relaxed. She carried the younger one and I carried the older one. I have to confess that her daughter was not very light. I followed her with the child in my arms. She first opened the screen door, then unlocked the main door and turned to me to say, 'Please come in.'

I followed her into the living room where she stopped and then addressed me again: 'Could you please put Sarjna on the couch? I'll be back in a few minutes.' She then very politely asked me not to follow her any further. While she took her younger one off into her bedroom, I put Sarjna down on the couch. She was fast asleep. I was not used to carrying children, and my neck protested at the strain. While I stretched, easing my spine, an attractive mahogany cabinet with clear glass sliding doors caught my attention. Several big and small photos occupied the first and second shelves of this cabinet – each one a proud record of some moment or other. There was a picture of her looking younger and with a smile all over her face; photographs of her with her daughters – one with the older one, another with the younger one, one with both of them; one with her and her husband and one with all of them together. They all looked so happy in those frames. If by any means these pictures could talk or think, they would surely have asked me the reason for my fixed stare. Why the hell *was* I staring at all of them? I asked myself. Then I realised that, on those two shelves, her family was intact, complete and in the same place, together in her mahogany cabinet. But in reality, outside those frames, they were all separated.

Separate: I could tell by the sound of cups and the microwave that she was in the kitchen, her older daughter Sarjna was sleeping on the couch in the living room, the younger one must be asleep upstairs . . . and her husband was there in the cabinet!

'Would you like to have some coffee? I've made it anyway so you really can't say "no" unless you are rude – and I know that you are not rude.'

Her voice had startled me. She stood there, right in front of me, holding a tray with coffee mugs. For the first time, I really looked at her. She had a fair complexion. Her lips were thin and her eyes were neither very big, nor were they small. But those eyes mirrored every expression on her face and also everything that was in her thoughts. Her eyes were loquacious. They would smile even before her lips smiled.

You shouldn't look at her like this, an inner voice warned me. I obeyed the voice of that stranger in my heart and started drinking the coffee in quick sips, my eyes aimed downwards, away from her and at her cream carpet, but they soon tired of that. Disregarding my inner warning, I glanced up again to see what she was doing while we both were immersed in silence. Her forefinger played with the rim of her mug and she appeared lost in thought. Suddenly, out of the blue, she threw a question at me.

'You were mentioning to that other doctor that you were not sure how much one could communicate by blinking one's eyelids.'

'Oh, I didn't mean it the way you interpreted it,' I clarified. 'My research area is the development of new and better human-computer interface technology. This technology uses sensory inputs from the human body as an information system to monitor the human response, and can also be used for the betterment of impaired human performance. This field is called Bio-Cybernetics. I specialise in something similar to electro-occulography where we use eye movements to develop this kind of interface. I need a certain type of eye movement to conduct experiments and this was why I was inquiring about the quantity of blinking which is used for communication. It is interesting the way we talk by blinking . . .'

She cut short my sentence, saying, 'I will be back in a few minutes.'

She was indeed back after a short time with a bamboo bag, which contained paper slips. She started showing them to me. I tried to read the contents of the paper slips. Some of them were clasped in her fingers, some had fallen down and some of them were still in the bag.

One said *Songs by Loreena McKennitt*; one said *Our wedding album*; one said *Books on Helen Keller*. Some had long sentences written on them.

'All this is written by our blinking conversations,' she informed me. 'You know how? It is done through Morse code. Blink the eye once and it is a dot, blink it twice and it is a dash. Even Sarjna has learned it now. Sound is nothing but vibrations of particles, isn't it? Vibrations of particles scattered in a medium. But it forms so much of human communication that we forget that it is the medium which helps us to talk; otherwise it would be just similar to talking through actions, which can also be blinking eyes.'

She suddenly burst into a bitter kind of laughter, which then changed into sobbing. I was stupefied – I had no idea what to do. I simply gaped at her.

She finally wiped her tears and managed to say: 'You must be thinking that I'm crazy. But believe me, it has been a really long time since I've cried like this in front of someone.'

'Don't worry,' I said. 'Crying helps . . . it relieves the mind, eases pressure. Sometimes when I am very tense, even *I* cry. I do it in front of the mirror.'

She laughed at that. It was loud and genuine, like a waterfall without any traces of sadness to contaminate it. I loved the way she laughed and felt an impulsive need to be with her all the time and make her laugh constantly, the way I had done then.

'So, your thesis . . .' she said. 'Have you done substantial work on that already, or will you start it after you collect the data from here?'

Her voice had wavered on the word 'data'. I knew what it meant for her. I felt like a fisherman, baiting the fish not for need but to kill for leisure. The need of one species for food had been transformed into the need for pleasure of the other. Her husband was indeed one object of my studies, a source of data for my research, as she had pointed out, and if only I had not met her, how easy it would have been to define things that way. I didn't feel I could answer her question right then.

I had finished my coffee. And so had she. I put my mug on the coffee table and got up, saying, 'I would like to talk to you about it some other day, but I am afraid I have to leave now.'

She nodded, picked up my mug and placed it gently inside her own mug. Those two mugs in her small, cupped palms looked like a pair of little birds in a nest. A shiver from nowhere shook me for no obvious reason. I had to get rid of it and I quickly shot a question at her. 'You don't drive?'

'Oh yes, I do drive.'

'Then why do you take the bus?'

'Oh, I never drive with the kids.'

'Why?'

'It's just that . . .' Her voice was damp and scared, and then she fumbled for words.

*

That day when I returned home, I was confused and distracted, not my usual self. There was a painful throbbing inside me. It had no name, no form, and no shape. There was no resolving it, no escape, and even if there was I didn't want it. She had pulled something out of me which had been protected so far, and in so doing had made me vulnerable, liable and responsible! It was as though someone had built up a huge pile of books, placing one on top of another, making a minaret out of them, and then some other person unknowingly pulled the first book from the bottom, the one that supported the entire structure, and the whole minaret just collapsed with a thud! I wondered whether I had similarly pulled out a book from her minaret, and if she felt that 'thud' the same way I did.

No, no way, I should stay away from her, I said to myself.

Next time I was at the Disabled Care Centre, I didn't see her. I collected a few papers, talked to her husband's doctors, spoke to her husband in Morse code, explained my project to him and stayed there to collect information on different cases of human disability associated with spinal-cord injuries.

I saw her on the stairs when I was returning to the car after completing my work. She was helping her younger daughter to climb the stairs, one step at a time. Her older daughter Sarjna was racing up and down the stairs and giggled when she saw me. 'Mamma – look who is here!'

She glanced up in response to her daughter's cry and smiled on spotting me, as if she had known me from long ago. 'Hello! I wasn't aware you were here too.'

'Mamma, would he give us a ride today as well?' Sarjna asked.

'No, beta, you shouldn't ask . . .' Her mother gave me an embarrassed look as she struggled to put the whole conversation back in place.

I couldn't take my eyes off her. She looked simple yet stunning with her strange look and untidy hair. For a few moments, her eyes were locked with mine in a minute space in this grand universe. Her embarrassment vanished, only to be replaced by confusion. She wanted to know why I was looking at her in that way. When you blink your eye in Morse code it means something; but when you try to communicate with your eyes *without* blinking it doesn't mean anything. She probably thought this as she jerked her head a little, before dropping her gaze.

I ended up giving them a ride home that day as well. I also had dinner at their place. Her food was simple, like her. Sarjna refused to eat anything at first until I promised to take her to McDonald's the next time I came, and only then did she relent. The little girl was bright and talkative. She always had questions to ask and she didn't mind if you told her that you didn't know. Then she would come up with her own answers.

Slowly I started to become part of her family, as integrated as one of the rooms of her house. I became best friends with her daughters Sarjna and Anuja. Even better than their dad! They confessed this to me one day after making me promise that I would never, ever tell their mother. I also got to know her better. I knew about her fear of driving the car with the kids, I knew about her fear of motorways and particularly the one where the accident had happened.

'Parimal was very active. He was full of life and energy. He would never sit still and always found something to occupy himself with. I used to tell him that one day, I would tie him down so that he couldn't go anywhere. And you see, I did tie him down, didn't I? In the cruellest way possible!' Her voice had broken after that.

Parimal, her husband, was quadriplegic because of a cervical injury. His C2 vertebra had been damaged in the accident, paralysing him below the neck, making his body unresponsive. He could hear and he could see but he could not talk. His brain worked; he thought, he dreamed – he had a vivid imagination, but he was on a ventilator, which helped him to breathe. He conveyed his thoughts by blinking his eyes using Morse code. He was a computer engineer and had played cricket and tennis before the accident. He was fond of delicious food and even with the loss that he had suffered I found him very cheerful and inspiring. His eye movement was wonderful. He could convey a lot of things that way – much more than I had thought. I hoped that if everything went well, I might be successful in developing an advanced interface, which would make better use of Parimal's brain and imagination. He had strength even when he lay there looking frail, weak and pitiful. He had the strength of willpower. I often wondered where it came from!

'There were these huge trucks either side of the motorway and I felt strong currents of wind pulling my car between them,' she told me. 'I became nervous and lost control. I don't know what happened next. All I remember is the screams – Parimal's voice screaming in the background, saying *"What are you doing?"*; the kids screaming *"Mamma, Mamma . . ."* and when I opened my eyes I was in the hospital. The kids only had minor bruises luckily, but Parimal . . .' Tears streamed down her cheeks.

'Life has shaken me upside down; I had become used to it being calm. It has been not only difficult but burdensome to handle all this. I swear, if I didn't have children, I would not have dared to live. Friends were there for me, but nobody could share my guilt, my loss. In their own way they tried to console me but they could only be with me for just so long. People here keep so very busy. Everyone has their own set of problems to resolve. Yet I decided not to go back to India. There are lots of difficulties here but at least no one launches into constant tirades against me. I have never understood why people have to be so bitter and abusive when it comes to blaming others. It was traumatic being on the receiving end of this, even on the phone. How can that attitude help me or Parimal? How can people be so ruthless as to think that it was only Parimal who suffered loss? I accept that the accident was my fault, but am I supposed to carry it with me like a cross for the rest of my life? I want to move on, even if I was wrong. I want to come out of it. I want to smile like I did before all this happened, without questioning whether it is OK to laugh, smile, and be happy.'

And then she looked at me with a lot of affection; an affection which was transparent through her tears and sparkled like morning dew does on the delicate petals of a flower. I wanted to be close to her, close enough to wipe away her tears; close enough to share all her hardships and burdens; close enough to restore her faith in life and the beauty which surrounds it. I knew she was reading me through my eyes for she whispered sadly, 'No, Shaashwat, just stay where you are. You will, won't you?'

An unknown bond had bound me to her and I knew that even though she would deny it, she felt bound to me in the same way. I also knew that she tried very hard each moment to break it, destroy it and deny it with the shaky conviction that nothing existed in the first place. But she was also equally convinced that her cultivated bitterness for me was the sweetest thing in her life.

She always talked to me about Parimal, about his likes, dislikes, his ambitions. But I observed that she had started to dress well, even when she was not going to see Parimal. She had become conscious of her appearance and I could see that a smile would light up her face whenever she saw me. Two pairs of eyes would cross the boundaries, and somewhere in the nothingness of this universe they would meet, bloom, play and return to their own little worlds, bringing back what they called happiness.

Whenever she had to take her daughters to see Parimal I would drive them to the hospital in my car and give them a lift back home. She would talk to Parimal in Morse code; her hands would tenderly hold him, his hair, his face, and his cheeks. I would make notes on Parimal's perception, his behaviour, his eye movements and the other sensory inputs that he could provide me with now or in the future. He would listen to me talk about my work with interest, giving helpful tips about how computers could misinterpret the bio-signals and also offering innovative suggestions on how the closed loop corrective systems could be developed for impaired human performance if the bio-signals were to become weak for some reason.

Many a time I felt like a thief who intended to take something which belonged to someone else. But a second thought would tell me that feelings and emotions are not normal 'things'. You can preserve them or discard them, but you cannot steal them because they don't belong to anyone else. They belong to you, they are yours and they are personal.

One day she was particularly happy and elated. She took everyone's picture in the Disability Centre. She took a picture of Parimal, a picture of Parimal and me, a picture of me and her daughters, Sarjna and Anuja. And then she boldly took a picture which was just of me, alone, with no one else. That day, Parimal had told her that whatever had happened had been an accident and that it could have happened to anyone, any time. It was just chance that she had been driving the car that day. He had said that it was not her fault, and that these things were part of life.

I had told her the same thing in different words at different times, but whatever I said never really made an impact on her. It was Parimal whose views gave her a new perspective and it was his thoughts that renewed her energy for life. I felt jealous and hopeless. What was my significance in her life? Nothing. But then why did she look at me with those melancholic eyes and then look away after giving a deep sigh? What kind of relationship was this? Broken yet connected somewhere; connected but broken everywhere. It was transient, ephemeral; it lacked stability, it wasn't meant to last forever. It was delicate – and unlike other fragile objects, no attempts were made to save it.

I knew that if need be, she would deny everything she felt for me including even my presence, my existence – because accepting it was wrong, forbidden. Our relationship didn't have a name, and if it did have a name it was too derogatory a word to be associated with it. And even if she didn't care about any of those things, she would not accept our relationship because she loved Parimal. He was not only her husband but her child too, now. He was the father of her children, her shelter, and she was his refuge.

I was a prisoner in a cage. There were no gates in this cage and I could fly whenever I wanted to. Surprisingly, I didn't want to be free, I didn't want to fly. I was desolate, confused and tired. So when we returned that day from the Disability Centre I didn't speak much. She too was unusually quiet. When we reached home, she asked me if I was coming in and said that I should have dinner before I left.

'No,' I said. 'I need to go.' My voice was choked, a bit heavy. She had black sunglasses over her eyes. And even though I could not see what she was thinking, apparently she could still read the desolation in my eyes.

She opened my car door as if she had the right to and spoke firmly: it was almost a command. 'I want you to come in and have dinner.'

I followed her like an obedient child. I played with her daughters while she cooked, trying not to think of that moment when after dinner I would have to tell her, as I had every other time, 'I guess I should go now.' And then like every other time she would nod her head in affirmation and wave me goodbye.

Her daughters fell asleep after dinner and she talked to me about some tax-related issues. I answered her questions and her doubts, and then I grew weary of them. On a nasty impulse, I suddenly demanded, 'Where did the accident happen?' She was startled by the question but sensing my restlessness, she answered whatever I asked her. 'Where did the accident happen?' I repeated. 'How far along the highway was it?' Then I got up in a fit of rage – or revenge, I don't know what to call it – and lifted her sleeping daughters one by one, carrying them out to my car.

'What are you doing? Where are you taking them?' She was pacing alongside me back and forth, as fast as she could, literally running at times.

When I got in the car, she jumped in and sat beside me. I knew she trusted me, otherwise she wouldn't have allowed me to do what I had done. She had locked the door of the house, she didn't call the police, she was not afraid of me. Now I was no longer angry, but I was driving the car on the same highway where the accident had happened. I could see that she was shivering now, and she kept saying, 'Shaashwat, let's go back. Shaashwat, where are we going? If you want to go for a drive we can go somewhere else.'

I went a little ahead of the site of the accident, a little further on from that spot which bothered her so much, and then I parked the car on the hard shoulder. I got out and asked her to take the driver's seat.

'What?' she exclaimed in disbelief.

'Yes. If you want to go back, you will have to drive this car, or else we can stay here all night. There's a chance that the cops might come, but you are free to tell them whatever you feel like. No matter the consequences, I am *not* driving back.'

She was afraid. She was afraid of the harsh tone of my voice. She started pleading. She was crying. Her voice was low so that it didn't wake up the kids.

'Please, Shaashwat, don't do this to me. Let's go home. I know something is bothering you. What is it? Tell me. This is no way to handle it. Don't force me to drive. Something could happen to all of us.'

'Wouldn't it be awesome if something did happen to us? It would be such a relief.' I don't know who put those words in my mouth. She looked shocked and angry. Angry because I had broken her trust. But I had become deaf; I could not hear the sound of anything breaking that night.

And then she had taken the driver's seat. I got in beside her. She drove and she sobbed silently like a child and like an adult. I tried not to look at her, didn't console her, and didn't apologise.

When we reached home, she went inside with a heavy tread and slumped on the couch. I carried her daughters to their room, and when I got back she stood there with her eyes spitting fire.

'You shouldn't have done what you did today, Shaashwat! Now will you please leave me alone. Henceforth do not . . .' The rest of the sentence was lost in her attempt to stay firm and strong. But I knew what she meant in that sentence which she didn't complete, which she couldn't complete. She had separated me from herself.

I took whatever was necessary for my thesis and research from her house. It was time to go back; back to my studies, to finish my research. The very thought of never seeing her again filled me with agony. I had become used to seeing her every day. I dreaded her absence, and the thought that my absence would not make her sad or affect her in any way was driving me crazy, to the point that I mocked myself.

Right now, as I write this, I am thinking about her. There was a message this morning on my answering machine. It was from her. Her voice was husky and tired as if she had been crying for hours.

'What's wrong? Why haven't you come to see me? It has been five days. Ever since you left I have been visiting Parimal every day. I go by car and I take Sarjna and Anuja with me. Don't tell me that this surprises you. I also took them on that part of the motorway where the accident happened. Sarjna remembered – she recounted the whole accident. She also asked me why you were not coming to see us. You see, we've got used to having you around.'

She went on: 'In the last five days I have realised how easy it is for me to be with Parimal if I miss him. How simple and straightforward it is to go to him, to touch him, to sit by his side and comfort him. But when it comes to you, even your thoughts demand that I justify myself. And despite all the reproach that I have for myself, I still cannot stop thinking about you. It has taken a while for me to accept this, but finally, I have.

'I have received the prints of those photographs I took that day. They came out well. And whether you come to see me or not, I have framed them and placed them on those shelves of ours with everyone else. There's one where both you and Parimal are smiling about something, there's another one in which you are holding Sarjna and Anuja's plaits, and there's one in which it's just you, looking straight at the photographer. I am sorry for whatever I said . . .'

Her message was cut short by my answering machine, which could not record very long messages.

I decided I would call her before I left this place. I would also give her my address and my telephone number. Then she could contact me whenever she needed me. How can something which thrives on love, solicitude and faith, and which nurtures emotional strength and compassion, be wrong? And why does it have to end? Why should it be terminated simply because it is not fragile enough to die on its own?

Now she can drive her car without any fear. She is not scared of the roads. She is slowly getting rid of the guilt which was eating her inside, and she is accepting life the way it comes.

She talks to Parimal in Morse code. She can surely talk to me on the phone.

Things Are Not Always What They Seem

Archana Painuly

Copenhagen, Denmark, 2002

'Ready?'

'Yes, Dad,' I replied, fastening the laces of my skates.

I picked up my hat and gloves and followed Dad who, in all his walking gear, had already reached the front door of our house. It was typical Danish weather – the sky was overcast and a cold wind was blowing. I wanted to be indoors, snuggled up in a warm blanket on our comfortable couch, watching a good movie and eating popcorn. But I had to take this walk every evening after dinner: I had no choice. The walk had become a rite for us ever since Mum's death. An integral part of our daily life, like taking a shower, or brushing one's teeth.

Every evening when Dad returned from work, he cooked dinner for both of us. Sometimes, on my insistence, he ordered pizza from the Pakistani pizzeria in our neighbourhood. Then he would drag me out into the fresh 'nourishing' air for an hour-long evening walk. He had three or four walking routes and each time we followed a different one, me on my skates and Dad walking briskly or sometimes jogging to keep up with me.

It was the beginning of December and the Christmas lights had begun to adorn the city.

'We shall celebrate Christmas this year,' Dad suddenly announced, pacing along at my side.

I looked at him, surprised.

'Yes, we will,' he said firmly.

When Mum was alive Dad did not let me celebrate Christmas. He used to say that it was not our festival. We had Diwali. I used to argue back that no one in Denmark knew when Diwali was, except for a few Indians who had moved here. Five or six Indian families would huddle in someone's house to celebrate: the day would pass without much ado. But when Christmas came, the whole country embraced the festive spirit. There were Christmas decorations, carols on the radio; shops remained open for longer and on all seven days of the week.

My friends would get presents from their parents and grandparents. I wanted to be like them and get gifts from my parents, and I also yearned to decorate a Christmas tree – one of our very own. My longing melted Mum's heart, but not Dad's. Mum would argue with him on my behalf: 'If Neha wants to celebrate Christmas in the Danish style, why don't we let her? Growing up in Europe, this is the only festival that is familiar to her.'

Looking at me, Dad would reply gravely: 'Although we live in a foreign country, and study and work with multi-ethnic people, our cultural heritage is our personal identity. A Christmas tree would not sit well in our house. That belongs to Christians.'

Mum sighed. I felt frustrated. Whenever Dad couldn't think of an answer he would bring our Indian culture into the discussion. But now he himself was suggesting that we could celebrate Christmas.

Wow – what a surprise! How people's opinions change! Actually, after Mum's death Dad had started doing things that pleased me.

*

Mum had died a year ago because of breast cancer. First a growth of cancer cells formed in her left breast and then it secretly invaded nearby tissues and spread to her liver, other organs and bones through the blood and lymphatic systems. By the time she discovered the lump in her breast and had a mammogram, it was too late. She had stage four breast cancer. The doctors treated her with a combination of surgery, chemotherapy and radiotherapy, but in vain. She was diagnosed in the month of March and in November she passed away. People said that she was fortunate as she did not suffer much. Her days of being hale and healthy were now a distant memory. All I remembered was her sickness and how, after a few weeks of treatment, she had looked like a nightmare – hairless, exhausted, depressed.

Mum's body lay in the morgue for a week, as Dad waited for our relatives to arrive: they were coming from India for the funeral. Mum's brother, his wife, and Dad's nephew came from India while Bua, Dad's older sister, lived in Copenhagen. She was the one who had initially sponsored Dad's stay in Denmark, and had later helped him to settle down here.

After Mum's death, Bua moved in with us for a while. She slept next to me, not letting me out of her sight, except when I needed to go to the bathroom or toilet. On the appointed day of the funeral I travelled to Bispierge Crematorium in a car with Bua and my maternal uncle's wife. Dad, his nephew and Mamaji – Mum's brother – had left even before I got up, to make the necessary arrangements. In the short car journey from my home to the funeral I learned that Indians living in Copenhagen cremated their dead in Bispierge Crematorium.

When we arrived, a crowd had already assembled there, waiting to enter the church, where a brief funeral service was due to take place. As soon as they saw me, there was a sudden hush and many eyes welled up with tears.

'They are saying that we must wait outside,' someone in the gathering informed us.

I waited there with everyone, trying hard to ignore the penetrating looks of those around me. Then, after a while, Mamaji emerged from the church and motioned for the immediate family to come inside. Accompanied by Bua and Mamaji, I entered the Bispierge Crematorium Church. Mum was lying in a casket in the centre. She was dressed in a new red sari and had make-up on her face. Who had done all this for her, I did not know. She had started turning blue but was looking neat and at peace. I cried seeing her lying still, like a log in the casket. Bua and Mamaji enveloped me in their gentle embrace.

Shortly afterwards, the other men and women were also permitted to enter the church. It was filled to capacity. I was the only child there – eleven years old. Every eye was upon me.

Most of the people were from our Indian community, but there were some white people also. They were our neighbours and Mum's colleagues at work.

Several people gave eulogies, praised Mum, and mentioned their noteworthy experiences with her. I learned several things about Mum that day: that she was a kind, open and warm person. She was a generous host. She always offered a wonderful welcome and hospitality to the people who visited us, and she had been very helpful to newly-arrived Indians settling down in Denmark.

Thereafter the hall echoed with the chanting of Hindu Vedic hymns: *Gayatri Mantra: Om Bhurva Bhuv Suvah* . . . People came forward to pay their last tributes to Mum. And then four men – Dad, my cousin, my maternal uncle and Bua's husband – lifted the casket and marched towards the fellowship building for the cremation. I followed them, but was held back by Bua. She hissed, 'Girls don't go in there.'

I suddenly realised that Mum had been taken away from my sight forever. That I would never, ever see her again – not alive, not dead. I cried fiercely at the cruelty of my fate. Many women leaped towards me, hugged me and consoled me, saying that I might have lost one mother but there were several mothers for me in the world. They all were mums to me.

*

No matter how difficult the days are, they slip by. Time does not stop. Our relatives who had come from India returned there, and Bua also went back to her own home. Dad and I, two lonely souls, were left in the house. We slept in the same room, next to each other, for a few days. He started taking special care of me and was trying his hardest to become my mother, my protector and my friend.

One evening after dinner he called me: 'Neha . . .' Then he paused.

'What?' I asked, looking at him.

He continued hesitantly, 'Er . . . I'm not sure how much you know about puberty. When a girl turns twelve or thirteen she starts getting her period. Do you know about that?'

'Yes, I do know all about it. My science teacher explained everything about puberty to us at school. Besides, Mum had told me too.'

'Mum had told you?' he wondered, and gave a slightly sad smile.

'Yes, the day she got her biopsy results and it was confirmed that she had a malignant tumour.'

'Oh!' Dad sighed.

Mum's biggest worry had been that she was dying when I was on the verge of puberty. Holding my hands, she had told me vehemently, 'Neha, I might not be here to see you become a woman, but I'll tell you all about it.' Then she explained to me in layman's language the phases and processes involved in a girl's coming of age. She then telephoned all her friends and acquaintances one by one, and giving gruesome details of her critical illness begged them to take care of me after her death.

Neither Dad nor I liked Mum broadcasting her illness to the world, but we noticed that it gave her some relief. So we did not stop her. And at her funeral, people in our

Indian community said that this was the biggest funeral gathering they had ever seen.

*

'Who should we invite to the Christmas party?' Dad asked me now, breaking into my reverie and filling the silence that had settled between us.

Still dazed, I could not think of a reply. He suggested the families with whom we were friendly and who had children, particularly girls of my age.

'Today is the fifth of December, right?' I said, and counted. 'There are nineteen days left before Christmas.' This was the first time that we had talked about a celebration since Mum's death. During the entire walk we talked pleasantly about the planning for the Christmas party. 'Yay!' Thrilled, in my excitement I skated faster and faster. Dad ran after me. Noticing that he was becoming breathless, I slowed down.

Ten days later, on a sunny Saturday morning, Dad and I went to the town square, where a number of Christmas trees of all sizes were displayed for sale. We chose a medium-sized, lush green tree. On the way home we stopped at the Føtex supermarket to buy decorations.

Ribbons, paper chains, tinsel, baubles, garlands – Dad did not stop me from picking up whatever I wanted from the shelves. Then, by chance, we bumped into Manju-auntie, who had also come there to shop. Manju-auntie was one of a few single Indian females among our acquaintances in Copenhagen who had suddenly developed an interest in us after Mum's death. She talked to me regularly on the phone, enquired about my health, how school was going, and at the end she would always ask me to convey her regards to Dad.

She beamed at us. 'Christmas shopping!' she said, looking inquisitively at our baskets. A series of questions followed. 'How are you guys doing? How are things? The weather is so bad, isn't it?' In between, she kept inspecting our hairstyles, outfits and shoes. I noticed Dad talking to her jovially, in between flashing her a shy smile and blushing hotly. At times I felt sorry for him. 'My poor pop!' I whispered inwardly.

When he had finished talking with Manju-auntie, he walked towards a section where the different hair dyes were kept. I followed him.

'Which colour would suit me, Neha?' he asked, seeking my advice.

I scanned his hair. At forty-one, three-quarters of his hair had turned grey. He bought the hair dye I selected.

On reaching home we placed the tree in our living room, positioned so that it could be seen from the hallway and from the front door. Then we decorated it enthusiastically, in our best artistic manner.

Dad was looking quite happy. He kept humming a song from a Bollywood movie. When we had finished with the decorations, he took out the dye and read the instructions. They were in Danish, and my Danish was better than his, so I helped him to mix the different chemicals in the right proportions in a glass bowl. Then I volunteered to apply the dye to his hair.

Wrapping Mum's old duppatta around his shoulders, he sat on a low stool before me.

'Dad,' I said, while applying the dye to his hair.

'Yes, sweetie?'

'Shall I tell you one thing . . . I think Manju-auntie has a crush on you. She was staring at you very fondly in the supermarket.'

'Really!' he exclaimed, and laughed uproariously.

Then, checking his laugh, he said with a tinge of pride, 'Many white ladies at my work also take an interest in me. Now that I'm single, they probably think I might be available.' He grinned and told me in a friendly manner about some divorcees who also seemed interested in him. I listened intently. For the first time in my life I realised that Dad needed me more than I needed him.

*

Christmas Eve turned into a grand celebration in our home. Dad invited five Indian families, including Bua and her husband. Bua came in the morning to cook food for the guests, while I took charge of the activities: I organised Christmas games, made people sing Christmas carols, dance around the tree and exchange gifts.

With its lights switched on, our dazzling Christmas tree uplifted everyone's spirits. It was a cosy evening. Our guests enjoyed chatting with each other and relished the delicious food prepared by Bua. They realised that celebrating any festival is good for the soul. I even heard them saying to Dad that he should hold a Christmas celebration at our home every year, as we had a relatively spacious house and our living room was particularly large.

The party lasted until past midnight. Bua stayed back as there was still a lot of clearing up to do. When the guests had departed, she and Dad, pleasantly tired from the party, sat together in a relaxed way around the tree and discussed the evening, the people who had come, and the happiness and enjoyment we had shared with them.

Suddenly Bua said to Papa, 'Sunil, have you thought about your future? You are only forty-one, and these days that is considered nothing for a man.'

Dad immediately shot a glance at me. I was sitting on the carpet, counting the gifts that I had received. Bua also looked at me. She said, 'Neha is growing up. She needs a female companion at home. Do you have anyone in mind?'

I looked at Dad. He shook his head – no. But what about Manju-auntie? I liked her, and Dad also seemed to like her, so why was he not admitting that?

'Dad, you like Manju-auntie, don't you?' I could not stop myself from intervening.

'No,' Dad said shyly, like a boy.

'Yes, you do,' I argued.

Dad gave me a disapproving look.

Bua looked at me, and then at Dad. 'Who?' she asked, curious.

Dad explained. 'She is talking about Malhotra's wife – Malhotra, who died in that car crash.'

'Oh . . . Manju Jain!' Bua exclaimed reproachfully. 'She is a widow with three kids. Who will take care of them? She will be a liability.'

Then Bua continued, looking at me, 'Why marry a widow with three kids when we can find a "single girl" for your dad?' She then suggested a woman who was a distant relative to her by marriage. Her name was Sunita. She was thirty-eight, divorced but childless, and was teaching economics at a college in New Delhi. Bua said she would be a perfect match for Dad.

Dad seemed to give his silent acceptance. I suddenly felt that people were forgetting about my mother.

That night, while I tried to sleep, I felt uneasy, with many thoughts running through my mind – of the Christmas party, the lovely presents I'd received, and Bua's suggesting a woman to Dad.

*

'Neha, where are you? Are you lost? You are not paying attention!'

Mrs Olsen was my science teacher – and also my class teacher. My parents had put me in an international school attended by students of many countries. They did not send me to a Danish school, in case I should feel like an outsider. Also, when they had been students themselves studying in Danish schools, they felt as if they had lost their cultural identity. Mrs Olsen herself was an African, married to a Dane.

'Can a woman have a baby at thirty-eight?' I asked her.

The whole class burst into loud laughter. And then I realised that I had said my thoughts aloud.

All my schoolteachers, knowing that I'd recently lost my mother, were sympathetic towards me.

Mrs Olsen made the students be quiet, and then asked, without sounding cross, 'Why are you asking such a question, when we are studying a totally different topic?'

Blushing furiously now, I just shrugged. 'Oh! Sorry. Never mind . . .'

She gave me a kindly smile and carried on with her lesson.

*

Three months later, while I was at school, I got my first period. I knew all about it, but it still scared me. I told my friends; they in turn informed Mrs Olsen. She wanted to call Dad, but Dad was not in Copenhagen. He had gone to India to meet the prospective wife that Bua had mentioned to him.

'Are you home alone?' Mrs Olsen asked, surprised.

'No, I've an aunt here. I've been staying with her until my dad returns from India.'

Mrs Olsen took Bua's telephone number from me and informed her about my period.

It was springtime; the days had become bright and slightly warm. Bua came to school to pick me up. She looked at me with new eyes, and gave me an affectionate hug. Taking my heavy school-bag from my hand, she placed it on the back seat of the car then informed me that we were going on an outing.

She drove me to H&M, a clothes shop, and asked me to choose a dress for myself. I chose a pretty, girlish dress. Then she drove me to McDonald's.

I ordered a milkshake, chicken nuggets and an apple pie. Bua did not let me buy Coke. She said in a stern voice: 'Healthy eating is very important for adolescent girls, to support the physical growth of the body and to prevent future health problems. Teenagers need additional calories, proteins, iron and calcium.'

Anyway, I was hungry, and I gobbled down the nuggets and pie. Bua watched me eat. 'Some families in India celebrate extravagantly when their daughters get their first period,' she said, 'but we are in a foreign country – we can't keep up with all our cultures and customs.'

She then briefed me on how Dad was getting on with the girl in India. He was seeing her every day. They were visiting places together. He liked her and seemed willing to marry her. I would have a mother now at home.

'I had only one mother, and she has died,' I snapped. 'No other woman can ever take her place in my life. A mother might have several children but a child can have only one mother.'

'No one is denying your mother's importance, but now she is with the Lord, and your dad has to move on with his life. He has suffered and grieved a lot, and now he deserves some happiness,' Bua said, agitated, and after a pause she warned me, 'You shouldn't create any more problems for him.'

I stopped eating. Bua watched me mutely for a moment, and then asked, 'Why aren't you eating?'

I pushed the plate away, my eyes filling with tears. A moment later I began to cry uncontrollably. Bua came rushing round the table and embraced me.

'Oh Neha,' she said, 'I did not bring you here to make you cry. Calm down, darling. Calm down. I know what you are going through. It's very difficult to experience the loss of a parent in adolescence. I'm your mother. I'll always be there for you . . .'

Nestling my head on Bua's breast, I cried for a long time. Bua kept patting me. I missed Mum a lot that day.

*

When Dad returned from India, he was filled with a new vigour and excitement. He started dressing smartly and acted about ten years younger. By contrast, I became all the more subdued. I had begun to think that I was going to lose him too. He had surrendered himself to a woman whom I did not know. After Mum's death I had thought that Dad's and my loss was the same, but now I realised that Dad's loss was restorable – but mine wasn't.

I often wore my mother's scarf or her cardigan to remind Dad of her, but it did not help. Either he was too obsessed with that new woman to notice, or he simply ignored me.

For six months Dad communicated with his fiancée through phone calls, emails and cards, and then he went to India to marry her. I joined him. And so the first wedding I ever attended was my dad's.

Whenever I visited India I did not feel myself to be Indian, and back in Copenhagen I never felt myself a Dane. Technically I was Danish and ethnically I was Indian, but in fact I was neither. However, mixing with my cousins and their friends, I discovered that young people in India at the age of fourteen or fifteen dated and smoked and did almost everything that children did in Denmark. The one major difference was that everything was done behind their parents' backs. It was a big surprise to me, because my parents had given me a different picture of India.

They were hypocritical, I thought crossly.

I also came to realise that a wedding is a big event in India and takes a lot of organisation. Regardless, Dad got married very splendidly. He wore a sherwani and an elaborate turban around his head. Accompanied by a band and a big procession, he left for the wedding venue riding a decorated horse.

But as we entered the wedding venue, every eye was upon me instead of Dad. I was just over thirteen. I had grown very tall and was quite developed already. There were many ceremonies. Everyone was in a happy frame of mind. Sitting beside his new bride in the ornate wedding canopy, Dad was trying to be himself.

Bua suddenly grabbed my hand and dragged me towards the canopy in order to introduce me to the bride. The bride looked at me, trying to muster up a smile. I wanted to say 'Hello' to her, but the word would not come. For several minutes our eyes remained locked, but there was restraint in our looks.

She is my stepmother. The thought stirred within me. I fervently believed that she was thinking the same about me – that I was her stepdaughter. Then a couple of guests climbed up to the canopy to congratulate the couple, and I silently clambered down.

The marriage rites were solemnised one by one . . . and Dad was remarried. He had a wife again. But did I have a mother?

*

A few days after Dad's wedding, we flew back to Copenhagen. Sunita, my stepmother, could not join us immediately. She needed to receive a residence permit from the Danish government. However, she and her family came to the airport to see us off. She was in tears while she said goodbye to Dad. I saw him squeezing her hand and reassuring her that she would join him in Denmark as soon as it became possible.

After returning to Copenhagen, I resumed my daily routine as if going to India and attending Dad's wedding there had just been a dream. Sunita's arrival in Denmark was not in Dad's hands. The immigration service was processing her visa application in their usual bureaucratic way. He could not do anything except wait.

I had started praying unwittingly in my heart that the Danish Embassy would not grant her a visa, so that she could never come to Copenhagen. That was the foolish wish of a teenage girl. Sunita met all the requirements that the new Danish law had stipulated for the spouses of immigrants entering Denmark at the time, and three months after the wedding, she was granted the visa. I was disappointed and agitated.

'Why did the Danish Embassy give her a visa?' I grumbled.

But incidentally, her arrival in Denmark coincided with my school's ski-trip. I was relieved. We went to Arosa in Switzerland. I had lots of fun for ten days with my school friends, and completely forgot about her. We skied on the snow-laden mountains. I was very close to one of my classmates, called Jing. Originally Jing was from China, but like me she had been born and brought up in Denmark. I told her about my feelings towards my stepmother. She consoled me, saying that not all stepmothers were bad, and that I should be glad for my dad that he had someone in his life.

Whenever I talked to Dad on the phone from Arosa, I did not enquire about Sunita and whether she had arrived in Denmark or not. He too made no mention of her.

After the ten-day ski-trip I boarded the bus with the other students to return to Copenhagen. By now we had started feeling homesick and wanted to go home. But I was a bit anxious at the prospect of seeing Sunita. Throughout the bus journey, with my fingers crossed, I prayed that she had not come from India. But to my utter disappointment, as I alighted from the bus in front of my school she was standing there with Dad and the other parents. She was slim and tall. She did not look thirty-nine, she looked much younger. Clad in a sari and wearing a bindi on her forehead, she stood out in the crowd.

'Neha!' Dad yelled as soon as he saw me.

'Dad, I'm back!' I hugged Dad and ignored Sunita completely.

As Dad opened the car doors, I jumped into the seat beside him. Sunita silently sat in the rear seat.

When we reached home, Sunita took out the keys from her jacket pocket and opened the door of our house, which my parents had bought together. As I entered the house it looked different to me. She had changed everything, and had given it a completely new look. It was neat, more organised, but strange. As she was a teacher it seemed more academic – jute baskets filled with colourful magazines, racks with collections of books. I roamed around the house. Dad kept following me, reading my facial expressions. I slowly entered his bedroom.

The phrase *Dear Mum & Dad, I love you very much – Neha* still hung on the wall above the bed. I had written it when I was in second grade and had just begun to write sentences. I sighed, for she had not removed it. But alas, she had changed their bedroom. Dad did not sleep with her in the same room he used to sleep in with Mum. They had made the guest room their bedroom.

That night, after Dad and his second wife had gone to sleep, I went into that room – the one that used to be my mother and father's bedroom – and lay down and wept on the bed. I felt completely alone in the world. I felt as though I had been robbed of everything.

*

'Didi, Didi!' Nikhil's voice sounds through the PC. 'Didi, tell Mum she should let me go on the ski-trip with my school.' It's a Sunday ritual to talk to Nikhil and Aditya – my two half-brothers – on Skype. Every Sunday, at 11 a.m. New York time and 5 p.m. in Denmark, I'll get to my computer, put the headset on and fix the video camera. After a while Nikhil's voice echoes in my ears.

First I'll talk to Nikhil, then to Aditya, and then to her, my stepmother. It feels nice chatting to them. Meyung, my husband, listens to me talking. Sometimes he also joins in, when they ask, 'Didi, how's Jiju? Get him on the line.' Then I'll hand over the headset to Meyung.

We live life in different patterns. No pattern of our life is permanent. We carry only memories from our past life and propel ourselves into the future. Now I am twenty-nine. From a girl I have become a woman. I dated a few guys, until I met Meyung. He is sober and gorgeous; he has all the qualities that a woman adores in a man.

Currently I am living in New York City with Meyung, who is originally from South Korea. He is a second-generation immigrant in the USA, as I am in Denmark. I work in New York in the finance department of the United Nations Development Programme, and Meyung is an IT executive in Goldman Sachs. I met Meyung on a ferry-boat tour to the Statue of Liberty about three years ago, and after one year of seeing each other we got married.

The years between age thirteen and twenty-nine are just a blur. The time passed quickly. I did not know then that when my stepmother came to Denmark from India to live with us, she was already three months' pregnant. Nikhil did not even stay the full nine months in his mother's womb. He came out a month before the due date. I remember, Dad took me to the hospital to see him the day he was born. It was Rakhi Day. Dad had bought a glittering rakhi for me from an Indian store to tie on his hand. I was amused by all these new developments and new relations. Nikhil was wrapped in a towel. I tied the rakhi on his new soft and tiny hand. He yawned. We all laughed. Papa said that this was his acknowledgement of my rakhi. My stepmother let me hold him.

The following year, Aditya was born. Then suddenly Dad realised that he had to guide me in my studies to help me into a good, rewarding career. With a growing family he had perhaps become financially insecure. His sons were still in diapers and on feeding bottles. They would take years to grow up. I had turned fifteen and was his best hope. So he turned his attention away from his sons for a while and focused it on me.

'Neha,' he would say to me, 'we are immigrants from a third-world nation here. For us, there is only one way to accomplish something – through hard work. Choose the slower streams, where the flow is less and the jobs are more. Choosing faster streams means you have to compete with white Danes, where it might be harder to shine.'

I remember Dad teaching me up to midnight, helping me in my maths assignments and exploring universities for me. When I turned eighteen, my birthday was celebrated lavishly. I had become *voksen*, an adult. Over the years, Sunita, whom I had inadvertently begun to call Mummy, became quite friendly with me. She even told me stories about her ex-husband, and about how cruel he was.

'It's good that you left him and married my dad,' I said to her.

She smiled, and hugged me.

*

And then one day Dad and my stepmother sent me off to the London School of Economics. Nikhil, Aditya, and my parents all came to the airport to see me off. Parting from them was indeed painful. I sobbed, Dad sobbed, we all sobbed. But I was glad that at least Dad was not alone. He had his family with him.

From London, I moved to Geneva, and then to New York, where I have been living for the last four years. Sadly, Dad passed away last year. He too died of a malign cancer – a liver cancer which started in the right lobe of his liver and spread. But he was able to see me getting married. His last words to me – 'Neha, look after your brothers' – are on my mind constantly.

My two half-brothers are the closest blood relations I have in this world now. As I recall that teenage girl sobbing on her dead mother's bed nearly sixteen years ago I realise that instead of losing everything I gained a new family. Things aren't always what they seem. I was a raging mass of hormones at that time, too young to understand things in their proper perspective. Dad's second marriage was certainly to my advantage. Nikhil is now fifteen and Aditya is almost fourteen years old. They call me every week, tell me what is going on in their lives. After a long and interesting Skype conversation with them, 'Didi, Didi' echoes in my ears for a long time.

My stepmother invites me every year to Copenhagen. She says that married daughters need proper invitations from their parents to visit them. I visit them twice a year, sometimes alone and sometimes with Meyung. During every visit my stepmother loads me up with home-made traditional Indian sweets and savouries.

Last summer I invited them to visit us. We were all very depressed about Dad's death and needed a change. They were here with me for about two weeks. We laughed, we cried. We had a wonderful time, visiting New York, Boston, Washington and the Niagara Falls. My stepmother felt very grateful.

Lately, she has been insisting that I should plan for a baby now, and that for the birth I should be in Copenhagen, with her, under her tender care.

Unsaid

Aruna Sabharwal

Birmingham, UK, 2009

It was Friday, almost midday. He should have been here. Nurse Daisy kept on looking at the clock. It carried on ticking, but there was no sign of him – and yet he usually got here early. *I hope he's not having a fit,* she thought to herself. The other day, his social worker had mentioned that ever since he had started coming to her clinic, he couldn't wait to come back here. Nowadays, he sang and danced; he listened to the instructions and followed them. He had been completely transformed.

He came to the surgery every Friday to see the doctor and Nurse Daisy alternately for a general medical check-up. Whether he had an appointment with her or not, he made sure that she saw him. He would gently knock at her door, and without waiting for an answer, would quietly pop his Mongolian face round, with his two small Chinese eyes and a nose like a ping pong ball, giving her the thumbs-up and saying, 'OK, miss?' with a big smile before leaving. Just seeing her made his eyes light up. He spread the happiness of his beautiful smile throughout the surgery.

Daisy could not stop thinking about his innocent face and his carefree laughter, which sounded as if life's mischief had never touched him. Ever since she had completed her State Registered Nurse training in Chennai, South India, it had been her dream to work with children and young people who needed special education. Such persons were usually kept hidden in dark corners across India. Suddenly, she looked at her watch and saw that it was well past twelve o'clock now. She was getting worried.

After finishing her to-do list she went to reception and asked: 'Liz, have you seen George today?'

'He's not on the appointment register today,' the other woman replied.

'But it's Friday – he should have been here by now.'

'Miss Daisy, last week George never even came in – he left the surgery without seeing the doctor. Around eleven thirty, I heard a lot of noise. When I went outside, there was George, sitting on the floor throwing a tantrum just like a spoilt brat, and refusing to come in. He kept saying, "I do not want to go in . . . I do not want to go in!" His social worker Miss Williams tried to persuade him, but he would not budge an inch. He just carried on saying, "I do not want to go in . . . I don't like it here".'

'But don't you want to see your friend Miss Daisy?' Mrs Williams had asked.

'No – she is not my friend,' he had argued, sounding frustrated.

'But you like her,' the woman went on, plainly baffled.

'No, not now . . . I don't like her any more,' he answered and started to cry.

'Please, George, let's go in – she is waiting for you.'

'I don't care! I hate her now and I don't like this place any more.'

He had started pushing everyone; at that moment it felt as though a twelve-year-old boy was trapped in the body of a twenty-five-year-old man who was now starting to rebel.

*

George was tall and well-built. He was always ready to help anyone, anywhere and at any time. He was polite and lovable. No matter how much pain he was in, he never failed to spread happiness to others. But even though he had a wonderful personality, somehow he had been cheated. God had been unfair to him, had made him differently from other children. He was born with Down's syndrome and nowadays lived in an Adult Training Centre (ATC), where doctors and staff worked together to improve the lives of their disabled youngsters.

George had come to the surgery for the first time with his social worker. While they were sitting in the waiting room, Miss Williams read the newspaper and George rocked back and forth on his chair, his hands clenched between his thighs.

'George Thomas,' Nurse Daisy called.

'Yes, miss.' He hesitantly raised his hand as a primary schoolchild might, and then very quickly put his hand back between his thighs.

'Good morning, George,' Miss Daisy greeted him.

Still sitting all hunched up, he reluctantly nodded his head and mumbled, 'Good morning, miss.'

'Come in, George, please sit down,' she said, pointing to the chair. He quickly sat down and made himself as small as possible, casting his eyes downwards.

'George, if you are going to be so shy, how can we be friends?' she asked, smiling.

'Doctor, will you be my friend?' he whispered.

'Yes . . . why not?' She had already studied his medical notes. 'George, please pull up your sleeve. Let me check your blood pressure.'

'OK, miss.' He nodded his head.

Miss Daisy checked his blood pressure, then told him, 'George, you can go now, but before you leave make sure that you make another appointment at the reception desk.'

He was still sitting with his head cast down as they left. He walked slowly, with his eyes focused on the floor, and shyly said, 'Bye, miss.'

Over the next few weeks, George started to open up, like a book. He became friendlier and more familiar with the routine. One day he came in all dressed up.

'You're looking very smart today, George.'

'Thank you, miss,' he said with a smile.

'Come in, let us check your weight.'

The minute he got onto the scales, he started reading the numbers and queried: 'Miss, why are there two different numbers?'

'One is for kilograms and the other is for pounds.'

'Pounds? Money pounds?' he asked innocently.

'No. These pounds are measurement of weight.'

He looked puzzled. It was time for him to go. Daisy told Miss Williams, 'George has become quite independent. From now on, there is no need for you to accompany him.'

'As you wish, Miss Daisy. I will wait outside.'

Since then, George had been coming on his own to see Miss Daisy for check-ups. A fortnight later, there was a gentle knock on the door.

'Come in, George – take a seat.'

While Miss Daisy was checking his blood pressure he became curious, and then amazed at how the pressure went up and down. When she had finished, he asked, 'Miss, can I hold this?'

'Why not. But make sure you don't touch any buttons.'

Since then, George had started to bring things he had made at the ATC to show her. One day he brought a book, and said, 'Miss, I can read this.'

'Very good – you are becoming very clever.' The second she had finished her sentence, he started reading all the posters stuck to the wall. He was overjoyed to hear her praise; who wouldn't be?

'Miss Daisy, one day I will become a doctor like you, you'll see.'

'That would make me very happy. Then I can come to *you* for my check-ups.'

'Yes, miss,' he smiled.

'OK. See you next week, George.'

As usual he put his thumbs up and said, 'Bye, miss.'

After he left, she started thinking. He was now able to express his feelings, desires and emotions. His life was beginning to get back on track.

When she arrived home after finishing at the clinic, Peter, her fiancé, said, 'You are looking happy today.'

'Well, do you know that today George was talking about becoming a doctor. He is beginning to have goals. Seeing him happy and confident gives me a great sense of achievement, great satisfaction.'

'Please Daisy, not now. Let's talk about us. We are getting married in three months' time and there is still so much to be done.'

The whole weekend, Peter and Daisy busied themselves decorating their flat. Winter was approaching. Monday was a walk-in day at the surgery, when no appointment was needed, and patients could come in for their flu jab. The surgery was packed. Suddenly there was a gentle knock on the door.

'Come in, George,' Daisy called out, recognising that knock.

As soon as he entered the room, he put his right hand forward, shook hands and said, 'Good morning, miss.' His left hand remained in his pocket, as if glued to his side. After twice trying to take blood from his right hand with no success, she spoke to him.

'George, may I have your left hand, please?'

But instead of putting out his left hand, he clutched his arm even more tightly to his body.

'Please, George.' After a lot of persuasion he reluctantly stretched out his hand.

'George, relax – open your fist. I need a vein.' He finally opened his fist, and out fell a small bunch of wild daisies. With his head still down and his eyes focused on the floor, he muttered, 'This is for you, miss.'

'Thank you, George, they are beautiful. Where did you get them from so early in the morning?'

'From the ATC's garden, miss.'

George's gesture touched her heart even more today. He left the surgery spreading his smile like the daisies. After surgery she met Peter at the flat to talk about guest seating arrangements.

'Hi Peter, sorry I'm a bit late – the traffic was bad.'

'Daisy, what is it? You're smiling – has something made you happy?'

'Yes, it has – you're right, Peter. You see, today I got a beautiful bunch of flowers from my admirer.'

'Oh . . . and who is this rival, trying to enter my territory?'

'Here they are.' She showed him the little posy of daisies.

Peter started to laugh and made fun of the flowers, saying, 'Is this what you call a beautiful bunch of flowers?'

'Peter! Please don't laugh at George; it is the thought that counts. Just think what lengths he must have gone to to pick these flowers early in the morning.'

'OK, OK, don't get all touchy and emotional – he is just another patient. Come on, let's get going.'

Over the weekend they worked in the flat until it was finished; only the furniture was still to be delivered.

George was making rapid progress. On his arrival the following Friday Miss Daisy said, 'Today we will check your full report on the computer.' While she was struggling on the computer, George watched her curiously.

'Miss, I know how to do that,' he said.

She hesitated, due to issues of confidentiality, and said, 'Let me try once more.' But she still couldn't make it work. Computers had always been her weak point. 'All right,' she sighed. 'You have a go, George.'

To her surprise, the minute he touched the computer, it started to work.

Triumphantly, George began to clap and kept saying, 'I did it . . . I did it!' He was always trying to impress her with little gestures, Nurse Daisy had noticed. His sense of achievement was reflected through his whole body. It was as though he had conquered Everest.

*

Time passed, and now there were only a few weeks left until the wedding. The wedding dress was not quite ready, there was confusion over the cake order and even the church service was not yet confirmed. What's more, the flowers still had to be ordered. And to top it all, Nurse Daisy still had a full-time job to do.

That Friday was the last time she was due to see George before her wedding leave. It was past eleven and there was no sign of him. She went to reception to collect him and asked at the desk, 'Liz, have you seen George?'

'He was here just a few minutes ago, as usual.'

'Maybe he has gone to the toilet.'

'Daisy, do you know that George is in an extra-happy mood today. He has been humming since he arrived. When I asked him why, he told me excitedly that he would only tell Miss Daisy.'

'OK, well, when he appears, send him to my room.' But as she started to move away, she could hear him coming, recognised the rhythm of his heavy footsteps.

'Hello,' she greeted him. 'I heard that you were very happy today. Do you want to share the good news with me?'

George became very shy.

'Have you won the lottery?' she beamed.

'No, Miss Daisy. Playing the lottery is gambling, and that is not good.'

'Then what is it, George?'

'Miss Daisy, do you know what Miss Williams told the Authority? That I am a very good boy now. She said that I have become more confident and independent. They say that I can live alone now and can look after myself. I am going to get a flat and they will take me out shopping. They will show me how to cook, clean and look after myself. I can sleep when I like now and I can eat what and how much I like. I will be able to watch television whenever I like too.' He paused for a moment and then added shyly, 'Miss, if I cook for you, will you come for dinner?'

'Yes, of course. What will you cook for me?'

'Beans on toast.' He kept playing with his fingers, still having something on his mind. 'Miss, can I say something?'

'Go right ahead,' Miss Daisy encouraged.

'Miss, you are very nice,' he said nervously, and then fell silent.

'Thank you. Why did you say that, George?' she asked.

After a long pause, still playing with his fingers, he said, 'Miss, you treat me like a man.' His voice was full of emotion. He quickly left the room.

The moment she saw this, Miss Daisy was put on the alert. She questioned herself. What did he mean? What was he thinking? Had she been getting his hopes up? She decided to transfer him to another colleague as soon as she returned from her leave.

*

At the Adult Training Centre, George was only getting nominal pay for his work, and had limited freedom to go out. But he was excited, and many joyful feelings were churning in his heart. For him, Miss Daisy was a ray of sunshine; she brought a smile to his face and set his heart and soul a-flutter. He started dreaming. He became very calm and collected; he even stopped having fits.

It was Friday the next day. George was over the moon. After four weeks apart, he was going to see Miss Daisy. He went shopping, picked up his suit from the dry cleaners, bought a new shirt and a matching tie and a beautiful bunch of flowers. He put everything in his old suitcase as he wanted to hide it all from everyone at the ATC.

The next day he got up early, had a bath, put on his suit, and his new shirt and tie. To make sure that he did not forget anything, he checked his list three times, ticking off every item which he had to take with him. A small red box, a bunch of flowers and a welcoming card.

On the dot of eleven o'clock, he tapped out the usual gentle knock on her door.

'Come in, George! It's lovely to see you,' Nurse Daisy said sincerely.

'Me . . . too. Nice to see you too,' he stuttered.

'Wow, George, you look very smart – very dashing indeed. Dark suit, blue shirt and matching tie . . . very nice. Are you going on a date? Who's the lucky girl?'

He kept quiet. The bunch of flowers was hidden behind his back.

'Sit down, George, let's check your blood pressure and take some blood. Both tests are due now.'

After checking his blood pressure she used her left hand to look for a vein to take his blood. George spotted the wedding ring on her finger. He got very confused.

He couldn't understand what was happening. It didn't make sense. He checked the little red box in his pocket.

As she got up to wash her hands, George saw a wedding picture with Daisy in it. He looked at the picture closely again and again, and thought to himself, *Is that me? No, no – it's not me.* He was puzzled; a knot of emotion was stuck in his throat.

'George, you are very quiet today,' she said. As she turned around, all she saw was her wedding photo tipped over on her desk, a crushed bouquet of flowers and a Welcome Home card. A rolled-gold ring poking out of a small, half-open red box was lying on the floor.

George himself had vanished.

The Encounter

Chaand Chazelle

Brentford, UK, 2012

'It seems that my PA failed to fill out some details in the form yesterday,' said Sheena Raampal, marching into the Headmaster's room unannounced. 'I thought I should rectify the mistake in person – it will save you a lot of to-ing and fro-ing.' She put the form on his desk, right under his nose, and examined the expression on his face.

Mr Srivastav stood up, looking very confused. He stuttered incoherently: 'I-I-I just wanted to . . .'

'Yes? You wanted?' Not waiting for him to offer her a seat, she sank into a comfortable armchair in the corner of the big room. Her presence had completely unnerved him. She asked again: 'Which column is left unfilled, Mr Srivastav?'

He picked up the glass of water lying on his desk and, with shaking hands, took a tiny sip.

'Do sit down, Headmaster. After all, it's your own office.' She smiled as she pointed to his seat.

'Would you care for some cold . . . or some . . .' He could barely get the words out; his throat had gone dry. He took another sip of water then repeated: 'Can I get you some tea or . . .'

Sheena cut him short, reminding him that he was still on his feet. 'Please do sit down. It'll be much easier to converse, won't it?' she said smoothly.

He was still trying to gather his thoughts, and his expression betrayed a sense of unease; the awareness that his position and status could be in jeopardy if he made a wrong move. He sat down, but remained perched on the very edge of his seat, trying to avoid her gaze.

'So, what seems to be the problem with the form?' she demanded.

He opened the right-hand drawer of his table, fished a fresh form out and put his finger in the middle, where it said: *Father's name.*

'This bit is not quite . . .' His voice sounded far away, as though he was deep in the belly of a cave.

'Haven't you noticed? It is duly filled in, Headmaster.'

'But . . .'

'But what?'

'This is not . . .'

'Go on, finish your sentence, please.'

'That is not his father's name.'

'Good, so no one here needs reading lessons, do they?'

'But this is *your* name, madam. It should be . . .'

'. . . his father's name? Is that all? Well, I am both mother and father to my child. Is that OK with you, Mr Srivastav? Have I made things clear?'

'But the law and the school rules require . . .'

'First of all, these forms.' She stood up and came over, picked up the form and put it back on the desk with contempt. 'I, as a mother, raise my son and pay for his upkeep. I'm his mother and his father, I fulfil both those roles. Why isn't there an entry for *Mother's name* on these forms, may I ask? As for the rules! Rules, Mr Srivastav, should change as society changes, isn't that true?' She looked at him for his reaction and continued: '*Parent* is a perfectly good word, isn't it? Why can't you write *Parent* instead of *Father*? *Parent* could refer to a father or a mother, whoever is the paymaster and has the custody of the child.'

Ignoring his confused expression, she went on: 'In many other countries around the world, where I have had the privilege of spending several years of my life, single parenthood is not such a big deal. For India, and maybe for you, it might be time to catch up.'

'In India our traditions . . .' he spluttered, about to defend his position.

'Traditions, tradition, traditions – those traditions which drag us down should be dispensed with. If India wants to stand up and be counted on the world stage and wishes to keep up with the twenty-first century then I think you should have all these forms destroyed and order new ones to be printed. But please make sure that this time,' she pointed towards the form, 'the word *Father* is replaced. It's a very small step, but every long journey starts with a first small step.'

She seemed determined to educate him. 'Don't you know that during the Second World War, when men were being killed on the front lines, it was the women here who ran the factories and hospitals – and they still managed to raise their children as well. Women can not only cook and clean, they can also earn as good a living as a man can.'

It seemed as if the Headmaster had lost his voice completely now, for he put forward no more arguments to defend his policy. Instead, he unconsciously started to crack his knuckles, making a ghastly racket.

As Sheena got up to leave, she looked at him intently and said, 'Life is not a stagnant pond. There should be dynamism and courage like a strong river which washes away all the dirt and filth. Despite the millions of dead bodies in the Ganges, she is supposed to still be pious and pure ...'

The Headmaster now started to scratch hard with his pen on a piece of paper lying on his table, and with every scratch the paper screamed silently as it was reduced to shreds.

Sheena, her hand already on the door handle, ignored him as he rushed over to open it for her. She gave him a piercing look and said, 'I should not have bothered you, nor for that matter have wasted my own time.' And without waiting for his response, she stalked out of his room.

As soon as Sheena had gone, the Headmaster sagged into his chair, emptied the glass of water and set it down with a bang. He then loosened his tie, took a deep breath and rested his head on the back of the chair. As he closed his eyes he muttered, 'These bloody women!'

*

Walking along the corridor, she moved past the staff room where many of the teachers were sitting, chatting or marking the children's homework. She heard a faint

'Who does she think she is? She doesn't give a damn about anyone else's opinion.' Sheena was all too aware of the jealousy that these women nurtured. Their remarks always amused her – she could easily disregard such useless tittle-tattle. The comments of people who had no connection with her life were of no interest to her.

She had learnt her lesson long ago: you should never try to please others, for they will always find some way to criticise you. For example, her single status always caused a little flurry over here in the UK – how they would love to know the name of the father! When she had lived in Europe and America, single parenthood was commonplace, not something to be gossiped about.

She smiled as she approached her official car, which sported an Ashoka emblem of India. As the chauffeur in his black and gold uniform stood to attention and held the car door open for her, she was reminded of the pathetic state that the Headmaster had been reduced to. She was the Chief Commissioner of the province – every department, including the education department, was answerable to her. Maybe Mr Srivastav feared that his job was in jeopardy after his behaviour the previous day, when her son Vishal had entered his school as a new admission.

She wanted to be a pioneer rather than a follower. She was ambitious, very ambitious. Some of her friends teased her, making prophesies that she would be the future Prime Minister of India. She herself nurtured a wish to be the High Commissioner of India to the United Kingdom, the country which had colonised India. The British still called the war of 1857 a 'Mutiny', but for Indians it was truly a War of Independence. And the British had not left India for another ninety years! It would be an honour for her to represent India abroad.

She also wanted to be an ambassador to the United States, the so-called most powerful country on earth, which had no healthcare system to speak of and whose financial rating had now dropped from AAA+ to BBB+. She remembered her last visit to Los Angeles: how she had felt sick to her stomach when she'd seen a black man lying at a bus stop. His entire leg was one long wound, exposed to the elements, leaking with pus and covered with flies. *This is America,* she thought, *where people from far and wide want to come, to live the American Dream!* What about this poor man's dream, he who had probably been born in this so-called Land of Plenty!

She herself had never felt hindered by archaic conventions or outdated customs. Looking back was not in her nature. 'If you keep turning your head back, you might not spot the ditch in front of you that could swallow you whole.' Although born in a Hindu-Brahmin family, her family was thankfully not overtly religious. No forced attendance in temples or Sunday congregations for her! She was a confirmed atheist. Religion had caused a lot of bloodshed in this world. Weren't we better off without it?

Her staff not only respected her but looked upon her with deep affection as she was acutely sensitive and aware of their needs. She was a sharp-minded woman who handled her complicated job with great insight. She was kind to her staff. When her peon's daughter got married, she surprised him by visiting his family personally rather than sending the wedding presents with a servant. When her junior clerk fell ill, she visited him in hospital; on his return to work, he found his workload considerably decreased.

She hated being interrogated. She did not allow even her friends or parents to interfere in her personal choices and decisions. She had worked very hard to get where she was. Having finished her MSc in Physics, she had entered the Indian Administrative Service competition at a national level, aged twenty-one, and qualified at her second attempt. Lots of her Indian Foreign Service friends were posted abroad, so she often travelled around the world in her holidays and stayed with them. She learnt a lot about other cultures from visits to Europe, America, Canada and Australia.

Despite her successful career, when she was the Deputy Commissioner of a big district, her parents, especially her father, were very keen to marry her off. She kept putting it off for a long time. Finally she agreed to an arrangement that her father had made – she was to meet up with another IAS officer who worked as a Deputy Secretary in a small district. She went through the usual drills. But she always thought that the way Indian girls of a marriageable age were paraded in their finery in front of the entire family of the groom was like being presented in a cattle market. The bride should be pretty and fit, with a good figure, must be able to cook and sew, her house-keeping must be meticulous, and so on and so on . . . and of course she must be fair-skinned!

Sheena had refused to put on the 'special sari' that her father had purchased for the occasion. She dressed casually, as she usually did – no gold jewellery either. She had always hated gold bangles – they seemed to her like golden shackles. She had never ever bought a single gold bangle in her life!

She vividly remembered that day; it was carved in her memory.

Her prospective father- and mother-in-law, accompanied by the prospective groom's sister and a maternal uncle, were gathered in her father's very lavish drawing room. She herself did not enter with the tea tray and refreshments, offering it to each one of the visitors as they examined her suitability. The servant of the house, poor dear, had relieved her of that humiliating and painful duty. The mother of the prospective groom stared at her, hawk-eyed. The dutiful son let his mother take over the proceedings and sat meekly, waiting for her to do the talking. She was already impressed by Sheena's light complexion.

The woman took the initiative, saying: 'Your daughter is pretty, and an IAS officer. Good, very good, that suits us really well, but . . .'

Sheena's father raised an eyebrow and looked at her. What was that 'but' about, he wondered?

The woman went on: 'Your daughter must give up her post.'

Hesitantly, Sheena said, 'Sorry . . . ?' Her mother was also a bit concerned by such a demand, but she contained herself and politely urged the groom's mother to continue.

'What I mean is that my son will not leave his job; his posting is 200 miles away from here. Your daughter must give up her job to be with him.'

Sheena looked at her potential husband. He sat there quietly, seemingly agreeing with his mother's suggestion. Her parents looked baffled. Her father tried to explain.

'My daughter is the Deputy Commissioner of this province and your son is a Deputy Secretary in a much smaller district. It's much easier for him to find a similar post in the same organisation here. There are several Deputy Secretary positions available in this province, but there is only one Deputy Commissioner. My daughter won't be able to do the same job in your son's district.'

The boy's mother emphatically declared, 'My son will not give up his job.'

Sheena stood up and told them in no uncertain terms: 'Nor will I. Thank you for your visit. Now please will you leave our house quietly, without a fuss.' She briskly left the room.

The woman got up in a huff, outraged. 'How dare she speak to me like that?' She stared at Sheena's father and went on: 'Your daughter is not well-behaved, is she? She must have had a bad upbringing!'

Whenever Sheena thought of that incident, she was relieved. Choosing not to marry had been a logical and sensible decision, after all. Men could not cope with successful women and women's jealousy was even more poisonous!

However, Sheena had fond memories of another enchanted encounter six years ago . . .

Her school friend Shalu lived in Washington with her two children. Sheena often visited her, and as soon as she landed in Washington, Shalu herself breathed a sigh of relief. Her friend's arrival meant that she could live her own life for a short interval while Sheena took care of her kids. The young woman adored them; she never minded being their babysitter.

Like most couples in Europe, America and elsewhere in the Western World, Shalu and her husband Kundan never had enough time for each other – what with both of them working full-time, doing the housework, washing their car, decorating, keeping the garden tidy, looking after the kids, and a lot more. It seemed that life was just passing them by – and that they were just maintaining an existence. That was the price Western society had to pay for the luxuries of life. Shalu was also an IFS officer, but as she lived in America she did not have the material wealth and luxury that Sheena enjoyed in her position in India. So Sheena's arrival was always a welcome treat.

Shalu's children were very fond of their 'Aunt Shinu'. One day, Shalu invited her for Sunday lunch. They also invited one of their American friends, Nigel.

Sheena often baked cakes for the children. While they sat around the dining table, Shalu's son Neetu said, 'Aunt Shinu, do you bake such nice cakes for your son as well?'

'You are my son, aren't you?'

'No, I'm Mummy's son,' he said in his childish way, and put his arms around Shalu's neck.

Kundan could not let his wife bask in all that glory by herself. 'And what about Daddy?'

'Yes, and I'm Daddy's son – happy now?' Neetu got off his mum's lap and ran away to his playroom.

Something pulled hard at Sheena's heartstrings. A grey cloud of sadness came over her and she quietly left the table; the meal was nearly done. They all went to the sitting room and decided to have their coffee there. Before following her brother Neetu into the playroom, the younger one, Shagufta, jumped into Sheena's lap, hugged her tightly and kissed her on the cheek. To Sheena that felt like a cool breeze on the burning, undeclared desire that she kept close to her heart.

'I love you, Auntie,' Shagufta whispered, and the young woman felt the comfort of that hug smooth out her crumpled brow. As she was a frequent visitor to their house, the children had developed an intimacy with her that Sheena cherished. She enjoyed spending her leisure time with the kids; it diminished the pain of being away from her own family. A void which she refused to admit even to herself was filled.

Kundan asked Shagufta to leave her aunt alone. She made a face but obeyed her father without any fuss. Once she'd left, Kundan turned to Sheena – as ever the joker, he was constantly teasing her – and said: 'If you love kids so much, why don't you get married?'

Shalu rebuked her husband. 'Haven't you asked her often enough? Maybe she has not found someone suitable.'

'Why are women always criticised for their choices, or for not making a choice?' Sheena burst out. 'Men don't face such scrutiny. Look at the Indian Prime Minister Atal Bihari Bajpai or President A.P.J. Abdul Kalam – their singledom never bothered any of the 1.2 billion Indians. I'm pretty sure a woman in the same position would have attracted a lot of the conventional talk about marriage.'

It seemed Sheena was in a mood to vent her feelings, for she continued in a huff: 'When a sixteen-year-old girl is widowed, her head is shaved, as her hair is a symbol of sexuality. And it's not just in India: remember David Lean's film *Ryan's Daughter*? Sarah Miles' character has her hair cut short to humiliate her. And Anna Karenina

102

had to kill herself. She had to put up with a loveless marriage – she dared to love Count Vronsky! An Indian woman is condemned to stay clad in white for the rest of her life, without make-up; everything is denied to her. She exists, but only really in name. She is not allowed to be present at any auspicious occasion in the family, because she is a "cursed woman"; even her shadow is unlucky. Why are widowed Indian men not subjected to such customs? Why must women always suffer? Why is it that people in India think that everyone was born just to be married, as if it were the most important thing in life? And then they burn women for not bringing enough of a dowry! Female victims of domestic violence never get any support or justice in Indian society. If the matter *is* reported to the Indian Police, they too abuse them. And then there is foeticide . . . If female embryos carry on being destroyed at the current rate, where will Indian men and all those vicious mother-in-laws find female wombs to produce sons?'

In order to change the tone of the conversation, Shalu intervened, informing Sheena, 'Did you know, Nigel is learning Urdu.'

Sheena looked at him. Really looked at him. He had a handsome face, and he was smiling. 'Why?' she asked in a gentler tone. 'What for?'

'I'd like to go to India and visit some ashrams. I'm really keen to see the Khajuraho temples and the magnificent temples in the south. It's a great country with so much ancient history.'

Nigel looked at Sheena intently, and their eyes locked – she became self-conscious and walked away into the garden. Nigel followed her outside. It was a nice sunny day and the garden looked beautiful; there was a lovely manicured lawn and the flowerbeds were a riot of colour, with blooms of every shade. It had taken Kundan weeks and weeks to achieve this, and he was proud of his garden. He was about to go after Sheena too, but Shalu caught hold of his arm and stopped him, murmuring, 'Leave them alone.'

Sheena was always intrigued and impressed by people of European origin who were keen to learn something about India. She felt it created an instant bond; it suggested to her that the person was not as self-centred as most Americans were. They thought that America was the entire world and that nothing beyond it existed. She was reminded of the US Vice President Dan Quayle on his visit to Latin America, when he had announced that 'People in Latin America speak Latin.' A Vice President of the United States! And Bush Junior had been elected twice – a man who couldn't even string two sentences together. And what about Sarah Palin – who celebrated her stupidity and revelled in her ignorance?

Sheena wondered if the American electorate would once again show its true colours by not choosing the articulate and intelligent Obama, but instead Mitt Romney, a Mormon whose wealth shielded him from those adversities that many Americans and billions of other people in the rest of the world had to face. Although countries outside the United States couldn't choose the American President, he would be thrust upon the rest of the world – and the jolts would be felt everywhere. The Tea-Party brigade might win, after all. What would that say about the electorate's intelligence and morality? That would be proof enough of the disinterest of many

Americans in the world around them, not to mention their own 'have-nots'.

Sheena always found it irritating when Oprah addressed the audience of her famous TV show as 'Americans', or when she said 'Hello America!' or 'This or that is for Americans . . .' She had made her billions by selling her show to 160 other countries. Sheena wished she would acknowledge their presence and their huge contribution to her coffers.

Sheena kept walking to the other end of the very large garden and sat on the garden bench; it was not visible from the French doors of the sitting room, which opened onto the garden. She was still absorbed in her thoughts – but for the first time in a very long time the focus of those thoughts switched to a man. How bewitching Nigel's smile was, she said to herself. Magnetic and enchanting. He seemed intelligent and kind too.

Nigel caught up with her and at a gesture from her, sat down beside her. 'Why are you so surprised that I want to visit India and learn Urdu?' he asked.

'Surprised? No, I'm just intrigued.'

'Is it because you think Americans are self-absorbed and self-centred?'

'No, not all of them obviously, but . . .'

'You are being polite – just be honest.'

Suddenly Sheena asked him, 'Why didn't you ever get married?'

'I'm not the marrying type. I don't subscribe to the view that people should own each other or be addressed as "the other half". Any institution which reduces a person to a "half" is not worth subscribing to.'

'Oh, like Oscar Wilde, you think that good institutions are not always worth being part of?'

'I can't stand the whys, whens and wheres of relationships. Going through each other's pockets! How can human beings endure such constraints? Such interrogation, day in and day out: "Where did you go? Who did you meet up with? What did you do?" My God . . . It's beyond me.'

Sheena agreed, adding: 'I know a woman who always went through her husband's pockets, checking his bank and credit card statements and his mobile phone bills, and querying every single call he made from the landline. Then she would empty the joint account with great gusto and, do you know what? She had never worked and did not have her own income!'

'See what I mean?' Nigel was pleased that he had her endorsement.

'I think that marriage is "a theatre for a day".' Sheena looked for his response.

'I agree with you – for women anyway.'

'But there's a price tag attached to freedom of that kind, isn't there?' she pondered.

'Sure is, but it's worth it, isn't it? I think I know what you are hinting at.'

'Which is?'

'That the price to pay is occasional loneliness – but it's a small price to pay, and everything in life has a price tag. At least being alone allows us to be ourselves and to explore the world. It's an informed choice, that's how I feel anyway. Nobody need agree with me.'

Yes, that was how Sheena felt. He echoed her feelings exactly. She never wanted to compromise herself for a short-lived liaison of any kind. After all, 50 per cent of marriages end in divorce. People marry three or four times. People like Liz Taylor and Joan Collins married seven or eight times, she had lost count. She was sure that at least 20 per cent of the population in Western countries chose not to marry, and together with the sizeable gay community, unmarried people were not such a minority, after all. She sighed.

Nigel edged closer to her and put one arm around her shoulders. She found herself looking deep into his eyes. Something special, very special, happened between those two strangers at that moment. Her raised face met his intense gaze, which penetrated deep down into her soul, making a connection with her inner being. He gently, very gently, caressed her lips.

Sheena treasured that enchanting smile for ever – and immortalised it within herself.

My Better Half

Divya Mathur

London, November 2013

Despite having been married to her husband Goldie for two years, Liz was still not sure whether he was serious about their relationship. His secretary Rachel had warned her several times that Goldie was an incorrigible flirt, and that at present he was romancing Leena Iyer, the new auditor at the Lloyds of London insurance company where they both worked. Liz generally laughed such rumours off, thinking that her friends were just jealous of her handsome and charming Indian husband. Most of them had problems with their own relationships; they were constantly bickering and breaking up with their partners. Anyway, what was she supposed to do? Follow him everywhere he went?

'Why won't you just accept that he is an awful flirt?' Rachel often asked, and in her heart of hearts Liz knew it was true. Goldie *did* chat up every woman who came his way, especially those with big breasts – and Leena did have a buxom chest. But then, if she were to confront him, Liz might end up losing him. Maybe he just couldn't help himself; maybe he meant no harm.

'Isn't it a bit much that he comes back to you every evening, insists on your accompanying him everywhere – and then flirts with the next girl who comes along?' As one of Liz's oldest friends, Rachel considered it her solemn duty to inform the other young woman about Goldie's goings-on.

'The other day, I saw him and Leena together in Westfield – and they were walking hand-in-hand!' she hissed excitedly into Liz's ear. '*Now* do you believe me?'

Liz knew that 'hand-in-hand' came from Rachel's own imagination, but her heart still ached. What was Goldie doing with Leena in the big shopping centre called Westfield? Was their married life truly over and done with? And how would she cope if Goldie left her for Leena? Even though he irritated her constantly, she still loved her husband. Part of her wanted to interrogate him about Leena, but for all she knew, Rachel might be mistaken and now she was just being paranoid. Also, she had heard on the grapevine that Rachel herself used to fancy Goldie.

'Meet my better half,' Goldie had said this morning, when introducing Liz to his new colleague, Henry Cox, who shook her hand and then politely kissed her on the cheek. At that moment, she felt like such a fool – especially when she saw their other colleagues smirking. She cringed every single time her husband used this expression, but did not have the courage to object. She often wondered whether the rumours about Goldie's affairs were true, because how could a husband who introduced his wife as 'my better half' not be serious about his marriage? Or had she been stupid to give him the benefit of the doubt for over a year now?

Until their first anniversary, everything had been fine. When friends and colleagues drew her attention to Goldie's lack of manners and his flirtatious behaviour, Liz refused to listen; she was totally infatuated by him. So what if girls followed him everywhere – he was hers alone. So what if he didn't say 'thank you', 'sorry', and 'excuse me' like everyone else in London – Indians don't believe in formality. So what if he ate his soup with a slurp – he appreciated her cooking. So what if he had never been serious about anything – he was an easy-going kind of guy. She tried hard to discover clues or traces of infidelity on Goldie's person, but there was nothing; his air of innocence made her feel guilty that she had ever listened to her friends, especially Rachel, who was a real gossip.

Things began to turn sour after their first visit to Baroda, Goldie's hometown in Gujarat, where everyone was talking about his philandering. India was a place where certain prejudices existed; most Westerners had learned about them from reading Kipling and more modern Indian writers, and from watching movies like *Slumdog Millionaire*, *A Passage to India* and *Bend It Like Beckham*. However, once Liz had fallen in love with an Indian man, everything about his country and his fellow Indians seemed rose-tinted. But the moment she arrived in India, and in Baroda specifically, she realised that not only did she have nothing in common with the country and its people, but that Goldie too was a far cry from the man he had seemed to be, back in London.

Goldie's mother, Santosh, had called her son her golden boy – 'Goldie' – in his childhood, and he liked everyone in the UK to call him that too. Goldie's parents had come over to London for his wedding and had stayed with the couple for more than a month. At that time, Santosh suddenly began calling Goldie by his proper name, Gopal.

'Now, I declare my son truly grown up,' she sighed regretfully, but kept treating him like a boy who should have married a desi girl from Baroda. 'Our desi girls serve their husbands hand and foot,' she'd tell Liz. 'A desi girl will get up at the crack of dawn, pray for her husband's long life, prepare breakfast and lunch before going to the office, and will not eat before everyone in the household has eaten.

'What would my Gopal like to eat for breakfast today?' she would croon, and before he had even replied she would start frying potato bhajias for everyone. 'Liz, beta, you must learn to cook his favourite foods,' she instructed her daughter-in-law. 'He does not like pizza and pasta. You can win your husband's heart with food, you know.'

'What about Liz's likes and dislikes?' his father dared to mention.

'She has been eating pizzas and roasts all her life,' his wife said firmly. 'Let her try real food now that she has married a desi boy. Indian food is the best, you know. I am told that our chicken tikka masala has been declared the British Dish of the Year.'

Before Santosh left London, she saw to it that Liz had learnt to cook all sorts of curries, chapatis, paranthas, savouries and sweets. Liz could not be disrespectful to her 'doting' mother-in-law and just say no; instead, she seemed to be cooking day-in and day-out. At the office, she ate sandwiches and chips in order to stay sane.

Twice during her in-laws' stay in London, Liz had had to work late at the office, and Santosh was quick to point out to her: 'Liz, beta, marriage is no guarantee that a boy will not stray. Our Gopal is a Krishan Kanhaiya, you know.'

The young woman enquired about Krishan Kanhaiya, and Santosh explained.

'Gopal is another name for Lord Krishna, who was a Don Juan. According to our Indian mythology, Krishna made love to hundreds of girls, including the beautiful Radha. She and Krishna were eternal lovers, who are still worshipped all over India.'

Liz knew that to be true as far as Goldie was concerned – he was quite a charmer. Of course, if someone were to ask her own mother about her, her mum might say the same sort of thing! Liz had had her own fair share of boyfriends announcing their lasting love for her, but she'd fallen for Goldie, who'd once been mad about her in return. And now she was beginning to rue the day they were wed.

'Girls used to line up for our Gopal, you know?' Santosh said, beaming. She seemed rather proud of her son's many relationships in Baroda. She also told Liz that before Goldie came to London, he had had a serious love affair with a local girl from his school days. By coincidence, she was called Radha.

'You know, Liz beta, Gopal and Radha were very close. Her parents approved, so the pair were together day and night. We all thought – actually everyone in Baroda took it for granted – that they were made for each other . . .' Santosh would get started on the story of their love affair whenever she found Liz on her own. 'We couldn't believe it when Gopal told us about you.

First we thought that it was just a fling, but when he told us that he was planning to get married, we had to inform Radha's parents. It was very difficult. They were devastated and we felt bad.'

'How could Gopal do this to our Radha?' the girl's mother had apparently moaned. The whole town was buzzing; how *could* Goldie abandon Radha like this, after a life-long friendship? The fables of Krishna and Radha were the hot topic in the neighbourhood.

'Lord Krishna also abandoned Radha when he left his hometown and went to live in Mathura,' Radha's grandmother had philosophised, claiming that history was repeating itself.

'Her parents forbade Radha to go out in daylight after that,' Santosh sighed. 'Such a shame brought on the family! Who is going to marry her now?'

'I don't understand. Why wouldn't anyone marry her?' Liz was horrified.

'In India, girls are not allowed to roam around with boys before they are married. Everyone blamed Radha's parents for allowing her to go out with Gopal unashamedly. You know what the womenfolk in Baroda thought?'

'No, and I don't want to know what they thought,' Liz replied silently, but Santosh carried on regardless.

'They thought that you had put a spell on our Gopal. Is it true that Angrez girls are attracted by our desi boys?' she asked a bewildered Liz. But before Liz could reply, she asked again: 'You prefer our dark boys to your fair ones?'

'But Goldie is quite fair,' Liz resisted.

'Not as fair as your boys,' Santosh said, ignoring her comment.

113

Liz wondered whether Goldie's complexion had unconsciously been a factor when she fell in love. Did she, in fact, prefer 'our dark boys'?

Although Santosh seemed to have quickly warmed to her new daughter-in-law, she worried constantly about poor jilted Radha.

'It's not just Gujarat, no one in the whole of our country will dare marry her now,' she fretted. 'We should have got him married to Radha before he left for England.'

'With such a stain on her character, she is destined to remain single,' her husband was quick to agree.

'What bad karma she must have, to suffer so much,' Santosh said pensively, looking up at the sky. The weird thing was that Goldie, who was sometimes present during these conversations, kept quiet as though none of it was anything to do with him.

Liz was relieved when her in-laws left for Baroda. She began to set her house right despite Goldie's objections: he preferred everything as his mother had kept it. He constantly criticised Liz, especially her cooking. But old habits die hard, and his young wife kept going back to the arrangements she had grown up with. At the weekends, she had to change into the Indian outfits Santosh had brought over for her. 'You look so pretty in Indian costume,' her husband would croon. 'Just like our desi girls.'

When Goldie and Liz visited Baroda after their marriage, he proposed to take her to meet Radha and her family. Radha was still unmarried, and her mother and grandmother had been telling their neighbours that she had taken a vow of celibacy. Obviously, a lot was at stake as far as Radha and her family were concerned, but Goldie seemed determined to take his English wife to call on them.

'Gopal beta, why do you want to go there? Her parents are still very annoyed with you.' Santosh was equally baffled.

'Why not, Mummy? If we don't pay them a visit, they will certainly mind. Radha and I were childhood friends. Radha has phoned me several times to say that we must drop by.'

From what Liz had heard, this sounded very strange. After what Goldie had done to her and her family, why should the other girl be interested in seeing him again? At least Goldie was frank about his affair, but if Radha had vowed to remain single, why did she keep calling him? Liz was perplexed.

Santosh insisted that Liz should dress up nicely in an expensive Indian dress and matching jewellery so that everyone would realise why Goldie had chosen her over Radha. Liz felt uncomfortable about the whole thing, but just as in London, here too she was supposed to follow instructions; no one bothered to ask her opinion.

'Meet my better half,' Goldie chuckled as he introduced Liz to his ex-girlfriend, and Liz felt as though he was poking fun at their relationship. She had been looking forward to meeting Radha. As someone smart and educated, who had just arrived from the West, she thought that she would have the upper hand – but Radha's laser-like gaze pierced through her, body and soul. This was not the shy young woman Liz had pictured, she thought, as the girls weighed each other up at close quarters.

Radha, it appeared, knew everything about Goldie and Liz. Had he been confiding in her about his married life? Was something still going on between them? Liz felt very insecure. Radha chatted with Goldie as though nothing had happened. They spoke about their college days and friends for hours on end, ignoring the English girl completely. They really must have been very close – or was Radha just showing off to rile Liz?

In fact, no one in the household spoke to Liz at all, and as she didn't understand a word of the conversation, she picked up a magazine and sat on a swing outside in the courtyard until she was summoned for tea, which was an elaborate affair. Liz had only seen such a variety of snacks at Neasden Temple in London, when they had celebrated Lord Krishna's birthday. Santosh had insisted that if they couldn't do the puja at home, they must go to the temple.

'Why are they celebrating Krishna, the philanderer?' she had asked sarcastically. Goldie stopped her there and then.

'Firstly, you should always address our gods with the suffix "ji".' Liz suddenly remembered that while praying to her God, Santosh used to address Jesus as 'Jesusji'.

'He was more than just a divine lover. Krishanji was a hero, a Supreme Being. On the battlefield, when Arjun preferred to renounce his kingdom rather than fight his kith and kin, Krishanji advised him that fighting was his dharma.'

'I know: everything is fair in love and war.'

'No, not exactly. He laid out a discourse which is compiled as the *Bhagavad Gita*, if you care to read it.' Talking about Krishanji, Liz found Goldie serious for once, and wondered why.

As is customary with Indians, the women attended to each and every whim of their men. In spite of

Goldie's telling them that Liz did not take sugar in her tea, during the visit to Radha, the other girl put whole spoonfuls in, and Liz felt like vomiting. Did her rival do it on purpose?

When they returned home, Liz felt really unwell. Santosh was sure that Radha's grandmother had put something in Liz's snacks. Taking some salt in her palm, she moved it around her daughter-in-law's face and then threw it in the sink, saying: 'Nothing can hurt you now.' Then she added: 'Why don't you have a baby quickly, Liz beti? That will keep Gopal busy.'

In spite of all her crazy quips, Liz had taken a liking to Santosh. 'Is that a good idea, Mum?' she grinned. 'I will be changing nappies while Goldie chats up some other girls.'

'I was telling his father the other day that Gopal's wife will have to keep on her toes day in and day out.' Santosh's words were prophetic, the young woman thought later, for their life in London revolved around Goldie, who sweet-talked her into doing almost everything, while he was useless around the house. He couldn't hoover, he couldn't put the washing out, he couldn't cook, he ate noisily and above all, he was miserly. Liz often asked herself why she had fallen for him.

*

While they were in Baroda, Radha had seemed to be free to join them anywhere, everywhere and at any hour. Liz's holiday was completely ruined. She had wanted to enjoy Gujarat's art and architecture, but she was constantly distracted by the others, who talked and laughed, showing little interest in their surroundings –

or her. Liz wanted to be left alone so she could make her own way around Gujarat, but Goldie would not hear of it. He and Radha had to tag along wherever she wanted to go.

Back in London, Goldie expected his wife to accompany him to meet colleagues from his department, and friends – especially Leena. Liz was so busy at work that she was always late getting to the pub, where they met more often than not these days. He wanted her to be friends with Leena, but Liz did not want to start a new friendship which she couldn't keep up. Leena kept phoning, asking her to go to a picnic or a film, and this made Liz really uncomfortable. When she kept coming up with some polite excuse, Goldie was annoyed.

'Honey, why can't you be nice to my friends?'

'Darling, I don't have time for my own friends and colleagues, how can you expect me to make time for yours?' Liz had been thinking this for a long time. She was fed up with his nagging pleas for her to accompany him to useless, boring parties.

'You are so anti-social,' he grumbled.

'Sorry, I just have too much going on at the moment.'

'Look, I work in the same company so I know how busy you are.'

'We may be working in the same company but our jobs are entirely different,' Liz snapped, then regretted it. She had recently been promoted, while Goldie had been passed over.

'How can I forget that?' Goldie scowled. As far as he was concerned, she had been promoted because she was a pretty white woman and the bosses were racist. 'They would never let an Indian like me be their boss!' But the truth was that she had passed all her actuarial exams and he hadn't. She was a fully-fledged actuary now while he still had to clear three more modules.

Liz had been trying to find a job in a different company so that she wouldn't have to listen to the gossip about Goldie. He was charming to everyone, and they just saw her as simply Goldie's wife. By now, Liz had come to realise that behind his initial charm, there was no substance. She was the one who had taken pity on him when he had first arrived. She had taught him the ways of the financial world – which shirt goes with which suit, about matching ties and cuff links. He used to buy his suits from Moss Bros like all Indians do, but he was working for Lloyds of London now and he had to follow their rules. What the CEO wore, his juniors couldn't; what auditors wore, actuaries couldn't – and what actuaries wore, trainees couldn't. She took him to TM Lewin to buy shirts and Roderick Charles to buy suits. Now, if someone asked, he pretended to know everything.

On their first wedding anniversary, Liz bought him an expensive Citizen watch, while Goldie gave her a blanket which he had bought from the Sunday market in Wembley. Even then, Liz was over the moon, and kept telling everyone how considerate he was – only last week she had mentioned that she liked to have a soft blanket over her knees while watching TV in the lounge.

Not once did Goldie thank her for her costly gift, nor did he mention it to any of his friends or colleagues. Liz kept all this in her heart. She considered it to be her own fault that he did not know how she felt, but these things were too unkind to be said out loud. If she started expressing her feelings, they would end up bickering like most couples do, and Liz did not want that. So the distance between them grew by the minute.

They had been so happy before they got married. But on moving in with Liz at Wembley, Goldie entered a new world, which his Indian friends called the 'gora ghetto'. They generally made fun of his gori wife and the couple's lifestyle, saying, 'If only you had married a desi girl!'

Liz came to know the local Indian community from close quarters. Both she and Goldie were disillusioned; they both had preconceived ideas about how their relationship would work. The shine of their marriage soon rubbed off, because they were no longer comfortable in each other's company. Goldie felt awkward at his wife's parents' house, and Liz, although she liked his family, was puzzled by his Indian friends, who mostly did not mean what they said. With a lot of understanding and effort, she tried to get along with her in-laws, but Goldie never ever bothered to try to be on cordial terms with her family; Liz started to make excuses and finally stopped visiting them at all.

Things between them went from bad to worse when Rachel informed her that Goldie kept chatting with a girl back in India. He had even asked Rachel to help that girl settle in the UK. Liz's heart sank. Was it Radha? Goldie had not mentioned any of this to her. *Bringing someone to the UK is not all that easy,* she thought crossly, *let him find out for himself.*

At dinner, Liz asked him outright if he had been trying to help Radha move to the UK.

'Yes, Radha is very unhappy in Baroda. I want to help her settle down here.'

Where did he find the time for all this? Liz was angry. She was working so hard that she barely had time to call her parents, and there he was, arranging to bring people over from India and help them acclimatise to this country. No wonder he had a reputation for not being fully committed to his job!

'You never said anything about this before,' she complained.

'What is there to tell?' Goldie shot back.

'This is not something you forget to mention. It's not like you inviting friends for dinner without telling me.' Liz thought she sounded like the bickering wife she had never meant to become.

'Good, you've reminded me: Dicky and his new wife Sara are coming for dinner this Saturday,' Goldie said, taking the conversation in a different direction.

'What? How could you forget that Papa has invited us to the theatre this Saturday?'

'Sweetheart, we can always visit your parents next weekend.' Goldie looked annoyed: who was going to cook for his guests?

'But next weekend your boss and his sister are coming. That's why I told Papa to book the theatre tickets for this Saturday. We haven't seen them in months.'

'For God's sake, you've lived with them your whole life . . .' Goldie started to lose his temper. He thought she would back down, but Liz felt it would be too rude not to go even if he didn't come along.

'Darling, I'm sorry but Pa booked these tickets far in advance. If you like, you can take your friends out for dinner.' Liz knew that Goldie could not cook if his life depended on it.

She was also aware that her father knew all about her predicament. She had been so close to him throughout her younger years. How she wished that her husband could share a pint of beer now and then with her father . . . Goldie hadn't said anything, but she knew that he felt intimidated by her father.

'I have invited them for dinner at home, not at a restaurant,' he sulked.

'Sorry darling, I wish I could stay and cook for them, but . . .' Liz surprised herself by standing tall and sticking up for herself.

'Then why don't you go and enjoy your time with *your parents*.' Goldie emphasised the last two words. 'I can manage.'

This was the first time in the last two years that Liz had accompanied her parents out in the evening on her own. They would have to sell Goldie's ticket.

'Doesn't your husband like our company?' Liz's mother had asked, several times.

'Mum, don't even go there. Goldie has such a lot of friends that . . .' Liz was so exasperated that she could not even complete her sentence.

*

Less than a month had passed when, to Liz's great surprise, Radha suddenly arrived in London. She had got a place at City University to study for an MBA as a private student. Had Goldie forgotten to mention this to 'his better half'?

Goldie insisted that Liz went with him to meet Radha, whose Aunt Susheela and Uncle Jayesh had a palatial house in Harrow. Goldie looked quite impressed by them, with their house in a posh area and the glittering objects all over their lounge, but to Liz the whole arrangement was a bit cheesy. There were marble tiles everywhere and tube lights in every room.

They were just leaving, when suddenly Susheela whispered in Goldie's ear, asking whether he would help them find a suitable boy for Radha.

'I thought she had come here to study,' Liz said, as Goldie seemed to be lost for words.

'Her parents want us to get her settled quickly,' Jayesh blurted out.

'What's the hurry? She can get married after completing her studies.' Goldie went into the lounge where Radha was sitting and asked her directly: 'Isn't that what you want, Radha?'

For a change, Radha looked a little lost – maybe she was jet-lagged, but she kept quiet. Goldie and Liz made their excuses and left immediately.

'These side table lamps do not give off enough light to read at night,' Goldie said before going to bed. Liz was horrified when he suggested that they too should consider putting tube lights in their lounge and bedrooms.

'You will have to sleep in the spare room if you want a tube light in your bedroom.' Liz was quick to stop him there and then. *Enough is enough*, she thought. When they were in Baroda, Goldie's relatives gave them bright glass and metal objects as wedding gifts. Liz tried to leave most of them behind, saying that they couldn't take such heavy objects on the flight. Goldie insisted on carrying some of them to London. He was quite annoyed when Liz kept them in their spare bedroom.

'If you don't like them, we can gift them to friends on special occasions,' he said.

'Honey, you can give them to *your* friends,' Liz said, and Goldie got the impression that these were not the kinds of gifts that were popular in England.

Whether they were about her marriage or her studies, Liz was fed up with the constant phone calls between Goldie and Radha. They chatted at odd hours. She had no idea what went on between them. She could hear Radha's agitated mumble while Goldie tried to reason with her. Not once did he apologise to Liz for getting up from the table and walking over to the balcony or lounge while breakfasts went limp and dinners grew cold.

Liz was almost at her wit's end one evening when she came home to find Radha sitting in their front garden waiting for Goldie to return, as he had obviously been delayed at the office. Liz served her tea, but Radha didn't say much to her. As soon as Goldie returned, the girl didn't stop talking. Apparently she was fed up with her aunt and uncle who forbade her to wear western clothes, go out in the evenings and return home late.

'Radha, can't you keep a low profile? Once you are on your own two feet, you can live independently,' Goldie said as he tried to calm her down.

'Then what, Goldie? Do you think they would leave me alone then?'

What did Radha mean by that? What hold did she have over Goldie? Liz wondered. Why was he so tolerant of her rants? Why wouldn't he confide in her, his wife? Whenever Liz approached the subject, he would shrug her off by saying, 'These Indian girls!' or 'Don't worry your pretty head, I can handle this.'

Liz felt so left out that she rang Rachel, asking if they could meet up in a nearby pub. She needed the comfort of a friend's presence, even though she knew that Rachel would immediately get onto her favourite subject. If only she had listened to her warnings, Liz thought sadly.

'Your job is to deal with major catastrophes for the company, Liz, so why can't you deal with this one?' The moment Rachel arrived at the pub she launched into an attack.

'What catastrophe?' Liz said, feigning ignorance.

'Oh come on, you can't deal with a problem unless you recognise it – but you seem to prefer to remain in denial.' Rachel was in a huff.

Liz tried to placate her; she had been a good friend. 'Rachel,' she replied, 'dealing with Hurricane Katrina in America is not quite the same as dealing with Radha or Leena.'

'Why not? It's the same thing! You raise the premiums or find ways to avoid paying for the consequences – isn't that what you're supposed to do?'

Suddenly, Liz's brain seemed to experience a hurricane of its own. She had been so foolish. Rachel was right – she should deal with it head on. And so she would – if not now, then later.

'Thanks, Rachel, you're right,' she said. 'I should have listened to you in the first place . . . but as you know, I was up to my ears with my studies and work.'

'Now you've finished your exams, tackle him. He definitely doesn't deserve you.' That was exactly what Liz's mum had said earlier that week.

'Whatever happens now, I will take life easier.'

'That's exactly your problem, taking life too easy,' Rachel disagreed. 'Take the bull by its horns, I'd say – starting this evening.'

Liz went home, determined to talk to Goldie about what his intentions were with regard to Radha, but all was quiet. She found Radha sleeping on the sofa and Goldie in their bed, also fast asleep. She herself lay awake for a long time. The next morning, when they left for the journey to work, Radha was still comatose.

'Don't wake her,' Goldie whispered in Liz's ear. 'That uncle and aunt of hers are making her life hell. They keep bringing her one boy after the other and she does not want to get married.'

'Has she come to stay for good?' Liz wanted to ask – but Goldie had hurried on ahead.

There was a Christmas do at the Dorchester Hotel in Park Lane that evening. Everyone had taken their change of clothes to the office. Liz was all dressed up in a red cocktail number and looked so gorgeous that, for the first time in a long time, Goldie felt insecure. Staff from rival insurance companies were paying extra attention to her, he saw, and Liz was ignoring him completely.

Liz had decided to really let her hair down and enjoy the party, and forget all about Goldie and Radha – whom Goldie had invited along. She had started drinking G&Ts to shake off all her worries and was feeling good. She and her friends and the other staff made a small group, slightly apart from where Goldie, Radha, Dick, Sara and Leena were sitting.

'Look at Goldie, he can't take his eyes off you,' Rachel breathed triumphantly into Liz's ear.

'Do I care?' Liz shrugged.

'That's my girl, this is how you can keep him on his toes.'

'But I don't want to keep him on his toes – or keep myself on my toes.'

'What? Radha has moved into your house and you aren't bothered?' Rachel was shocked.

'Exactly. Goldie is who and what he is, and I've come to understand that, with him, there will always be a Radha or a Leena. He will never be happy with me alone and I can't go on looking over my shoulder for the rest of my life, so I have decided to let him go.'

'Are you crazy? At least take what is owed to you!'

'It doesn't matter. Life is more than a house or money in the bank, Rachel.' Liz was a little tipsy already.

Just then, their handsome boss, Peter Hays, approached and bent over to kiss them both and wish them a Merry Christmas. Goldie could not take it any more. He bolted towards her.

'Are you all right, darling?' he asked.

'I'm fine, sweetheart. You stay over there with your little friend – you are made for each other,' Liz said and laughed.

'What are you talking about?'

'You know what she's talking about,' Rachel butted in. 'You've made her so unhappy, Goldie. It is Christmas, you know.'

'Darling, let's go somewhere private.' Goldie took his wife's arm and led her outside to the lounge, where he sat her down on the sofa and ordered coffee.

'Radha and I are *not* made for each other. How have you got this into your pretty head?' he asked, sitting down beside her.

'I don't know what is going on, but I want out. This marriage is over.' Liz knew that he would try to change her mind – the last thing she wanted.

'Darling, what do you mean? I accept that I am a male chauvinist pig who is too engrossed in sorting out a friend . . .' He leaned over and whispered something in her ear.

'What?' This was too much for Liz, especially after a few drinks.

'Radha is a lesbian and we have known it since our school days. In India, it is still taboo, you know. That's why her parents agreed to send her here, but her aunt and uncle are proving to be impossible, that's all.'

'So you haven't been having an affair with her all this time?'

'No, I was just trying to save her from shame and embarrassment.'

'But your mum said . . .'

'I promised Radha that I wouldn't tell a soul. I'm sorry, I should have told you.'

'So I really am your better half.'

'You really are.'

Liz laid her pounding head on Goldie's shoulder. She so wanted to throw her anxieties away but looked up and found Radha and Rachel standing behind them.

'What did you just say, Goldie?' Radha pulled Goldie's head round to face her. She was trembling with anger.

'Nothing, I just want to sort everything out nicely. You go back to your friends, Liz honey, I will be in very soon.' Goldie suddenly looked very vulnerable.

'He said that you were a lesbian, Radha.'

Rachel stood with her hands on her hips. Radha and Liz both looked at Goldie suspiciously.

128

'You know what? You are all madwomen. I am fed up with your accusations.' Goldie was holding his head in his hands, trying to find a way out of this mess.

'How dare you!' Radha shouted. 'My parents paid for your higher education, thinking that you would come back to marry me.'

'Shut up, Radha, you don't know what you are saying.' Goldie's nostrils flared in rage but Radha stood her ground.

'Why did you keep quiet for so long, Radha?' Liz needed to ask.

'Why do you think? This bastard told us that he was saving someone's reputation.'

'Whose reputation?' Liz's heart began to sink.

'Yours, who else?'

'What happened to my reputation?'

'He told us that you were tortured and raped by a thug . . . do you want me to give you all the gory details?'

At that moment, it dawned upon Liz why the women in Radha's family had looked down upon her in disgust during her visit. For an unmarried girl in a town like Baroda to be pregnant was a huge scandal; girls had no choice, they were either murdered or left to commit suicide. Liz felt so shocked, she had to turn away from Goldie to steady herself. A terrible anger surged through her body and burned into her brain.

'Darling, don't listen to her, she is mad – that's why I had to run away from Baroda to make a new life for myself.' Goldie again tried to clasp hold of his wife, but Rachel pushed him back violently.

'Get your hands off her! Leave her alone! In fact, leave both of them alone. The game is up, Goldie, you'd better go and hide your face somewhere dark.' Rachel held a shaking Liz in her arms.

'Liz, darling, she just wants to ruin our marriage. Listen to me before it is too late!' Goldie fell on his knees in front of her.

'You have not only ruined my life, you have also ruined my parents' reputation. I pray to God that you suffer a hundred times for each of your bad deeds.' Radha was in a frenzy as she cursed him.

'How can someone lie so much?' Liz was still in shock.

'You have survived the worst, both of you. Now is the time to have fun. Let us go in and forget all about this loser.' Rachel put an arm around each of them, and led them into the noisy, crowded hall.

Liz glanced around and saw Goldie sitting slumped in the corner looking as if a bomb had hit him. She turned and marched back up to him, and for one blissful moment, he thought she might have forgiven him – it was Christmas, after all. He half-rose to receive her in his arms with a 'sorry' on his lips.

'You *are* my better half,' he said hoarsely. 'I meant it, honey.'

'I never ever believed you were sincere when you kept introducing me as your "better half". Yes, I certainly *am* better than you – and don't need to put up with your lowlife tricks any longer. You will find your belongings in the front garden tomorrow morning. Goodbye.' And without waiting for a response, Liz walked away to a beaming Rachel, the saviour of the two wronged women.

Both Rachel and Radha had been waiting anxiously to see whether Liz would once more give in, believe Goldie's lies and go back to him.

Thank heavens, she had finally seen sense.

It was exactly midnight. Linking arms, the three young women had a group hug then began singing 'Merry Christmas' along with the crowd – and at the top of their voices.

The Table

Ila Prasad

Houston, USA, 2007

We finally had our new home fully organised, but couldn't find a place for the chowki – a low wooden stool. In the end, I decided to keep it out on the patio. There was already a complete set of four garden chairs and a table outside, so it wasn't really needed there either. But by doing so we got rid of it for a while.

Had we been in India, this stool would have been used for the deity during the Satyanarayan Puja and thus would have proved itself to be the most important article in the house. But a change in surroundings changes one's needs as well, and that's what happened with the fate of this stool. Here, in the USA, living in a carpeted house prevented us from planning such a Puja at home and all the festivals, such as Holi and Dewali, were celebrated in the temple.

So the stool no longer had a purpose.

No one questioned my decision to place it outside, but we all knew that it would gradually be ruined by exposure to the sun and the rain.

'OK, but paint it,' my husband Sachin said.

Once painted, it could be used as a fifth chair when needed – a good idea. I agreed to do so. But when I had painted it bottle green with the gloss paint we had available at home, Sachin was irritated. 'I thought you'd make it look better,' he complained. 'Beautiful, even! You could have decorated it with some colourful artwork – but now you've made it look even worse.'

I hadn't thought about it that way. I had simply painted it to protect it from the sun and the rain. The paint was like a shield. What had beauty to do with it?

But Sachin had his own way of doing things. He cared for practicality, yes, but searched for beauty too. From then on, he would cast contemplative glances at the stool every time he saw it, and then his gaze would turn to me.

'We could put a flower pot on it,' I suggested. 'The one with yellow flowers would look good, wouldn't it? Or I could put a plastic cover over it – that might look better. Or if you want to read newspapers, you could keep them on the top of it.'

Sachin was not impressed.

It was a hot summer that year in Texas, and on one such day we suddenly noticed a pair of blue birds on the tree in the neighbour's yard, facing our patio.

Blue birds are extremely beautiful! There are many species of blue bird in Houston, one of which is named the Blue Jay. This is a very beautiful, medium-sized bird with blue, black and white bars on its blue plumage. It has a blue-black ring around its neck, which reminded us of the colour called Neelkanth in India, after the legend of Lord Shiva.

Whenever one of the birds came down into our yard, glorious sky-like colours seemed to light up our garden from one side to the other. But the effect only lasted for a few seconds, after which the little creature would again hide itself in the surrounding trees.

I read in a book that Blue Jays love to play in water.

We thought then that the stool could be of some use.

'We can put a basin filled with water on it,' I said. 'The Blue Jay can take a bath.'

Sachin liked my revolutionary idea. But the timid Blue Jay would fly far above us, still not ready to come down onto the patio.

We waited for many days. Then we moved the water-filled basin to the top of a high steel stool that we placed at the back of the yard – and wow! After that, the Blue Jay would often fly down to the basin to drink some water. Spreading its lustrous blue plumage, the beautiful bird would sometimes start to play, splashing its feathers while we enjoyed watching it from inside the house.

The wooden stool remained unused. We found ourselves unable to decide what its fate should be.

*

Summer passed. Autumn arrived. The outdoor furniture set was folded away and kept in a corner now but the wooden stool was still out there on the patio. These days, it was very often covered with yellow-brown drying leaves. Whenever I sat on the patio, my first duty was to clear the pile of leaves off the stool and then to wipe it, adding extra work to my daily routine. Every time I dusted it, I thought, *Why do we still have this?*

The newer stool made of steel was too good to throw away either, so we continued to hang on to it. In Houston, there are heavy rains during the autumn months. The wooden stool started losing its colour very fast. 'Once it breaks, I will throw it away,' I told myself. Sachin probably thought along the same lines, because I noticed that whenever he came down to the patio, he gave the stool a kick just to emphasise that it was trash.

After autumn we had winter.

It hadn't been this cold in years, everyone said. There was sleet and rain. The leaves on the trees had ice ruffles. Meanwhile, the stool had become even more discoloured. The green glossy paint was losing its grip and the wood showed its original colour here and there. Now we didn't even like to look at it: as well as paint, it was also losing its place in our hearts.

On the other hand, the Blue Jay was the focus of all our attention. After the winter, when spring arrived, we didn't only have Blue Jays but Northern Cardinals, American Robins, Woodpeckers, and even yellow and white Parakeets.

'Let's keep some bird food outside,' I told my husband. 'They will stay here for longer if there is food. You know, I saw a House Finch yesterday.'

At first Sachin laughed at my childish excitement, but after giving it some thought he understood that since I was at home all day on my own, this would help to keep me occupied. So he drove me to the pet shop where we bought a bird-feeder along with a big sack of bird food.

The birds welcomed our decision. Only the Blue Jay was keeping away. I couldn't understand why. It would cast a highly suspicious glance at the bird food, swoop down to drink some water and then fly away. Yet the number of House Sparrows was increasing every day. We now faced a new problem. The squirrel had developed a liking for bird food. Very quietly, it would come, open the lid of the bird-feeder and steal as much of the contents as possible. That gave me one more duty – guarding the bird-feeder. Whenever I had time, I sat indoors, next to the patio door, and kept a watch through the transparent curtain. The squirrel was fast stealing all the nuts and seeds to create stores for winter, and we couldn't afford to keep buying bags of feed for the birds.

The House Finch occasionally gave a long twittering call. We had learned to understand its meaning: the feeder needed to be filled again. The squirrel had stolen all the food.

One day, there were heavy rains.

Rains like this bring so much water into the drainage system of the bayous that they flood the streets. Driving then becomes a challenge, and accidents happen. But at this particular time Sachin was at home on holiday so I didn't have to worry about him.

The heavy rains were relentless, showed no sign of stopping.

'The House Finch has given her twittering call so many times. When will you fill the bird-feeder?' I asked Sachin.

My husband watched the rain through the window, a frown on his face. 'If I go out, I'll get soaked,' he objected. Then: 'OK, I have an idea. I will take the umbrella and spread the bird food on the wooden stool.'

I looked at him in disbelief. But he was set on it – there was no point in saying anything. He went off to the patio and spread a handful of bird food on the stool.

A few minutes passed. Then three blue birds appeared on the tree in front of the patio.

'See? There are three of them.' I was overjoyed. 'That must be why they were not paying any heed to our bird food before. I have read that House Sparrows eat Blue Jays' eggs. We have helped them by feeding the House Sparrows. That's what they used to see from a distance and now they are here with their baby.' I had been trying to find all kinds of reasons and excuses for the Blue Jays' absence. I was so happy, excited . . . I pulled Sachin to the window.

Slowly the birds landed on the wooden stool.

'It's their dining table. Let them have their food in peace,' Sachin said quietly, smiling too – and yes, he was right! Within the next few minutes, a number of House Sparrows, Doves, a pair of Finches and a Red Cardinal – all were fighting and eating on their new dining table with the Blue Jays.

That day we really loved the partly broken, discoloured wooden stool. It was a stool no longer; it had become a glorious dining table.

The Unposted Letter

Kadambari Mehra

Surrey, UK, 2012

It was a bright and sunny morning, but the temperature outside was below freezing point. It had snowed in the night, and everything was buried under a thick mantle. The sky was blue and the earth was white. Nothing living could venture outdoors; even the birds were in hiding.

On my laptop was a message: *Happy Birthday! You are seventy today. It's time to give away all the unnecessary items in your household to charity. Sort out your papers and destroy the ones that are no longer relevant. Discard old letters. Your physical strength will deteriorate day by day, as you are not getting any younger. Spend what is left of your time keeping fit . . .*

My wife Nisha brought tea and a tray. What a lovely birthday treat. Breakfast in bed!

Normally she slept in late and I had to tread like a mouse for fear of disturbing her. I thought she deserved these late mornings now that she had retired from a demanding job, with a great deal of responsibility.

When I showed her the message on the computer, she smiled as if she had won a game of chess. I immediately realised that I had made a big mistake: she hates my habit of collecting and keeping paperwork. I know I'm lazy, but I don't want my progeny to find my tell-tale letters and photographs. So I decided to do something. Nisha offered to help.

Now in every household there are certain items which, in spite of being quite useless, stay forever. You have failed to get rid of them however hard you have tried over the years, as if they had a willpower stronger than your own. Just like the celestial Cobra that guards your ancestral home and lives under the floor of your courtyard. When you almost stop believing in its existence, it suddenly surfaces and you catch a glimpse. By the time you decide to strike, it has either already slithered away or disappears in the wink of an eye back to its hideout.

That particular letter and its accompanying photograph had a similarly permanent existence. Many a time I came across it but I could not post it, nor could I throw it away. A strange feeling of guilt forbade me – and back it went into the same folder and lay there, forgotten, for many years. Once I even wrote the address on its white envelope:

Girija Prashad Sharma
Station Master, Bus Stand
Katra, Jammu, India

As I did it, I realised that I was being foolish. What if he was not still there? After all, people do get promoted and move house; he might be living in a different town.

Doubts bothered me, and so I threw the letter back in with my other things in the bottom drawer of the filing cabinet, where it has since turned yellow with age.

Just my luck! Nisha came across it today. She opened the envelope, looked at the photograph and asked, 'Who is that?'

'Somebody you don't know.'

'A friend?'

'No. Just somebody. Even I don't know who they are.'

'That's very strange! There is a letter in here as well, about four pages long. If it is someone you don't know, why is it amongst your most personal documents?' Nisha sounded annoyed.

'For no particular reason, honestly! Someone once asked me for a favour and I obliged. This fellow is his father.'

In the picture, a stockily built, middle-aged man was playing with a brown cocker spaniel on his tiled patio in front of a French window. He wore blue jeans and a red pullover. He was fair, but definitely Indian. Nisha became so inquisitive that I had to tell her the whole story. As the saying goes, curiosity killed the cat.

*

About thirty years ago we took the kids to India over the summer holidays. It was the rainy season and the holy month of Sawan. The temples were celebrating the onset of the monsoon. On an impulse I decided to visit the Temple of Mata Vaishno Devi up north in the Himalayas near Jammu. We were a party of eight altogether. We took a flight to Jammu and then hired a car to Katra. From Katra it is a long and strenuous journey on foot or horseback, lasting two days, to the temple. All went well, but when we arrived in Katra the place was crawling with pilgrims from all over India. Every hotel was full. The journey needed a licensed pass as the authorities feared there would be a stampede up on the steep narrow track which circumnavigated the hills. It was two-way traffic with no warning signs about what lay ahead around the corners.

Going back was out of the question: cancellation would cost a bomb. We had to start climbing that very day but I could not obtain the all-important pass. I ran from one officer to another but to no avail.

Just then a young man tapped me on the shoulder and asked, 'What is the problem, uncle?'

When I told him about our plight, he said, 'You don't know these scoundrels, sir! You told them that you were from London, that's why they are pestering you. They are just looking to line their pockets, that's all. Wait here, and I'll try to help you.' I asked his name. He told me: 'Girija Prashad Sharma.'

He did help us. Within about two hours he returned with passes for climbing up that same day. We started soon after lunchtime. The next day, on our return, he approached me again.

'Namaste, uncle! *Jai Mata Di!* How did it go? Did you have a good Darshan when looking face-to-face with the idols?'

'Yes, brother. Thanks to you, we were able to offer our prayers. May Mata Rani fulfil all your wishes in life.'

I wanted to give him some money as a token of gratitude, but he refused.

'No, sir! It is my duty to look after the pilgrims. You are my seniors anyway. But I would like a favour from

141

you. If you really want to help me, please find my father, who lives somewhere in London. I have his old address and a photograph. If you locate him, please ask him why he has forsaken us. My mother and I have waited for him all these years. My grandparents pined for him and died heartbroken. Tell him we don't want his money. We want him to come home just once and meet his wife and son. He should accept us as his family. Everybody in this small town thinks I am the son of a banished wife. I don't have a respectable social status, uncle.'

Tears flowed down his cheeks. Girija must have been about thirty or so. He could speak English fluently and his manner was dignified and compassionate.

He showed me a faded photograph of his father which, he said, he always carried in his wallet. It was the only picture of his father he possessed: he had got it from his father's old workplace. Girija had had scores of copies made from some cheap studio, hence the faded print.

I was moved by his story. I have great regard for my parents and for a moment I imagined myself in his shoes. So I agreed to help him. I put the address and the picture carefully in my briefcase.

*

'Did you then keep your promise?'

'Well, put it this way: I couldn't escape.'

Girija had my address in London. He kept reminding me about it, and in the end I decided to act. I personally visited the address he had given me in Edgware. There I was told that the man in question, Devi Lal Sharma, Girija's father, had moved to some unknown address. So my next step was to explore the telephone directory of

London. There was more than one D. Sharma but no one with the initials D.L. Sharma. I investigated them all, but none of them was my man. So I widened my search area. At long last I found someone in Slough who had originally come from Jammu nearly three decades before. Slough is quite far west of London, so I needed a whole day for the trip.

I told him casually on the phone that I had a message for him from India. He was surprised to hear that, yet he gave me his address and invited me over to see him that very weekend. He owned a big house in an expensive area of Slough. It was very well-kept. He told me he was married to an Irish lady and they had two sons. As it was the weekend, his wife and children were in Wales with her family, who had moved there from Ireland. He had stayed behind to look after the dog and catch up with his paperwork. He politely hinted that I shouldn't take up too much of his time.

I started by telling him about my visit to the Vaishno Devi Mandir. His face lit up, and he joined his hands and bowed in the direction of the temple. It seemed to be a spontaneous gesture on the part of an habitual devotee. Then he told me how he was brought up at the feet of the Goddess. However, there had not been room for his big ideas and ambition in that village, ten miles away from the small town of Katra. So as soon as he could, he had left and travelled to the UK. Over the years he had set up a successful hardware business. He was proud of his two sons and his educated wife. As we spoke, the little dog hovered around us restlessly. Devi Lal said that the dog was jealous of me. We both laughed.

Then I came to the point. I asked boldly why had he forsaken his first wife and son. How could he have forgotten them so easily? At that he was taken aback. His face hardened and his smile disappeared. A shadow of foreboding loomed between us, and I could sense the heavy air coming from his nostrils. Before he could say anything, my hand reached for his photo in my front pocket.

Quite vehemently, he proclaimed that he had been married once and once only – and that was to his present wife, Ina. With that he turned his face away and stared into the distance just like a sulky child. I said if that was the case, why had he become angry and turned his face away? Was he not trying to hide something from me?

He did not answer. I then showed him his photo. He looked at it, first in amazement and then with an angry suspicion. How had I found it, he demanded – and who was I working for? So I explained simply that I was returning a favour to a good person who happened to be his son. His face went red with anger. He repeatedly denied having another family – but I refused to accept his pleas. I reminded him that if he believed in Mata Rani, telling lies was a sin. At that, he finally came down from his high horse. I told him about Girija Prashad, a young, healthy, married man of thirty with a respectable job and a pleasant manner, a son of whom he could be proud.

Devi Lal then informed me that Girija was not yet thirty, he was only twenty-eight. With a sigh, he said that he had made his escape from the stifling atmosphere of that place a long time ago, never to return. He did not want to know anyone from his past. Then, point blank, he asked me to leave.

I was equally adamant. How could I leave without accomplishing my mission? I calmed him down with some flattery and words of sympathy. I narrated the whole story of meeting Girija Prashad. Then I explained how I was obliged to return his favour in the name of Mata Rani. For the sake of my promise, he had to help. All I needed was a short message. I suggested he should write down whatever he wanted to tell Girija directly. If he wished to say that he did not want to remember his past, that all the people he knew then were as good as dead to him, he could do so frankly. But he could not let me down and leave me to sink in the quicksand of ingratitude. He should at least honour my promise to Mata Rani.

To my great relief, Devi Lal agreed. I asked him to supply a recent photograph as well. Then I thanked him, left him to it, then went window shopping on the local high street.

When I returned after a couple of hours, Devi Lal had everything ready. He looked relieved, and said he hoped it would be the last nail in the coffin. It was rather unpleasant to hear him say that, but as it was none of my business, with a word of thanks I said goodbye and left.

All through that week I was too busy to post the letter by airmail to India. At the weekend I decided to act. The trouble was that Devi Lal's picture was not inside the envelope and it was slightly too big. But there would be no harm in cutting it to size, I decided, and putting it into the envelope along with the letter. Off I went, fetched my scissors and sellotape and put the kettle on. After a minute or two on the steaming spout the glue softened and I opened the letter.

'Not only that – but I bet you read it too!' chirped Nisha tauntingly.

'Yes – and it was fortunate that I did,' I said with conviction. 'If I hadn't read it I would have posted it there and then – and it wouldn't be here today.'

'But why? You swore by Mata Rani,' Nisha said gravely.

'I am sure Mata Rani would forgive me. If you have any doubts, read it yourself.' I handed her the letter and went to have a shower.

The letter ran as follows:

Dear Girija Prashad,

Thirty years ago I graduated in the first division from a college in Jammu. My future was bright. I wanted to qualify for the Indian Administrative Services and was preparing for the exams. I was twenty-two years of age. However, my family wasn't faring well money-wise. There were three other children besides me for my parents to bring up. Being the eldest, it was my duty to find a job and help them.

Fortunately, one day our family priest Pandit Motaram Chaturvedi came to call at our house. Despite his name of Motaram – fat person – he was as thin as a rake and very energetic. He was a devotee of Kali Mata – the goddess of dark powers. Daily he walked up to Bhairon Mandir barefoot: Kali Mata is supposed to have appeared to him there. He would carry a plate of offerings in one hand and with the other he turned the beads of a Rudraksh Rosary, chanting nonstop the mystic Mantra of Kali – *Om Heem Kleem Chamundaaye Vichchai . . .* His back was straight as a plank as he climbed the steep path. People in our town had great respect for him. Regardless of the weather, he wore a thin white muslin dhoti and a handstitched kurta shirt. He covered his top with a yellow cotton shawl with Lord Shiva's name printed all over it. He had a large number of followers, male and female, who held a Keertan – prayer session – every Saturday in the courtyard of his house. There was loud melodious singing, with harmonium and percussion, for hours on end. These Keertans attracted dignitaries from miles around, which made Pandit Motaram a very influential person.

My mother was delighted to receive him that afternoon. As is customary, she wanted him to read my horoscope. She told him that she wanted me to earn some money rather than spend it. Pandit Motaram predicted a bright future starting in a short while. The very next month I got selected for a job in the administrative office of the local magistrate. We thanked him because he had used his influence. In my spare time I could continue with my studies.

Hardly a week or two passed when he dropped by again. Very unusual! It wasn't an auspicious day, so my parents were surprised. They offered him hospitality. Fresh fruit was brought in and an almond milkshake was prepared. He ate and drank to his heart's content. My father asked politely the reason for this visit.

He answered joyfully: 'I have brought good news. Your son should be getting married in the near future.'

My father was taken aback. None of us was prepared for my marriage yet. My father spoke in a sombre voice. 'But Panditji, my son is only twenty-two. He is studying for the Indian Administrative Services. Besides, he wants to go abroad before settling down.' My father had given his verdict.

Panditji said with authority, 'Of course, of course! Nobody can stop him from sailing across seven oceans, so his stars say. But, my brother, is it wise to send an unmarried young man to the land of free women? The unharnessed bull will only romp about and ruin the field. Put the yoke on him now.'

'Panditji, you are right, but where is the girl? It takes time to find a suitable person.'

'That's just the point! You see, I have already found a very nice girl. That is why I called. Praise be to Mata Rani!' With a loud burp he continued, 'This girl is no stranger. She is the lead singer in my Keertan meetings. You have seen her many times. You know how pretty she is – and as for her voice . . . My word, there is no comparison! So melodious . . . Aa ha ha! Only yesterday her mother sent for me to read her horoscope. She is already very worried about her marriage because the girl is seventeen. As soon as I saw her stars I knew this was the most suitable match for your son.'

Then he lowered his tone to a whisper and said in confidence, 'Her father is only moderately well off, but the girl is extremely lucky. You see, the devotees of Mata Rani lavish gifts and money upon her when she sings bhajans (devotional songs). They see the celestial form of the very Kanyaa Kumaaree (the Virgin Goddess) in her. Her parents don't touch that money as it is holy. She has quite a significant sum in the bank. All that is going to stay with her.'

My father couldn't ask for more. Within a few days I was married to this girl called Sandhya. Besides being beautiful, she was very obedient and hardworking. Everybody liked her, especially the ladies, because she was very polite and softly spoken.

Due to irregular eating during the wedding and the stress of leaving her home, she fell ill. First it was a cold and a fever, then came the vomiting and diarrhoea. She ran into the toilet every few minutes. Each time she had to wash and change, as my mother had strict rules about hygiene around the house and kitchen. We informed her parents, so they took her away and looked after her until she recovered, although I could not keep away from her so I would sneak out, almost daily, to meet her.

A month later, when she came back, she was pregnant. Our secret meetings became common knowledge. My mother was very happy. A child conceived during the first month of marriage is thought to be especially lucky. She was sure it would be a boy. Sandhya was very good at the household chores. My mother adored her. Pandit Motaram stopped coming to our house. On auspicious days he would send some junior trainee pandit to collect offerings from the family altar. My mother thought it was due to the old social custom of not accepting anything from a daughter's home. After all, Sandhya was from his own town and had been his disciple.

During the seventh month of her pregnancy, Sandhya suddenly went into labour. My mother became nervous. A premature child! Anything could happen. The baby and the mother were both in danger. She called the local midwife immediately.

The midwife was an experienced Muslim woman. Respected by Hindus and Muslims alike for her knowledge of herbal medicine, she was the only doctor for miles around for women and children. In villages a doctor was called only if a man fell ill. Women always went to her for treatment for their various ailments, and her concoctions seldom failed. People also called upon her for her wisdom, to settle personal disputes, so she earned the title Vakeelan, the Legal Adviser. Her word was honoured by everyone.

Mostly deliveries took place at home. Ours was no exception. At the far end of our long courtyard there was a cowshed. Adjacent to that was a storeroom. It was quickly cleaned and washed. Traditionally, it was used as the labour ward whenever a child was born. Sandhyaa gave birth to a boy at eleven o'clock at night. I was hiding behind the shed to be able to see my child being born. Vakeelan delivered the boy, but remained strangely quiet and sombre. My mother asked, 'Why are you so worried? If God has sent him into this world, He will give him long life and health as well.'

Vakeelan said nothing. She washed the newborn and wrapped him up in a cotton flannel blanket. My mother rocked him gently and sang traditional songs of welcome and prayers. Vakeelan congratulated her in low tone but I could sense that she was too tired to smile. She received a generous sum of money from my mother and asked for a rickshaw to take her home.

Vakeelan seldom travelled alone. She had a permanent companion, a cleaning lady called Shanno. Shanno's job was to remove soiled clothing and bedclothes. So she collected the lot in a huge bundle and came outside to join Vakeelan. The women waited in the dark for the rickshaw, just a few yards away from where I was still in hiding. I planned to go and see my wife after they had left: in those days it was forbidden.

The ladies had been chatting in low voices, but seeing no one around, Vakeelan burst out: 'I will have my face spat at if this child is said to be premature. I know better! I've delivered at least a hundred seven-month babies in my lifetime, and this one is so alert and healthy – and it must be about eight pounds in weight. This is a full-term baby, I am quite sure of that. What do you think?'

'Yes, Bibi. I'm glad you said it, rather than me. I noticed something too but I thought I had better keep quiet.'

'Come on, you can tell me,' urged Vakeelan.

'Well – is she not the same girl that Pandit Motaram brought to you for an abortion? Don't you remember her? She started screaming when she saw your knife. The pandit quickly took her back home in case the rumours spread. It would have ruined his reputation.'

'But of course! I could not put my finger on it. I thought the girl's face looked familiar. You are right. Oh, that impostor Motaram . . . He has defiled so many young girls. What foul practices he gets up to in the name of religion! That famous prayer session is just a cover-up. Afterwards he treats his influential friends with the money he collects from the altar. That marijuana drink "thandaai" is freely available, and when they get high they do all sorts of things – it is a sin to even mention them. Hundreds of times he has asked Karim's father, my husband, to cut meat close to the shrine. Then he gets a new lamb which had been killed as a sacrifice to God. In this case, I am sure, he has used this girl, and when she became pregnant, he found an innocent man and a decent family and married her off. Bastard! May he rot in Hell!'

She took a deep breath to control her anger, then spoke again: 'Think of the future now. Two nice respectable families will be ruined through no fault of their own. So we'd best keep quiet. We are small people; our word doesn't carry any weight. Besides, he is a spiteful man.

151

Remember two years ago, when he had the water supply to our colony cut off with the help of the District Collector? For months on end the taps remained dry until finally, the Minister's visit to canvass for the votes of the Untouchables was due.'

The rickshaw had arrived. Both ladies went on their way.

The very next day, I packed up my suitcase and told my mother that I was going to Delhi for a better-paid job. Inside, I was heartbroken. I did not go back to my village ever again. In Delhi I got a visa for the UK and left my country for good. I did not see the face of that newborn baby. Maybe it was you. But I do not regard myself as your father. For a while your mother was my beloved, my first love. But alas . . .

Forever regretful, Devi Lal Sharma

*

When Nisha finished the letter, her eyes were moist. It went in the shredder that same day.

The Swansong

Neena Paul

North of England, UK, 2009

It was make or break time for Sonal. The concert had sold out and was to be covered live on the local radio. At last she was going to make her father Kapil's dreams come true.

Every breath she took was laden with guilt: the guilt of having cut her dad out of her life. It was four long years since she had spoken a single word to him. The sound of her singing his music on the airwaves – of her 'angelic voice' as he always called it – would fill him with pride, she hoped, even though the poor man was knocking at death's door.

At this very moment, at his home in Mablethorpe, her father was bent double in a bout of severe coughing; breathing was painful. He had one hand on his chest and the other gripping the back of a chair for support. The moment he was able to hold his head a bit higher to breathe more easily, the cough took over again. Sonal had never seen her dad like this before. She had no idea what to do, how to react. Fortunately, her younger brother was much quicker on the uptake; he came running in with a glass of water in one hand and an inhaler in the other.

In spite of her differences with her father, the sight of him in this weakened state was very upsetting. Sonal had perfectly good reasons to bear a grudge against him. After all, when she had needed him the most, he had spurned them and walked away from everybody. He had thought only of himself. Without even bothering to see his children one final time and say goodbye to them, he had left the family home without a word of explanation.

How could she ever forgive him?

At the time, she had agonised over this betrayal. Questions had tumbled out of her like an avalanche, one following the other – but she had never received an adequate explanation from her mother about what exactly had happened. The resulting tension caused angry words to fly around, and even today, her memory of those evasive answers could still make her furious.

*

'Children, your dad wants both of you to spend the summer holidays with him at his house in Mablethorpe. I have promised him that you will go.'

'What? No one bothered to ask us what we wanted. Why should *he* have his way all the time?' Sonal objected.

'Sonal!' Her voice raised a decibel, her mum Anjali asserted, 'He's your father – surely he has some rights?'

'Rights? Mum, are you kidding me? How can you even mention that word? Did he think about our rights when he disappeared without a word? He left us at a very critical phase of my life. I was so embarrassed to tell my friends that he'd deserted us – so no, I am not going anywhere.'

'Listen to me, Sonal. At certain times, life will bring you to a crossroads, where you are forced to make decisions.'

'Without the slightest consideration for the hearts you break in the process? Mum, I am an adult now, and entitled to know why Dad left us all those years ago.'

No answer was forthcoming. Anjali just kept staring out of the kitchen window.

'Right then, I have taken my decision.' Struggling through her tears, the girl declared, 'I do not want to meet him, and I do not want to talk to him either.'

'You are so stubborn. You don't even bother to answer his phone calls.' Her eleven-year-old brother Chirag couldn't resist the chance to have a dig at his sister.

'It is none of your business – is that clear?' Sonal was furious.

'That is enough, both of you! No more of this madness.' The steel in Anjali's voice had the desired effect.

There was silence in the room, broken only by their mother, who said eventually: 'Sonal, you are right: you are not a child any more. You will be going to university after the summer, so why not spend this last holiday with your dad and then you can do whatever you want to.'

'Mum, Mablethorpe is near Skegness, isn't it?' Chirag said excitedly. 'Oh, come on, Sonal – it's going to be so cool! We'll be near the sea for two whole months. Think of all that spare time . . . racing against the waves with Dad.'

But Sonal just shrugged off his hand.

'Yes, my darling, your dad loves you a lot,' Anjali said, her voice low and mellow.

'That's just not true.' Sonal's voice was bitter. 'The only thing he loves is his music, and perhaps the mysterious woman he left us for. I hate his harmonium and tanpura. The day he disappeared from our lives, I swore never to sing again.'

'Sweetheart, these promises that we make, particularly those made in anger, never take the unforeseen into consideration. Life is too short. There is no time for regrets.'

*

Sonal certainly came to regret her decision. Neither time nor her indifference had diluted her dad's love for her. Finding her right in front of him, Kapil stood transfixed. His little doll had grown so tall in such a short time. The years had flown by.

In his mind's eye he could still clearly see himself pacing up and down outside the maternity ward, feeling so helpless, sweating out Anjali's pain.

'Mr Sinha, we have intravenously injected the required dose of Syntocinon to facilitate the delivery. We have the situation under control.' The doctor's words had calmed his taut nerves.

Kapil had bought himself a cup of tea from the vending machine and pulled up a chair in the waiting room. The night-long vigil then took its toll, because the moment he eased his tired body into a relaxed position, nature took over and he drifted off to sleep . . . He dreamed of a smiling lady, dressed in white, entering a fully lit room.

156

She was holding in her arms a baby wrapped in pink. She duly handed over the child to Kapil.

'Mr Sinha!' The nurse had shaken him awake. 'Congratulations! You are now the father of a beautiful daughter.'

'How is Anjali, Nurse?'

'Mother and daughter are both fine.' The nurse was all smiles.

'Am I allowed to see them?'

'Why not – come with me.'

'My dear angel!' Heart aflutter and hands trembling, Kapil had picked up his tiny daughter.

'Remember we have named her Sonal, not Angel,' Anjali softly admonished him.

'You call her whatever you want to, but to me she is an angel.' Kapil was overwhelmed with joy. 'Thank you for our beautiful daughter.' He bent over and planted a kiss on his wife's forehead. That took care of her mild protests.

*

At their first meeting in Mablethorpe after years of separation, he wanted to tell his daughter how much she meant to him. But Sonal had built an impregnable wall around her, keeping any emotional encroachments at a safe distance.

'Daddy!' Chirag's warm embrace brought him back to earth, but his eyes remained fixed on his daughter.

'Hello, Angel. How is my doll?'

'Now you've even forgotten my name. Let me jog your memory, Father. I am called Sonal, not Angel,' she snapped, and without pausing to embrace him, she walked straight past him. Kapil's open arms fell to his side, his tear-filled eyes revealing his pain.

'Give her some time, Dad,' Chirag advised gently. 'She is hurt. She will get over it.'

But time marches relentlessly on – only man shows its effects and slows down. Kapil's energy levels were falling too. Just a few minutes of work and he would be short of breath. These days he was totally focused on planning a huge stage show and was struggling to muster up the courage to ask Sonal to sing with him.

Kapil had seen the spark in Sonal's voice early on. Her melodious voice had all the signs of a child musical prodigy. Once, he had been teasing the keyboard with a new tune when his daughter broke into song; it left him gaping.

'Dad, I have composed a song,' she said gaily. 'Would you like to hear it?'

'Yes, my darling, let me hear what my Angel has come up with.'

Sonal started banging on the table to accompany her English song.

'What kind of a song is this?' he queried affectionately.

'Dad, these kinds of songs are getting rave reviews these days. Music-lovers are lapping them up.'

'Yes, darling, I will concede that it is a good song, but don't just go with the flow. Such songs fade away as quickly as they bloom. Time is the acid test: good melodies will always play on people's lips and find immortality in their hearts.'

'That kind of music doesn't exist these days, Daddy.'

'That is where you are wrong; such music is all around us, my darling. Every particle of nature is humming captivating musical notes. Listen to the bees caressing the flowers, the pigeons dancing to the morning light, the divine notes of the nightingale and the lark. That music will never cease to affect the soul. You too can make such music – for your voice has a touch of heartbreak that gradually rises to an ecstatic crescendo. All you need, my Angel, is the right direction.'

Kapil was rambling on as if in a trance. Sonal too was mesmerised. She thought, *Oh Lord! Daddy hears all that, so early in the morning . . .*

*

Behind closed doors, at this very moment Kapil was engrossed in his music – lost to the world, singing, swirling in his own private bubble. His voice, riding waves of sound, reached Sonal's ears. The words and the tune were familiar.

Without realising it, Kapil had delved deep into the past and started singing the song that he had used to help Sonal prepare for her school competition. Drawn instinctively to the music, she began humming along and was making an effort to blend her voice in with her dad's when Kapil's song was cut short by a prolonged bout of coughing. This shook Sonal out of her reverie. She felt as though she had been struck by a thunderbolt.

Kapil started again the moment the cough stopped, but then, unable to restrain herself any longer, the girl stormed straight into his room where he was rehearsing.

'Dad!' Her strident voice made him fall silent. 'Just what are you trying to do here? Whatever game you're playing, it won't work, I tell you. Now do us both a favour and refrain from performing one of our songs while I am here. It will be better for both of us.'

Unable to make his daughter unbend even a little to see his point of view, Kapil wondered whether he was running out of time.

When Chirag came out of the house, looking for his dad, he found him on the seashore enjoying the breeze, which was playing hide and seek with the waves. Such soothing scenarios could be deceptive, the sick man knew; for at any moment, a hurricane could roll in out of the blue and wreak terrible destruction.

The time-tested cure for Kapil when agitated was to take deep, slow breaths. He had an instinctive paternal understanding of his daughter's psyche, knowing that her rock-solid exterior concealed a tender, caring heart. She was someone who responded naturally to love.

Oblivious to the time passing, enraptured by the musical waves, he failed to notice the approach of two friends. A familiar voice brought him back to the present.

'These waves seem to be giving you inspiration for some new tunes,' the voice said, and he turned to find Peter, the local vicar, and Gautam, their mutual friend, standing behind him, both with broad smiles on their faces.

'Oh Lord, did the sun rise in the west this morning? Can my dear friends really be sacrificing their beauty sleep for a morning walk?' Kapil teased them.

'Old chap, we do not start our morning with a walk,' Peter said, and yawned.

'Ah, that reminds me, I need to ask you a favour,' Kapil said. 'Can I hold my rehearsals in the church? My children are here to spend some of their holidays with me, and I don't want to disturb their sleep.'

'Yes, why not?' Peter's response was immediate. 'But are you aware that there is a lot of building work in progress in the church? You will find a lot of plaster dust flying around, which might not be good for your asthma.'

'No problem. I will have finished in a few days, but at the moment I am in the middle of writing some new compositions that need immediate and sustained effort,' was Kapil's logic.

'Well, if you can survive in the dust, I am with you all the way,' Peter promised him.

'Look at my brave son approaching.' Kapil pointed to Chirag.

'Your children are certainly very brave. Yesterday the courage Sonal showed in saving that child was exemplary. Very few children are bothered about others these days.'

'Are you speaking about my Sonal? What did she do?' Kapil was all agog.

'Didn't you know? If Sonal hadn't reached that little boy so quickly, he would have been in big trouble. A five or six year old was riding a horse on the merry-go-round. The moment he spotted his mother in the crowd, he took one arm off to wave, lost his balance and was catapulted into the air. Sonal caught him and was all smiles despite the pain of her sprained wrist. Kapil, we all are so proud of your children.'

Chirag seized the emotionally charged moment to challenge his father to a race.

Kapil was no match for an eleven year old; he was huffing and puffing before the race had even started in earnest. He had not gone far before a seizure had him clutching at his chest. Pain distorted his face. There was a strange iron-like taste in his mouth, and wiping his mouth with his handkerchief, he found blood sprinkled all over it. Hurriedly he put the hankie out of Chirag's sight.

'You are too slow, Dad.'

'What can I do, son!' Kapil panted. 'Your dad is getting old now. Come on, tell me why Sonal was having a go at you this morning.' His diversionary tactics worked well.

'She was harping on about the same old things – "your room is so dirty, your clothes are thrown all over the place" – she went on and on. Do girls ever do anything other than cleaning and tidying up? I don't think they have the faintest idea how to enjoy life.'

'You are getting cocky, my boy. Now tell me, what is your sister's favourite colour?'

'Sky blue, of course. Why, Dad?'

'We will make something for her tomorrow, the two of us together, father and son.'

They both worked hard all of the next day. Kapil kept coughing every now and then but they did not stop until the deed was done.

'Wait, Sonal – stay where you are.' Chirag stopped his sister from entering her bedroom that evening. He was holding a pair of scissors.

'I am very tired,' she told him sternly, 'and in no mood for playing games.'

'This is not a game and I'm tired too,' Chirag said grumpily. 'I have been slogging away for you ever since this morning.'

'What do you mean?'

'Take this pair of scissors and cut this ribbon; only then can you enter your room.'

'Give them to me.' Sonal frowned at him. But as soon as she entered her room, she stopped dead in amazement. The walls were painted sky blue, and there were new curtains and new bed linen in the same colour.

'It was Dad's idea but I helped,' Chirag explained. Sonal was speechless.

The next morning, Sonal opened her eyes and found her dad standing by her bed. He was looking lovingly at her. Their eyes met, and she felt like embracing him but instead she looked away. Kapil went out sadly and Sonal sobbed.

Kapil himself had cried all those weeks ago when the doctor told him that he had cancer in his lungs, and that it had spread to other parts of his body.

'It means that I will not survive, doesn't it?' he had asked brokenly.

'You have left it too late, I am afraid. I can't do anything at this stage.'

'Tell me straight, how long do I have?'

'Not long.'

'Two months? Five months? How many days, Doctor?'

'I can't say for certain, Kapil. You may live for one year but it will be very hard . . .'

'I understand. Look, please don't tell this to anyone yet.'

'Until when? You can't hide it for ever.'

*

Children, like their parents too, cannot remain angry forever. Sonal was worried about Kapil's constant cough. She wondered why he did not sing that morning and felt bad about her hostile behaviour towards him. In

Mablethorpe, she could hear the birds chirping – unlike London, where no one had time to listen to birdsong. Noisy London, where the doors were always shut and the windows double-glazed.

Sonal put on her dressing gown and went to knock at her dad's room. He was not there, and his harmonium and tanpura had also disappeared.

In the afternoon, Kapil returned home from rehearsing in the church. Something smelled nice, he thought. He feared that he might have left something on the cooker – his memory had been playing games with him lately. However, when he entered the kitchen, he found Sonal frying pooris and Chirag enjoying the food.

'Hi, Dad, lunch is ready,' Sonal said, looking affectionately at him. Then she repeated: 'Come on, Daddy, don't let it get cold,' and Kapil was so surprised. She sat down with him and they all ate the meal in companionable peace and quiet. Father and daughter both secretly wanted to pour their hearts out. For the first time, Sonal really looked at her father properly and could see how very weak he was.

Kapil himself had drawn deeply from his reserves of willpower over these long years apart, but his courage was faltering now. 'Do I have enough breath left to give away my daughter in marriage when the time comes?' he wondered. 'Oh, why did fate have to conspire against me like this? By now I must surely have had more than my fair share of adversity. Chirag is so young, but I am not worried about him – Neeraj is there to look after him. It is Sonal that concerns me.'

The next day, Sonal had prepared lunch once again, but Kapil had not come home. Her dad's unexplained absence made the girl anxious. Feeling very hungry, Chirag had opened a packet of biscuits and was stuffing himself with them.

'Chirag, stop,' his sister said. 'Dad will be annoyed if he comes in and sees you. By the way, where is he?'

'Still in the church, I expect – where else? And I'm starving . . .'

Of course – the church, where Kapil was rehearsing for the big concert.

The moment she entered, Sonal could feel the curtain of dust all around her; it was hard to breathe. Kapil was sitting at the harmonium, composing, rushing to write down the notes before he furiously shook his head, and began trying out a different interpretation.

This routine continued for a while. Kapil worked on. He was humming a tune – but the moment he broke into a song, his cough took over. He tried to suck in a breath of fresh air, but instead he inhaled a lot of the plaster dust – which resulted in a violent spasm of coughing that forced him to bend over the harmonium. After a while, when he raised his hand, his hankie was soaked in blood.

'Daddy!' Sonal raced over to cushion Kapil's sagging head.

The man heard his daughter's piercing cry of – 'Oh Daddy, I'm so sorry!' – and then he became unconscious.

*

Kapil slowly regained his senses to find Sonal and Gautam sitting before him. 'How on earth did I get here?' he mumbled confusedly.

'How could you not tell us about your illness – it's cruel and unpardonable,' his daughter burst out. 'You have been going through all this on your own – we had no idea!'

'It's just a little cough,' he lied weakly. 'I'll be better soon.'

With a hand clamped over her lips, barely able to control her sobs, Sonal ran out of the room.

'Does Sonal know?' he asked Gautam.

'She is not a child any more,' his friend said gently. 'She found out about everything.'

His brow furrowed, Kapil asked, 'Pass me your mobile, Gautam. I need to make a call.'

When Anjali answered, he said: 'Hello, Anjali – yes, I am fine, but Sonal has found out about the cancer and it's upsetting her. I'd like you to come and take the children back with you as soon as you can.'

By now, Sonal had returned to the church with Chirag in tow. Overhearing her father's words, she asked to speak to her mother on the phone and put it on loudspeaker mode so that they could all hear what was said.

'Look, Mum, I am not going back to London with you,' she said.

'You will have to go, I can't stand your stubbornness any more,' Kapil spoke up, trying to sound firm.

'No! I know why you are doing this, Dad, and I'm not going anywhere. I refuse to leave you on your own.'

'Listen, my darling,' Anjali tenderly cajoled her. 'You will be starting at university soon. This is the beginning of a very important phase of your life. Please – don't let emotions ruin your career. If you like, you can spend all your summer holidays with your dad in future. Now, you have to come back home.'

'Why don't you understand? Dad needs me to see him through his illness. In any case, I am eighteen now. You cannot force your decisions on me.'

And before Anjali could recover from her daughter's outburst, Chirag himself chipped in with: 'I am not going to leave Sonal alone, Mum.'

'But term will be starting soon. What about your school, all your friends?'

'There are schools here in Mablethorpe too,' the boy shot back.

'This is getting ridiculous. Sonal, you bad girl, you are influencing your brother as well.' Back in London, Anjali felt overwhelmed and tearful. 'We have had enough drama for the time being,' she went on. 'Now pack up your bags and I shall drive up and collect you before nightfall.'

Sonal handed the phone back to her dad, saying kindly to her brother: 'Come on – I'll help you pack. You know very well that Mum cannot survive without you. I will join you as soon as Dad recovers.'

'There we are, Kapil,' Anjali was saying now. 'Didn't I tell you that her deep-rooted love for you would overcome all her resistance the moment she set eyes on you? I give up. If she is hell-bent on ruining her career, I'll let her get on with it. After all, she is eighteen now and must make her own decisions.'

*

There was not a shadow of a doubt in Sonal's mind that she needed to stay in Mablethorpe with her dad. What a paradox, that now Kapil had his daughter back, time was the only commodity he was short of – the sands of time were slipping away fast now. His health was getting worse by the day; he was compelled to stay in bed much of the time. Resting his hands on Sonal's shoulders, he tried to get to the seashore for short walks – but his stamina would fail him after a few steps. His body was fast being shrunk to a mere skeleton. Sonal did not leave him alone for a minute. Gautam tried his best to share the responsibilities with her.

Being so young, Sonal was in need of a lot of moral support as her reserves of courage began to run thin. Gautam was the only person who understood and shared her anxieties.

'Uncle, I am responsible for Dad's slow death. He is suffering because of my stupidity.'

'No, my child, you have no reason to indulge in such silly thoughts. On the contrary, can't you see the change in my friend? Your presence here has given him another lease of life.'

'Uncle, I want to do something profound so that Dad can feel proud of me. I want to give him an experience that he can happily carry with him to the world beyond this one.'

'I am sure that will be possible. Kapil has always insisted that the Goddess Saraswati has blessed you with a musical voice. The concert that your dad is preparing for – you must take it over.'

'How can I? I'm incapable of singing a song at the moment – I can barely even hum one. Moreover, in his present condition, Dad can't help me, and I will not be able to do it on my own. No, Uncle, I will have to cancel it. You must think of something else.'

'Are you aware how much happiness this would bring to him? There are still three more weeks before the concert. We should pray that he survives to hear you perform.'

Sonal's sobs were accompanied by free-flowing tears, and she sought solace against Gautam's broad chest.

After that day, Sonal started to work in earnest on her dad's music, vowing to herself that she would fulfil his dreams. Meanwhile, Kapil was moved into a hospice, as it was no longer possible to care for him at home. Gautam was always on hand to keep the sick man company while Sonal took time off to rehearse. The girl was aiming for one thing and one thing alone – to sing for her dad and win Uncle Gautam's approval.

*

The big day dawned – the concert was due to take place. Kapil was intermittently floating in and out of consciousness. The doctors had warned his family that Kapil could breathe his last at any moment. Hearing this news, Sonal had summoned Anjali, and she had come up from London.

'Kapil, you must hold on for a while. Don't you dare slip away.' Grief had made Gautam's voice hoarse. 'Your daughter is about to present you with the most beautiful gift of your life. Anjali, give him strength – you must not let him go yet. His daughter has worked so hard to prepare this for him.'

Anjali was finding it hard to hold back her tears. She switched on the radio at Kapil's bedside, the exact moment that his friend Gautam's voice came on the airwaves, telling the listeners:

'Most of you sitting here are aware that Mr Kapil Sinha is in hospital at the moment. The date of this concert was fixed a long time back, before he received the devastating news about his health. Bravely, he never let anyone know about his illness and carried on with his preparations. Naturally, his hopes for the concert were dealt a severe blow by this hurricane moving stealthily towards him. However, Mr Kapil's daughter has replaced him on the soundwaves to give voice to the music written by her dad. She will start the programme with his swansong. Ladies and gentlemen, put your hands together to welcome – Sonal!'

'Daddy!' Sonal's voice pierced through Kapil's half-closed lids – 'Daddy, your last song is going to be your Angel's first. Your daughter will keep your music alive. I give you my word that I will take your music all around the world. I love you, Daddy, I love you . . . so much.'

She started humming the tune to deafening applause. But as the music picked up, you could hear a pin drop in the hall. As if in a trance, she entered a musical world of her own. Each word came straight from the heart. She felt as though her dad was playing the harmonium. The lilting words pulled at the audience's heartstrings and many eyes were filled with tears. In the hospice, the dying man's pride shone through his eyes.

Afterwards, members of the audience surrounded Angel, trying to congratulate her, wishing to talk to her. But all she wanted to do was to get away and rush back to her daddy's bedside.

In the hospice, night was falling and Anjali was desperately chatting away to Kapil, trying to keep him awake. The doctors had been concerned that once he went into a deep slumber, he might slip away into the unknown this time. Anjali was waiting for Kapil's Angel, not Sonal. She paused for a moment and was astonished to see her husband strive to speak. She bent close to listen.

'Neeraj, how is Neeraj?' Kapil said weakly.

'Why would you think of Neeraj at this critical moment,' she breathed, 'when he caused you so much torture? What kind of a man are you?'

'You looked so happy that day.' Kapil was barely audible.

'Ah, that day when we came out of the hotel arm-in-arm, to find you standing right before us! The horror in your eyes has kept me sleepless many a time – I wake up sweating all over. If you had punished me for my infidelity, it would have been justly deserved. And I would have been able to cope better. The ease with which you forgave us was the worst punishment that you could have inflicted on me.'

'You are a very good mother, Anjali,' the sick man gasped. Then, 'Please. You must be careful. My Angel must never find out about this.'

But it was too late. Because Sonal, his Angel, was already at the door of his room – and she had heard every word.

'I cannot believe this,' she whispered. 'It was you all along, Mum. *All the time, it was you.*'

The Flight

Purnima Varman

Sharjah, United Arab Emirates, 2011
After grabbing a quick cup of coffee, Sakshi entered her classroom, where the first group was about to end their presentation. Good – that meant that she had time to finish her coffee. Waving a quick good morning to her lecturer, Ms Ana Gavassa, the girl started mentally rehearsing her PowerPoint presentation. Sahar Masood, her teammate, was busy connecting the projector to the laptop and getting everything ready for them. He was relieved to see Sakshi's arrival.

'Everything OK?' she asked.

'*Akeed* – yeah,' he replied, with a thumbs-up.

After the first presentation had finished, Ms Gavassa returned to her office for a five-minute break. Sakshi and Masood were on next.

Their presentation went well. The newly-added SVG (Scalable Vector Graphics) were amazing. Masood had managed to find these in the French library overnight, and had converted the text into English. The SWF movie at the end made a real impact. He had done a great job, and throughout Sakshi's English narration was both clear and impressive.

When the opposing team assaulted them with questions, Sakshi replied with eloquent and thought-provoking answers. Ana Gavassa was pleased with their work. Afterwards, Sahar Masood hi-fived his partner. The tricky technical parts had been his responsibility, while Sakshi's job had been to ensure that the presentation was of high quality. The two of them had planned and rehearsed it all thoroughly and deserved their high marks.

Sakshi decided to stay back and thank Masood; it was because of him that they had done so well, she thought. She fully intended to help him clear up, but all of a sudden she just walked out and left, abandoning him in the classroom with all the packing away to do.

It was an ordinary morning at the American University of Sharjah. Every day, aspiring to make the world a smaller place, teachers and students came together to try to eliminate barriers of language, cuisine, lifestyle and any other possible cultural divide. Right now, some students had gone to the canteen for a quick snack. The next two groups were preparing for their presentations and those who had finished were sitting outside, chatting on a bench.

It had been a successful morning, so Sakshi thought it would be a good idea to pick up her favourite movie on her drive home.

Making her way slowly down the stairs, she reached the car park – then remembered that today, there had not been any spaces available in her department's area. Perhaps the third-year students had some function on and thus had occupied all the available spaces. She had had to park at a distance and walk the rest of the way. She reached the car – a Jaguar – turned on the engine and drove off, leaving through the university's main gate.

*

When driving the powerful car, Sakshi felt as if she was flying. In fact, she aimed to fly in every aspect of her life. Flight – *udaan* – was in her blood. She longed to leave everything behind, to fly somewhere out of this world, to a place where only she existed . . . That was why she had completed her 50-hour driving course in just 30 hours and within a month had become the proud owner of a driving licence.

Her father, Sandeshmal Saraf, was clever enough not to allow his daughter to drive a car for the next three months. As a rule, if someone had an accident within the first three months of procuring their driving licence, their licence was cancelled and they had to retake their tests. It was said that in the Emirates, buying a car was cheaper than actually procuring a licence! To get a driving licence for the second time would have meant shelling out another AED5,000. Mr Saraf was a rich man, but not so rich that he would turn his three kids into spoilt brats. He had raised three responsible children and his two elder sons had settled down in America. After the three months had passed he gave Sakshi the best luxury sedan that he could afford, and the girl was one step closer to embarking on her flight with a Jaguar's aggressive leap.

At this moment, Sakshi was driving the Jaguar down a wide, vacant road, her mind finally free of all the pressure of exams. In her haste she had not had anything to eat that morning. From the dashboard she picked up her mobile phone and dialled her home number.

'Mum, I'm starving! Can you cook some rajma chawal? You know it's my favourite.'

'How was the test, sweetie?'

'Superb!'

As the needle on Sakshi's speedometer rose to over 120kmh, her mum heard the beeping and said anxiously, 'Are you talking on your mobile phone again while driving? I told you not to.'

'Oh come on, Mum! There's no surveillance camera in this area. OK, I'll hang up now.' And Sakshi disconnected the phone. The girl knew very well where the speed cameras were and where she could drive without worrying about getting a fine. She had to take care though, because her dad would pay the fine, but not without giving her a good lecture.

After about 300 metres the road turned onto a motorway, signalled by a blue notice board. Sakshi checked in both directions and then accelerated onto the motorway.

When she reached home, she rang the doorbell repeatedly, but no one came to answer. Frustrated, she started banging at the door. Even then there was no response. She took out her mobile phone and dialled the landline number; she could hear the phone ringing inside but no one picked it up. Dad was supposed to be home for lunch at around this time, Sakshi thought, and just a few minutes ago, she had spoken to her mum. What had happened?

Sakshi lived in a twenty-one-storey building with two penthouses on the top floor. One belonged to her father, Mr Sandeshmal Saraf, and the nameplate for the other flat read *Dr Valery Kolotov and Dr Yulia Kolotov*. They were an old Russian couple who had been resident surgeons in Zulekha Hospital for a long time now. They spent most of their time at the hospital and so their apartment was silent all day long. Their key was left with the cleaning staff, who usually came for an hour or so around noon. Just then, the Kolotovs' door opened and the cleaner, Ali, came out, carrying the vacuum cleaner and humming his favourite melody.

'Hey, Ali,' Sakshi greeted him. 'Have my mum and dad gone somewhere? No one's answering the door.'

'Mrs Saraf is inside, madam. I know because I handed her a packet of rajma just half an hour ago.'

'I wonder what's wrong? I have been ringing the doorbell for the last fifteen minutes, and I've banged on the door a zillion times, but there's still no answer. I've even called on the landline, but had no luck with that either.' The girl was becoming agitated.

'Have you come to meet Madam Saraf or Ms Sakshi, madam?' he enquired.

'What nonsense! Can't you recognise me? I *am* Sakshi!'

'Oh, so your name is Sakshi too? Wow! Sir and Madam Saraf also have a daughter named Sakshi. She went to university this morning but she isn't home yet. Are you a college friend of hers?' he asked.

'How long have you been working here?' she demanded in a frustrated whisper.

'For two years, madam,' he replied politely.

'So how can you forget a face that you've been seeing every single day for the last two years? I leave for university in the morning – and by noon you've forgotten my face? Don't you get it? It's me – Sakshi! Can't you recognise me?'

Seeing her reaction, Ali was a little scared. He stared at her from head to toe and murmured to himself, 'You are not Sakshi.' More loudly, he said: 'Let me ring the doorbell. Mr and Mrs Saraf must be inside.'

Ali rang the bell once and the door opened.

It was Sakshi's dad.

Nearly in tears and a little angry, Sakshi entered the drawing room without saying anything. She passed the dining table and sat on the sofa.

'For God's sake, Dad, I have been banging at the door for half an hour, ringing the doorbell, calling on the landline, and you never answered! You guys scared me to death!'

The man maintained a neutral expression, then his brow lifted in surprise. 'You are calling me Dad?' he said. 'Yes, I'm of your father's age undoubtedly, but which address did you want to go to? Who are you looking for?'

'Don't be silly, Dad. I have come home and I'm talking to you, my one-and-only father. My test was excellent today.'

'Well done, my dear. Are your parents staying in the building too?' Mr Saraf asked her pleasantly.

'What are you saying? Don't you recognise me, Dad? It's me – Sakshi! Your one and only daughter!' She broke down in tears and couldn't say anything further.

'Hey, Kalindi! Come and see who is here.' Mr Saraf went inside, calling his wife. 'This young lady appears to be from a good family, though she's saying strange things and seems to be mentally unstable. God knows

177

'where she wanted to go and where she thinks she has ended up.' He was obviously concerned.

'Didn't she say where she came from?' asked Kalindi.

'No, she insists only that her name is Sakshi, and she keeps calling me Dad.'

'How does she know Sakshi? Maybe it's a friend of hers who's visited before.'

'I don't think so. Why don't you come and talk to her?'

Sakshi clearly heard the muted conversation as she sat in the drawing room. She was tired, hungry and heartbroken by this strange treatment – and in her very own home!

'Oh God, what are they thinking? What the hell is happening here?' she whispered to herself. She felt a strong urge to run to her room, hide her face in the pillow, and cry her heart out. She got up and started walking towards her bedroom.

'Where are you going, my dear?' Sakshi's mum came out and stopped her.

'I want to go to my bedroom, Ma. Please stop whatever you are doing. Is this some kind of prank you are all playing on me? It's NOT funny, so please stop it right now. Please! How many times do I have to tell you? I AM your daughter, you both are my parents!'

Oh! There is indeed something wrong with this poor girl, Kalindi thought, wiping her hands on a kitchen towel.

I hope we don't get into any sort of trouble, thought Mr Saraf.

'You are right. This is Sakshi's room, but she isn't home yet.' Kalindi was trying to stay as calm as possible.

'That's enough! This is the absolute limit!' Sakshi burst into tears. Whatever was wrong with everyone?

She was really worried. Had her dad found out about that day last week when she had bunked off her classes and gone for a day out with Jimmy to Umm-al-quwain? It was just to pass the time – she didn't have a serious relationship with Jimmy, but as a result of all the texting and chatting on their mobile phones, she had ended up spending a whole day at Umm-al-quwain with him.

She knew that her dad had already arranged her marriage to another boy; after all, she had helped to choose him as well. Then . . . then how could she have run off with another boy for a full day? Shit – why did she do these stupid things? If she had thought it through, she would never have done it in the first place. She knew that her dad would kill her if he found out – but strangely, he didn't seem angry. Was this silence his revenge? Was he planning to disown her? If so, what would she do? Where would she go?

Her pulse accelerated in fear. Somehow she controlled herself. No, this couldn't be happening. Her dad might do such a thing, but her mum . . . her mum could never behave indifferently towards her. She could never act like this, with anger growing in her face. Instead of consoling her, her parents were standing there like strangers, shocked and helpless.

'Don't you recognise your own daughter?' she begged.

'You are not Sakshi.'

'Of course I am Sakshi, I am your daughter!' She stood her ground, looking her mother straight in the eye.

'No, you aren't,' her mum sighed.

'I just called you from my mobile phone to say that I was hungry, and to ask you to please prepare some rajma chawal for me, and hearing my speedometer beep you even scolded me.'

'Were you in Sakshi's car at the time?' her mum asked doubtfully.

Mr Saraf quietly got up and sat down on a sofa slightly further away. A frown surfaced on his face. 'Please just tell us what you want,' he said. 'Why have you come here?'

'Oh, now you are talking to me as if I'm some kind of blackmailer. Why am I here? This is my home! Where else am I supposed to go?'

'This is not your home, and we do not know you,' Kalindi said kindly. 'Look – it's getting dark now. Try to remember your address and we will help you to get there. It's not advisable to wander around in the dark alone. If you wish to leave, you should do so right away while there is still light outside.'

'Oh Mum . . . where am I to go? There is no one else I can go to other than Dad and you!' Sakshi's voice choked and she started crying inconsolably, covering her face with her palms.

Ignoring her, Mrs Kalindi continued with her kitchen chores while Mr Saraf opened up the newspaper. No one paid any attention to Sakshi, but seeing the darkness falling, Mrs Kalindi eventually got a bit worried. Seeing her mum looking so anxious, Sakshi wiped away her tears, got up quietly and dragged herself out into the lobby, where she pressed the lift button.

Going downwards, the lift stopped and Shibu, who lived on the fourteenth floor, got in. Although she was a student in her third year at the university, she looked at Sakshi without recognition. Shibu, who never tired of calling her 'sis', stood there silently all the way down to the ground floor. Sakshi finally began to think that maybe she wasn't really Sakshi, and her legs started trembling. Walking past the supermarket downstairs, where she purchased her food every day, no one smiled at her or said hello.

She walked towards the seashore and sat down on a bench to watch the white birds that had migrated in winter enjoying their routine. She felt disconnected from everything: the material world, her family, the city, the earth itself . . .

All of a sudden, her emotions were lifted away: there was no more pain in her heart, no tears in her eyes and her mind was serene. She felt weightless, lighter than air – as if she were a kite, as if someone had cut her strings. And now she was flying with a big group of the white cranes, just like them, swimming in the air . . . One of the cranes turned his long neck to look at her, as if he recognised her. Oh! They all recognised her, all of them. Where had she come from, she wondered, and where was she flying to? She kept on flying . . . far, far away . . . just far, far away . . .

*

Next day in the local newspaper, the *Gulf News*, there was an article about a fatal accident the previous afternoon between a car and a truck at the junction of the main road to the American University of Sharjah.

Whenever there is an accident on the roads in the Emirates, the police usually take no more than ten minutes to free the traffic. The ambulance arrives, the road is cleaned, and the insurance claim is issued in no time.

Having collected up all his belongings after the presentation, Sahar Masood was driving home when he saw the wrecked Jaguar on the road. For a minute his heart skipped a beat. A girl was lying on a stretcher which was being carried to an ambulance. Was it Sakshi? If so, was she dead or alive?

Masood immediately pulled in next to the crash – but passers-by were forbidden to stop at the scene of an accident, unless the police themselves called for assistance. If only he could remember Sakshi's licence-plate number! He tried to find out by looking at the yellow-taped scene from all the mirrors of his car for as long as he could, but it was no use. He did manage to get a glimpse of the girl's face, but it was unrecognisable.

Sakshi wasn't a friend of long standing, it was true. It had only been a few months since their admission to the university, after all, and Arabian and Indian students didn't usually hang around together. The two of them had only really got to know each other a week or so ago, when they had formed their little team to prepare a presentation for the class. All the same, it was a terrible shock.

*

A memorial was organised within the department.

'Good teachers always want to see their students rising high on the ladder of success, not departing like this,' Ana Gavassa said in a choked voice during her speech. Sakshi's friends had tears in their eyes too – but Sahar Masood broke down completely. In the canteen his friends tried in vain to console him.

Virgin Meera

Dr Pushpa Saxena
Translated by Anila S Fadnavis

New York, 2009

'Aunty, have you been to any bars here?' my nephew Pratik asked me on our long drive after dinner.

'Why should I?' I replied. 'I don't drink.'

'What – you are visiting the USA and you have never been to a bar – not even entered one? You really are missing something. Let's go and have a Coke at least. Is that a problem for you, Uncle Sunil?'

My husband shrugged. 'Not at all – but I don't have my wallet with me.'

'And I am not dressed for the evening,' I said.

'Don't worry, Aunty, you look fine. And Uncle, I think I can just about spare a few dollars to spend on my own relatives,' Pratik joked as he drove towards a bar.

The twinkling lights of the restaurant were visible from a distance. As we grew closer, I could see that the place was full of smartly dressed young men and

183

women. The youngsters I usually saw wore casual T-shirts and shorts, and went around with backpacks on their shoulders.

The restaurant was a little noisy but lively and cheerful.

As we went in, Pratik teased me, saying, 'Are you twenty-one, Aunty? If not, we won't be allowed in.'

'Yes, I know – I should have brought my ID, like you and Debashish,' I said, joining in the joke. As we entered, I thought how it was nothing like my Indian idea of a bar. There was soothing music and the people around were all gazing into each other's eyes. Embracing and kissing in public places was no longer a new sight to me these days.

The table where we sat was in the middle so we could see every corner of the bar. A girl sitting near the window looked as though she was in a melancholy trance, I thought. She seemed very sad and completely separate from the world around her.

Sunil and Pratik ordered Pepsis for the four of us. I could not stop myself asking about the girl near the window. 'Why is she is sitting so quietly in a place like this, Pratik?' I asked.

'That's Virginia. She is waiting for one of our Indian brothers who will never return,' he said.

'Has she lost her beloved and doesn't know about it?' I asked.

'No, that's not it. Aunty, do you know the story of Ahalya, the most beautiful woman in Hindu mythology, who was seduced and then cursed and abandoned? Well, that Indian brother I spoke of cursed Virginia in the same way.'

My nephew could see I was curious, and he asked me if I wanted to meet her. 'Aunty, you should try to make her talk and hear her story. Come, I will introduce you.'

We left Sunil and our other nephew Debashish for a few moments while Pratik dragged me over to where the young woman was sitting. 'Hi, Virginia,' he said. 'Meet my aunty from India.'

She looked at me, starting slightly at the word 'India', then dropped her gaze again. Without her consent, Pratik brought over an extra chair for me, and we sat down beside her, although her expression was not particularly welcoming.

'Do you know, Virginia, Aunty is a writer; she has interviewed many students for her work and now she has come to talk to you,' said Pratik.

'Nice meeting you, but I've got to go,' she muttered, and got up from the table, leaving her drink.

Pratik was embarrassed. He tried to explain. 'Virginia is very emotional; it's tragic, but she just wants to be alone since Ravi left. And yet she was once the life and soul of every party. Do you think, Aunty, that any Indian girl takes love affairs this seriously?'

Pratik spoke more about Virginia on our way back, but Debashish tried to change the subject, saying that it was ruining his mood. The discussion then turned to various Indian bars, cafes and restaurants, but I was still lost in Virginia, her pale mysterious glance: I just could not erase her image from my mind.

'Who was Ravi? Where did he go?' I asked.

'Are you still thinking about her, Aunty?' said Pratik.

'Yes: you spoke of the cursed Goddess Ahalya, didn't you?' I asked.

'Yes, Aunty, but the person who cursed her was neither a mahatma nor a saint, he was just a cowardly, evil-hearted person,' said Pratik.

Apparently this Ravi had arrived in Albany, New York as a PhD student, with his Desi brand of toothpaste and his copies of the sacred books of *Ramayana* and *Bhagawat Gita*. His father was the priest at a temple in Benares. One of his disciples had bought Ravi's ticket to America. Like other university students, the young man soon found ways to earn his living – he and some of his hostel friends started washing cars after college hours. They used to charge three dollars per car and find customers at the traffic lights.

One day at the lights, Ravi asked Virginia politely whether she would like her car washed. His polite gestures, the way he was dressed – in simple Kurta pyjamas – and his attractive, warm skin colour appealed to the girl.

'Where do I take the car?' she asked.

'Just behind that building there.' Ravi was very happy to get a customer. She asked him to jump in and at the green light she turned towards the building.

The boys had set up their car wash beside a volleyball ground near their hostel. Virginia was asked to park in the shade under some trees. She watched as the boys toiled away, and was particularly drawn to Ravi. She offered him a two-dollar tip as she paid for the car wash, but Ravi politely declined, with thanks. As she walked back towards her car she asked him more about his college and about the subjects he was studying.

'I am here to get a PhD in Indian Religion and Philosophy,' Ravi said.

'I'd love to know more about Indian philosophy,' Virginia said enthusiastically. 'Would you be able to help me with that?'

'Would you really be interested?' Ravi didn't believe her.

'What's the matter? I'm a student of English Literature, and Tagore and Arobindo are my favourite authors.'

'I don't think that I can spare time for this, miss. You see, I have to work after college hours,' Ravi said helplessly.

'I will pay you for the time you spend with me – it's my responsibility,' Virginia added.

Ravi was shocked. 'How can I charge for teaching our religion?' he said.

Virginia smiled at his confusion. 'See, we Americans are straightforward – you are giving me your time and I have to pay for it. I think it could work, don't you, Ravi?'

He thought about it and then agreed. What she said made sense.

Virginia was a beautiful girl. The daughter of an industrialist, she had a cheerful, carefree nature and was a great party person. Most young people could only dream of having such a friend. Ravi started teaching her about his father's priesthood in the modern age. He told her stories of Rama, Sita, Krishna, Meera and Radha. The pair went to nearby temples, and Ravi prayed to the idols and involved Virginia in their age-old stories.

'Look at the Ram-Sita idols with faith, Virginia, and they will start talking to you. The smiling Bhagawan Ram is blessing you.' He closed his eyes and became engrossed in prayer.

Ravi used to sing the *Ramayana* and *Krishna Leela* and other epic poems in his sweet voice, explaining the meaning of each of them. Virginia was overwhelmed by the powerful, age-old stories, and believed each word that Ravi said. Particularly when he told her that Rama married Sita and never looked at any other woman ever again.

Virginia asked whether Indian men were all like Rama. She also asked Ravi about his own relationships, and he replied confidently, 'Yes, as I am an Indian man, I too am just like Rama.' He added to this by saying that Indian women, too, were so selfless that they would not continue living after their husbands died. They used to practise self-immolation in the good old days. Sita went into the forest for fourteen years, in exile with her husband leaving her castle. In Rajasthan women still performed Jauhar – suicide – after their husband's death.

God knows how many stories Ravi told Virginia about Radha-Krishna and the platonic love of Meera and Krishna, and many other heroic and selfless women who accepted death at their own hands after their husbands died.

Virginia started going to the temple with Ravi regularly. She updated her learning and read books on Indian philosophy and religion. Ravi was stunned to see her become a vegetarian. 'How will you survive, Virginia?' he asked.

'If Sita can live on roots and fruit for fourteen years in the jungle, why can't I?' she answered. She had started reading books on Hindu mythology too.

One day she was chanting Bhajan in the temple when Ravi said, 'Virginia, I feel that you are the soul of Meera. You have been reborn here. We Indians believe in rebirth. Otherwise why would you be carving out this knowledge of our philosophy and religion thousands of miles from India?' Thus Ravi placed Meera in Virginia's mind.

'Really, Ravi, is it possible? And are you Meera's Krishna? Is that the reason why we met?' Virginia was excited.

'It was not easy for Meera to be with Krishna. How will it work for us? Who am I to you, Virginia?' he asked.

'Don't you know, Ravi? You are my God, my destination, the last word for me,' the infatuated girl answered.

'What if I am no longer here?' said Ravi.

'Then I will enter the fire like Sati.' Virginia was serious.

'Oh! No, don't be foolish, Virginia.' Ravi laughed at this.

'Aren't you going to take me with you? Let's go to India.'

'But there are such scarcities; how will you survive there?' asked Ravi.

'The place where Rama, Krishna, Gautam, Arobindo, Meera lived – how can you say that such a sacred land is a place of scarcity?' She sighed. 'I wish I had been born in India.'

'All right then, as soon as we can, we'll go to India, to my small house near Ganga, and you will love it,' Ravi promised.

'Will your family accept me even if I am not from the right caste or religion?' Virginia asked.

'Yes, Virginia, with the sprinkle of Gangajal my father will purify you,' Ravi told her.

'Do you think that water can bring purity? Am I not pure? What magic would it perform?' Virginia asked, aghast.

'It's divine water for Indians. A drop of Gangajal on your deathbed takes your soul to heaven.' Ravi narrated the story of Bhagiratha in detail.

Virginia was more and more attracted to Indian religious rituals. Whether it was Ravi's story-telling skills or whether Indian philosophy alone was enough of a draw for her, remained a mystery.

On Ravi's completion of his PhD, Virginia invited many friends and professors to their party. She was dressed in an Indian outfit. She had learned to cook Indian food, which was a real surprise to Ravi. The food was vegetarian, too. Enjoying the party, he said, 'Wow! Thank you, Virginia, for all that you've done. I think you have all the skills and knowledge to be an Indian daughter-in-law now.'

The party ended, and Ravi lost himself: he crossed the boundaries that he himself had set, and tried to take Virginia to bed. She stopped him.

'This is not fair, Ravi! As you yourself said, we can't go to bed before marriage, can we?'

'What's the matter, Virginia darling? Come on. I want you . . .' Ravi was on fire.

Virginia stopped him, coldly. 'No, Ravi! This will spoil our heavenly love.'

'Don't be silly, Virginia,' Ravi pleaded.

'Do you think that Meera and Krishna were not actually in love, as they didn't come together?' Virginia retold him his own story. 'I don't think you are a man of principle.'

Ravi left that night more ashamed than insulted.

The next day, there was an urgent message from India about Ravi's father's serious illness. The only son had to be near his father and was asked to fly home immediately. Ravi was worried, but Virginia assured him that he should keep his faith in God; she would accompany him to India, she said, and she was ready to take care of his father.

Ravi said, 'I am sure my father will accept you for me, but I don't want you to be cursed by other family members, Virginia.'

Virginia was not bothered about the possible taunts of his family, but she said sadly, 'Very well. I don't want to be blamed if anything goes wrong, so I think it's best if I don't meet your father.'

'True – it will cause more problems if I take you right now, but I will call you as soon as I reach India,' Ravi assured her.

*

Back in the bar, Pratik continued his story. 'So Virginia paid for his ticket, Aunty, and Ravi left for India.'

'What happened to Ravi after that? Is he no more?' I asked.

Pratik sighed, then continued. 'Nearly one month later, there was still no word from Ravi, and no sign of him. I met up with Virginia many times, and I used to tell her not to worry. I thought that Ravi's father must be in hospital; at times I even thought that perhaps his father was no more, and that Ravi had had to perform rituals, which as we know takes nearly a month. So I told her I assumed he must be busy taking care of these matters and of the family. Virginia was anxious to go out to him; she wanted to be at his side. She decided to leave for India, to look for Ravi and to help him, as she thought of it as her duty.'

'And did she?' I asked.

'No. Before she left for India, I got a letter from Ravi in which he tried to justify himself for not contacting Virginia. He was such a coward and a cheat, Aunty. He wrote that the message he had received about his father turned out to be false. His father had come to know about Virginia and Ravi's affair and had said that it was against their religion and family rules. The daughter of one of his disciples was ready to get married to an American PhD holder, and Ravi was the ideal groom. It was the girl's father who had funded Ravi's education. Ravi said he had tried to explain the situation, but his father remained inflexible in his values and beliefs. In fact, he threatened to go on a fast until death if a foreign girl from a foreign religion came to his house as a daughter-in-law. So Ravi wrote that it was not in his power to make his own choices and go against his father's wishes.

'Poor Virginia was keeping a fast for Ravi's father's health on the very same day that the scoundrel Ravi was getting married to the disciple's daughter! It was Ravi who had emphasised the importance of keeping a fast for someone, and the selfish, ruthless, coward . . .' Pratik could not stop himself from abusing Ravi. 'Aunty, at one time I thought I would tell her that Ravi was dead – but I was sure that Virginia would have gone to India to perform those last sacred deeds for her so-called husband in the Ganges. But it was true that the Ravi whom she loved was dead, and he remained only as the son-in-law of a rich man.

'Finally, I told her the truth, and like a wounded bird she drove herself to the bar and drank as much as she could. Following the so-called philosopher's ideas about female behaviour, she had stopped drinking during her time with Ravi.

'No one could stop her; she never allowed anyone to get close to her again.' Pratik sighed once more. 'Now she comes and sits in that place looking as though it is the end of the world. Several of us have tried to befriend her, but she has turned herself into the deaf and dumb stone of "Ahalya".

'Poor Virginia,' he concluded. 'I doubt now that she will ever allow any Rama to appear in her life.'

No, I thought. You are wrong. She is not Ahalya: she is a Virgin Meera.

Good Morning, Mrs Singh

Shail Agrawal

Abergavenny, Wales, UK, 1997

'Good morning, Mrs Singh!' I said.

But there was no response. The woman lying in front of me on the bed was just a heap of bones. I felt scared even to turn her over, let alone try to wash her or change her clothes, in case she fell apart – in case she just crumpled in my hands like a dead flower-head.

I should have understood the situation from the moment when my good friend Barbara rang me first thing one morning, saying: 'Please, Shai, come and help us. There is an Indian woman here, staying in one of the rooms in our Crisis Centre, who hasn't eaten anything for a week now. She hasn't washed or brushed her hair during that time, and she won't talk to anyone or let anyone come near her. She just lies on the bed, with her eyes closed – she has completely withdrawn into herself. We are all extremely concerned about her.'

Barbara sounded quite agitated. She went on: 'Maybe you can do something for her where we have failed?

Perhaps she doesn't understand English . . . She might be less withdrawn with another Indian lady and you may be able to help her.'

Perhaps I will, I thought, and sighed, suspecting that it wasn't just a question of a language or communication barrier. I felt sure it would be something much more deep-rooted. It sounded to me as if this woman had lost the will to live, and had no interest in herself or in her surroundings.

*

When I saw the state of the woman in question, I was lost for words. How can someone be called back from that Land of the Dead?

Looking at her, it was difficult to tell if she was sleeping or awake, conscious or unconscious – but one thing was clear: she had cut herself off from this world and no longer cared what happened to her.

The air in the room was heavy and suffocating. There was a definite stink of death and decay. It was difficult to breathe. I opened the curtains and windows first. We both badly needed some fresh air.

There was a slight movement in that heap of a dirty and crumpled sari, and those bony legs silently folded themselves up towards her chest. I shook out her untouched blanket and tenderly covered her cold, frail body. The blanket started to heave with each of her tiny sobs. So she wasn't unconscious, after all.

Gathering all my strength, I put my hands on her shoulders and said gently, 'Perhaps I can help you, if you let me share your pain.'

There was no reply. Even her sobs had subsided now.

I sat silently by her side, stroking her dry, uncombed hair. She needed to take her own time, I knew that. It is not easy to open up, particularly when one is so knotted inside. I tried once again to reach her.

'Where do you come from?'

'From here in Abergavenny.' Her voice was hoarse and sad, as if she had been crying forever and had not spoken for many days.

'No, I'm not talking about this country, I meant back home. Where do you originally come from?'

I don't know whether it was the words 'back home' or my kindly, caring touch, but she opened her eyes and was looking at me now, revealing a most beautiful round face and big brown eyes. She really was lovely to look at.

'What is your name?' I asked.

'Kanak Lata. I'm from Bhagalpur Bihar.' Her English was flawless.

Now she wasn't just listening to me but understanding and answering. Her sindoor and bindi were sure signs that not only was she married, but that her husband was alive and well. I responded with an affectionate smile.

'Where is your husband and what is his name?'

'Harry Prasad Singh.'

'Harry Prasad?' I repeated the name in astonishment.

Then for the first time I saw a twinkle in her eyes, and a cheeky pink glow spread all over her face.

'Yes, you are right. My in-laws named him Hari. But once he arrived in this country, he told everybody that his name was Harry. All his patients call him Doctor Harry.'

'Patients . . . ' My interest was mounting now. 'What does he do? I mean profession-wise?'

'He is a GP here in Abergavenny.'

'Why didn't you tell me before, that you were the wife of Dr Singh?' Dr Singh, that famous psychologist and successful professional – and here was his wife in this terrible condition? I refused to believe it.

'No, I'm not his wife, I'm just married to him in name,' she replied bitterly. 'The one who shares his life and his bed is called Alva.'

'Who is this Alva?' I was finding it difficult to conceal my curiosity.

'The Other One!' she replied in a trembling whisper.

'Why do you call her the "Other One"? Why not call her his second wife or even his mistress?' I asked, feeling intrusive.

'Because there is no love or commitment there; no vows were taken, no promises made. She is just an opportunist; she doesn't give anything in that relationship – just takes and takes. Anyway, what difference does it make now?'

She tightened her lips, as if she didn't want to tell me any more, as if she didn't trust me enough yet.

But then she burst out: 'You see, they didn't even exchange rings. It is just a simple, convenient agreement. *Be my employee in the day and share my bed at night and I will repay you. Be my partner in sin for the rest of my life.*' Her face had gone bright red now in anger and disgust, and her sorrow disturbed me.

'Why didn't you put a stop to all this, or stand up for yourself?'

'Yes, I could have done that – if I had been allowed to. You see, I was over in India in Motihari at my in-laws' house, bringing up our son Rakesh. Waiting for those necessary papers, a passport and visa, my husband's sponsorship, and dreaming day and night with open eyes about our future life together here in the UK, a constant game of Happy Families.'

Then she paused for a moment and wiped her streaming tears. She proudly showed me a photograph of a seven- or eight-year-old healthy and handsome boy, which she had kept hidden inside her blouse, so that it was close to her heart.

'But when my family came to know that Hari had got another woman here and that she was expecting his child as well, out of wedlock, there was anger and abuse for him from all quarters. But I calmed them down. You see, my son's future was in question.

'Within weeks I was here with my father-in-law, who threatened Hari, saying: "You have married this woman in the presence of the whole community. These bonds cannot be broken so easily. My son, you have got to give her her rightful place in your life!"

'And so, you see, I *did* get my rightful place – in the corner of his servants' quarter, cooking and cleaning for them, away from my family, away from my son.' She spoke in harsh tones, as if it hurt her to say the words.

'This was my work, my duty and my door to heaven. My father's princess Kanak Lata was reduced to a domestic maid, and only paid in food and lodging. But I accepted all this as my fate because in return my husband promised to send money regularly to educate and look after my son. He is studying in the prestigious Mountview School in Bangalore now,' she told me proudly, wiping her tears away with her palloo. A smile illuminated her face as she thought about her son.

'And how did all *this* happen?' I had seen the wounds and scars on her arms and the back of her neck as she moved on the bed; they were deeply shocking.

Her lips quivered with a tearful smile. 'Oh, these injuries are the perks of my job. An everyday occurrence. Sometimes when I have accidentally dropped something or was unable to do the housework because of illness or some other minor or major problem, I would be beaten with belt buckles or whatever was handy. Can't you see what a thick skin I have developed now? I am surviving it all. But it didn't stop there.'

She kept on talking, in an uninterrupted flow now, as if I wasn't there, as if she would never get another chance.

'One day I bumped into a woman I knew from home in the local supermarket while doing some shopping for the household. Sheila used to be my brother's classmate at medical school in India. She and her husband had come over to the UK only a few months before, and had made their home here in Abergavenny. Sheila immediately said that they would like to pay me a friendly visit sometime soon. How could I say no to them?' Kanak Lata shuddered. 'And so they came one day and saw everything! In his shock, her husband fell into a frenzy: he is a doctor too – an upright man – and he challenged Hari about his irresponsible and unethical behaviour. He even threatened him, warning him that if he didn't mend his ways towards me he would take him to court for living in sin with two women at the same time, since this is not allowed in law, nor in our religion. The scandal would ruin both his reputation and his career.

'Sheila's husband told Hari again and again that he had brought shame on a noble profession. For me, however, it just made matters a hundred times worse: it was the opening of Pandora's box. After that day, my beatings became regular and more severe. I was not allowed to go out or visit or talk to anyone, and Hari used to lock me in my room at night in case I tried to escape. One day, when Sheila and her husband came round again, uninvited this time, they found out how I was living. Then their anger became out of control. They used foul words against him. The moment they left, Hari became wild with rage. He kicked and punched me until I fainted.

'You probably know the rest of the story. I was brought here by some kind person who wants to save my life, but I have no wish to carry on living . . . '

Kanak was looking very tired and frail now. It wasn't good for her to get this worked up. I helped her to get washed, found her clean night-clothes and settled her into the bed. After that, I went and warmed some vegetable broth in the kitchen at the Crisis Centre. It took some persuasion to get her to sip even a few spoonfuls.

'You must rest now, Kanak,' I told her. 'I will come and see you again tomorrow, I promise. If the pain from your injuries becomes severe, then take two of these tablets – but no more.' Putting a jug of water and a little bottle containing six painkillers on her bedside table, I said again, 'Remember, no more than two, all right?'

She smiled and just said, 'Goodbye, and thank you.'

'Don't forget to ring me anytime if you feel like it or want anything. Here is my phone number.'

She just waved this time, unable to speak, but her eyes, despite brimming with tears, were full of affection and gratitude.

She was so weak, so vulnerable and lonely.

*

The phone rang early the next morning. It was Barbara again, all in a panic.

'Shai, come straight here,' she said. 'It's an emergency. I will tell you everything once you get here.'

She put the phone down without even waiting for my response. I drove straight to the Crisis Centre and was there within a few minutes.

Barbara was waiting for me at the door. She and the other staff were looking very distressed. She pointed wordlessly upstairs, towards Kanak's room.

The lift didn't come, and I just ran towards the stairs. I couldn't bear to wait any longer. What had happened to Kanak now? She had been getting so much better – or had she? I flung the door open and saw one of the nurses busy at the bedside.

'Good morning, Mrs Singh, Kanak!' I said breathlessly. But there was no response. Had she fallen back into her depressive mood? But she was looking so peaceful. I turned to ask the nurse attendant, Lee.

'I'm afraid that she passed away last night. It was probably an overdose. We found this on her floor.' Lee blurted all this out in one long breath.

In utter shock and horror I looked at the bottle in Lee's outstretched palm. Yes, it was that same fateful little pot of painkillers that I had given her last night.

But the half-dozen I had left inside were not nearly enough to kill someone.

'I don't know how she got hold of these, since we keep all the medicines locked up, even the ordinary painkillers.' Lee was puzzled, and remained so when I had explained about the painkillers I had given her.

'Why, Kanak?' I implored the dead woman, full of grief. 'Why, when we would have helped you to make your life so much better?'

I felt angry and despairing. What a waste! She'd been so young and so beautiful! And to die, just when everything was about to improve in her life. Only yesterday, a few hours ago, I had been thinking of suggesting that she train as a nurse or social worker – once she felt better and had come out of her depression, of course. Because she herself had gone through so much, I felt sure she would understand the pain and suffering of others – and would have made an excellent and understanding nurse. She could have started a new life with her son, a real Happy Family, away from that monster of a man.

Lying still on the bed, she looked so serene and peaceful; there was no trace of bitterness on her face, as if she had forgiven them all.

With a heavy heart, I dragged myself back to the office.

'These are her belongings,' Barbara said. 'I don't know what to do with them. Perhaps you can help?'

She handed me the photograph of Kanak's son and of course that sindoor, which she wore so proudly on her forehead. The two objects in her life that she had loved and valued most. But they represented the two people who were always beyond her reach.

My thoughts turned to her son. I couldn't help Kanak Lata any more, but I should find and inform Rakesh, and make sure that his education was not interrupted. Suddenly I felt responsible for him. She had told me that he was studying in Mountview School in Bangalore and that Dr Hari Singh was paying for him.

I researched the number and rang the school – only to be told that there was no boy of that name in the school, nor had there been for many years. What treachery was this? So she had worked like a slave for nothing! My tears betrayed the turmoil beneath my cool, controlled exterior.

'Sleep peacefully, Kanak,' I whispered. 'I promise you that I won't let your son's life be neglected and wasted like yours. He will get all the things a child deserves in life.' Wiping those tears away with steely determination, I realised that my promise had been made not to her (for she had gone beyond either promises or betrayals) – but to myself. And immediately after her funeral, I got busy on the phone, booking my flight to India, and organising a trip to Motihari, Bihar.

My heart remained full of hope.

Rude Awakening

Sneh Thakore

Written in Toronto, Canada, 2000

Boom! There was a loud explosion, and hilltop debris danced in the air before finally depositing itself on the ground. There had been a time when the glorious reflection of the hills in the River Ganges had been a sight for sore eyes, but now those hills were being destroyed one by one, to make room for industry. What a price to pay for so-called progress!

And Dhara's life had shattered, she thought, just like the hill across from her house.

It was a hot, humid day. A fragment of sunshine, perched on the arm of her chair, jumped onto the windowsill and was getting ready to jump from there too.

Dhara was feeling dizzy. The walls were closing in and the ceiling placed a crushing pressure on her shoulders. Like that fragment of sunshine, she too wanted to jump from the window. Inside her, pain stretched from one end to the other, remorselessly, like the straight line on a heart-monitor screen when the heart stops, flat-lining, just *beep-beep-beep* . . . the monotone signal of death. The only difference was that she must be alive, for she was experiencing excruciating pain. If she were dead, would she have felt such agony?

Dhara had learned a long time ago to close the doors on hurtful memories. That was the only way to live a relatively peaceful life. Then why this restlessness today? Why was Sheila's insensitivity disturbing her so? The other woman hadn't said anything out loud, yet the language of her unspoken words said a great deal. Sometimes you don't need a ladder of words to reach the heart. The mere sight of the scratch on Dhara's arm had made Sheila flinch, as if a huge, poisonous snake had reared up to strike at her.

Dhara had not yet recovered from the shock of being diagnosed HIV-positive. Beyond the physical symptoms, she was also enduring a barrage of emotions within herself. And now, this social rejection! Sheila wasn't the first person who had made her feel as though she was untouchable.

Questions, questions . . . everywhere a daunting wall of questions. And in her search for answers she found only more questions. A fog of thoughts flew over her in a thick black cloud, and loneliness was choking her.

Evening was getting ready to surrender to the arms of night. Beyond the horizon, a train passed with thunderous noise, breaking Dhara's concentration. Lights from the compartment windows shimmered on the river's surface. The young woman's deep sigh made the bird perched on the windowsill flutter her wings, but seeing no sign of danger, the bird comfortably burrowed her head deep into her breast.

As Dhara got up and went to the bathroom, her footsteps echoed in the silence of the room. A stubborn tear was still hanging from the bottom of her eyelashes. With the back of her hand she swiped that tear away, destroying its very existence. She washed her face determinedly, as if to wash away all the sad thoughts. While she washed, she muttered to herself, though her voice sounded as if it was coming from a distance and belonged to somebody else. *Words,* she thought, *are just sounds until we pour our emotions into them; only then do they become meaningful.*

By now Dhara was ready. Her thoughts gathered strength, her voice became clear and her words had gained meaning.

Why should I be upset or punished for things I haven't done?

Why should I behave like a criminal when I am not one?

Why was I put in the witness box when it was no fault of mine?

Why should I bow to those who are inhumane, insensitive and ignorant – and want to remain that way?

*

By the time the young woman reached Vasudha's house, however, her self-confidence started wavering, eventually collapsing like a sandcastle. The hurtful memory had penetrated her brain like a leech, and she found that the beautiful Amaltas flowers in the front yard and the colourful bunches of bougainvillea entwined in the verandah's trellis had lost their usual mesmerising charm.

She shouldn't have come, Dhara thought. Yet every time she refused to attend these meetings due to the nature of her illness, Vasudha insisted that it was particularly important, given the nature of her illness and for the sake of her illness, that she *should* attend.

'Dhara, you are HIV-positive – you don't have AIDS. You know that there is a big difference between the two. An HIV-positive person doesn't necessarily become an AIDS patient. HIV can remain in the body for years. Though some HIV-positive people may show signs of AIDS-related illnesses, they may not be life-threatening.

'Having AIDS *is* life-threatening, but being HIV-positive is not. As you know, AIDS means Acquired Immune Deficiency Syndrome. You develop AIDS when the body's defence system declines so much that it's unable to fight the infection.'

A still-depressed Dhara mumbled, 'I could develop AIDS at any time.'

'Yes, you could. Anything can happen at any time. Who can see or predict the future? Do you know what the next moment holds for you? The possibilities are endless; you may slip on a banana skin and die. You can't live on assumptions. Even if you have AIDS, you can't pass it on to anybody by being at gatherings, touching hands, shaking hands or embracing somebody. This virus can only be transmitted through blood transfusions, semen and vaginal fluids. Sweat, saliva and other bodily fluids don't have a strong enough concentration of the virus to be contagious. On the other hand, using an AIDS patient's needle is highly contagious. It is important to know the high- and low-risk factors. Learning how to protect yourself and others from this illness is more important than creating a cocoon for yourself. You have a right to live, too.'

'If I have a right to live, then why did God give me AIDS?' Dhara's voice was bitter.

'I told you, you don't have AIDS!' the other woman interrupted her.

'Vasudha, not everybody is like you. You know how people cut me off! One more category has been added to the untouchable caste. People may not call us untouchable, but we are made to feel that way . . . '

'That is exactly why I asked you to participate. I understand your mental anguish, but people do this out of ignorance. You have to educate them – if not for yourself, then for future generations. People think it is a serious illness, which it is until the cure is found. But on the other hand, there is so much misunderstanding about how it spreads: we *have* to address this so that people will stop behaving so inhumanely.'

Dhara cried, 'How can two women teach the whole of society?'

'Women are not as powerless as you think. We are not decorative toys. Whenever a woman has fought for justice, society has stood by her. Don't consider yourself weak or lonely. Drain this sea of tears that is clouding your judgement. We have to stand up against the ignorance about AIDS and prevent the spread of the virus. If we are not able to do this, and do not educate the masses about it, HIV and AIDS sufferers will clam up when they see and suffer mistreatment, and this cruel and criminal behaviour will continue. They will conceal the disease to protect themselves, which will be disastrous. We have to create understanding and trust amongst ourselves. Open conversation and education are the only solutions. We can't hide our heads in the sand like an ostrich, we have to face reality. AIDS has started ticking like a time bomb. We need to defuse it collectively before it erupts into an epidemic.

'Dhara, do you remember that essay I read to you some time ago? I have the utmost respect for those people who have been fighting this disease for years. Because of their mental awareness they have warded off AIDS until now. They have learned to live with their condition, not in ignorance but on the basis of their knowledge. Being HIV-positive is not a death penalty for them, though who knows when death will snatch the life from any of us? Only God knows the time of our birth and death.'

Dhara was somewhat pacified by the conversation. 'Yes,' she replied quietly, 'I do remember that. All right, from now on you are my guru. I will do whatever you think is right.'

Then she added, with more heat: 'What irony, Vasudha! Our genetic families have become strangers to us, and strangers whom we have never met or heard of before have become as close as family. My own flesh and blood, for instance, have turned their backs on me. Betrayal by your own neither lets you live nor die in peace.

'I was brought up with so much love and care, like a delicate flower, yet now I have been discarded like a foul weed. They still feed me, maybe because they fear the wrath of society or because they have the remnants of a conscience which pricks them. But they are not even slightly concerned about my well-being, nor do they care how much their behaviour hurts me. The cruelty of my so-called "loved ones" burns me inside.

'It happened so fast. In the blink of an eye my life was destroyed, just as a storm uproots trees, lays waste to flowers and fruits and then deserts the land. Every day, a volcano erupts inside me, yet outside I remain like an iceberg. My heart is a dumping ground and my whole life is a living grave. How can I go on like this!'

Vasudha's throat swelled up with sympathy. She tried to console Dhara, but words failed her. Sometimes even a single word refused to come out from her vast vocabulary, but at other times words emerged in such a rush that they tangled together, and couldn't move, standing still like cars in a traffic jam. Words . . . what a strange commodity – powerful yet worthless. But unbeknownst to her, Vasudha's compassionate silence spoke louder than a million words.

Dhara felt suddenly empowered with understanding. Passionately, she said, 'Vasudha, I have been running away from everybody, even from myself, because I'm afraid of people. My life has become an empty shell without a trace of hope. If ever I do feel alive, it is for a fleeting moment, like lightning in the sky. My eyes have stopped dreaming, my words have died. I don't know how to start my life again. I'm like a woman who is knitting a sweater and halfway through realises that the pattern she has knitted is not to her liking. Now what should she do? Unravel it? Do I have time to start a new pattern in a new sweater? Or shall I carry on with this even though I don't like it? Do I knit another design on top of it?'

Like a tap from a full tank of water, Dhara's words kept on flowing. 'Vasudha, do you think the world will ever change its attitude? Are these moments of pain and sadness enough to shatter this unreal tranquillity?

Are these ripples sufficient to create bigger ripples and eventually huge waves, or will they just vanish unnoticed, leaving the sea's surface calm and untroubled? Will the silence of death prevail?'

And then Dhara began to sob, uncontrollably. She became like a tree, standing at the edge of a landslide, looking for support as the earth kept slipping from its roots. Vasudha opened her arms and Dhara's head found shelter on her chest.

After a while, the other woman lifted Dhara's face and looked into her sorrowful eyes. Two pairs of eyes gazed at each other, trying to clear the vast jungle of questions and answers.

When she eventually spoke, Vasudha's gentle voice was full of assurance. 'Time never stands still. The clock ticks at its own pace, oblivious to our feelings. For some of us, time may not move at all – it just stands still – but for others it soars in the sky. In fact, it is we who give the meaning to time with our happiness or tears of sorrow.

'Dhara,' she went on, 'you must understand one thing. Comparing your own sadness with someone else's does not help with the pain. There are vast differences in feelings. Don't measure yours with the same yardstick but keep on pushing for awareness. Sitting still is fruitless. People equate being HIV-positive with AIDS, and that's why they don't come forward. We have to support each other. AIDS doesn't spare anybody, regardless of their age, gender or nationality.

'Society's ignorance is not only unacceptable and dangerous for patients, it is equally damaging for the next generation. We have to tackle it socially, politically and individually, otherwise it will romp around like a wild animal wreaking havoc. If we allow this disease to become an epidemic because of ignorance, this small pond will turn into an ocean of devastating grief.'

Breathing heavily with the strength of her conviction, Vasudha continued: 'Nobody deserves to be sick with this illness! Nobody asked for it! How can we forget the huge number of innocent people suffering from it? Children from infected mothers who themselves were not aware of it, blood recipients and so on. Education is the first step.'

'You are right, Vasudha. Fear breeds fear. In fact, fear is spreading faster than the virus. In small villages, even the health professionals are not properly educated. Anamika was shocked by their behaviour when she was admitted. The oath they'd taken to help their patients evaporated like camphor. She understood their reasons, their ignorance about the disease, but it hurt just the same.

'HIV-positive people can live a normal life for ten to fifteen years at the moment, and that period is increasing all the time. And more and more health professionals are being trained to deal with it, although progress is admittedly slow.

'That is why we all have to pitch in. It's not a problem that's specific to one group. The key to dealing with it is a combination of research and learning from patients' experiences – and then incorporating this knowledge into the education system to change society's attitude. In societies where discussions about sex, homosexuality, drugs and AIDS are taboo, people form ill-conceived opinions.'

'Vasudha, your thoughts are a guiding light in my life's dark alley. You are absolutely right. I have to make people understand that I am just another face in the crowd. I not only want to live, I want to help, too.

'When Revati got married, she had no idea that her husband had AIDS. By the time she found out, she was the mother of an HIV-positive baby girl. Why don't we have blood-tests before marriage? Gajendra's parents arranged this marriage to stop his wandering eyes. Little did they know that in the process, they condemned two more lives!

'Gentle, simple Rahul had no idea that the blood he received through a transfusion was to prove a death sentence, since people not only shunned him, but the disease alienated his parents and siblings too.

'So many lives are affected, through no fault of their own. Instead of dreams, their days are filled with desperation.'

On a softer note Dhara asked, 'Was Divya a relative of yours?'

'I interviewed her as an AIDS patient. Later, friendship blossomed. Unfortunately, we think these people are just a chart to be updated. We don't want to be connected with them in any way, shape or form. We have created this image in our minds that only prostitutes, homosexual couples, drug abusers – so-called "bad" people – get AIDS. So we put them together in a pot and tighten the lid. We can justify ourselves for washing our hands of them. From Divya, I learned that this disease throws out its net like a cruel hunter upon any one of us. When we realise that we could all become an unlucky victim, perhaps then we will see reality more clearly and have more compassion.'

Vasudha's voice was filled with highly charged emotions which galvanised and inspired the other woman.

'I am with you all the way,' Dhara said steadily. 'We can't afford to lose a single moment. Even if I die, I know

I will be useful for somebody else. When the seed buries itself in the ground, only then does the new shoot open its eyes above the earth. By destroying itself, the seed gives birth to trees, fruit – and more seeds.'

Vasudha grasped Dhara's hand and raised it. Together, they formed a fist. The women's fingers, though weak individually, were powerful joined together.

Unmourned

Sudershen Priyadershini

Cleveland, Ohio, USA, 2008

I live in a development which is made up of small, medium-sized and even high-class condos. The name of the development is Tree-trail (we call it Mohalla back home). It is a beautiful name, and suitable too, since there is a long tree-trail weaving around our homes like a queen's necklace.

I sometimes take a drive just to enjoy the scenery and the landscaping that people here have created around their properties. I admire all the different kinds of flowers, bushes and trees – but sometimes, in my heart of hearts, I secretly criticise their arrangements, if they have the wrong colour combinations, uneven growth or a jumble of bushes and trees. I pause to watch the dancing daffodils in early spring, or the white lilies fluttering in the wind, giving immense joy to everybody. The flowers, birds, butterflies, trees – I believe that every creation of God has its own identity and can talk in its own language and share with its own world. I wish we too could communicate with Nature like that. In a way we can pick up a sense of Nature when we are outside, and it can touch us, entice us and give us a divine, celestial and unexplained joy every day.

On one such beautiful and serene morning, before I could even think of heading out to enjoy the weather and the natural world, I unfolded my blinds, opened the storm door and windows, and put my percolator on the hob for my morning coffee. Suddenly, my eyes were struck with an unexpected sight. Across the road, a funeral van was parked.

My hands trembled with shock, and for a split second my heart missed a beat. *Who, when* and *why* – these questions encircled my mind. Without stopping to think, I opened my front door, dashed out and was almost halfway towards the hearse when I came to a halt in the middle of the road. Where am I going? I asked myself. I don't know those people, and I don't even know who it is who has died. It was not like in India, where without knowing someone, you can walk into their house and ask anything and everything on humanitarian grounds.

While I stood there, perplexed, I spotted my next-door neighbour and hastened back towards him. I did not know him well either – only from that one night when I had arrived home late and discovered that I had locked all my house-keys, together with my bunch of car-keys, inside my car. Rick – I remembered his name now – had helped me to call a repair vehicle. After that day, we exchanged hellos and goodbyes whenever we saw each other.

Rick was standing in his porch looking bewildered, like me.

'What happened, and when?' I asked breathlessly.

He looked even more dumbstruck than before, and there was an expression in his eyes as if I had asked him a question which was both bizarre and stupid.

'I don't know,' was his dry response. 'The guy who lived there had been diagnosed with cancer. I know that, because his son was here one day talking to his friends, and I overheard him. I've never seen any of his other relatives.'

I was up against a brick wall and getting no information. I had never known the deceased, although I saw him sometimes in the mornings picking up his newspaper while I was collecting mine. And if by chance we made eye-contact, we waved at each other, exchanging silent but polite 'good mornings'.

'Did you go to visit him when you found out about his illness?' I enquired.

'Oh, no. I couldn't intrude in his private life.'

After this bland answer I had nothing else to say and went back to my house, wondering how on earth somebody's sickness could be a private matter? If I were in India, I would have raced over to the house immediately to meet everybody, and I would have stayed and helped till the end. And I definitely would have followed the funeral procession, ignoring all my daily chores, no matter how urgent they were.

Why, I asked myself, if he was so ill, had I never seen anybody around? Only yesterday, on my way home from work, I had noticed two people standing on his front porch, chatting casually to each other. As a passer-by, I had thought nothing of it; it had seemed perfectly normal to me.

Now I stood at my gate looking at the faces of the three people who were grouped on the verandah at the front of the house, holding coffee mugs in their hands. One was drinking while pacing back and forth, and the other two were sipping and talking to each other. One guy acknowledged me, since I had seen him yesterday smoking recklessly, right here on the porch.

Overall, there was a blank look on their faces which I put into the category of sadness. But in reality, there was no air of sorrow or loss. I wish I could have heard some part of their conversation to get a better insight into their state of mind. My impression so far was that their behaviour was detached, aloof and unsentimental compared to that belonging to my own background. It was as though they were sitting in a waiting room, and when the funeral team had finished with the body and everything was done, they could go home.

I felt helpless and also disturbed. I would have liked to convey some kind of condolence or sympathy to them – yet there was no opportunity. I convinced myself that the person was dead, and that he would never know if I was sad or not, or if I'd wanted to participate or not. But even then, I felt that we should perform the right rituals, despite the fact that there did not appear to be any moist eyes amongst those so-called relatives or friends.

I was fighting back my own tears – I don't know why. Perhaps because I felt strongly that I should say something at the demise of a man who was not even being mourned by his family, but I just couldn't find the right moment.

I returned to my house, since it felt rather awkward, standing in view of those people who wouldn't even spare me a glance and acknowledge me. In the meantime, my percolator had burned dry and the room was full of smoke. I put on the extractor fan, which took care of the smoke and also dimmed my inner storm a little. I then paced to and fro, killing time so that I would be ready when the funeral team came out to put the body in the van. I was waiting for some kind of wailing or sound of distress which would signal that it was time to go – but there was no sound of any kind.

I hurried back out to the hearse to have a final glimpse of that unknown person, but to my disappointment, they had already put the body in the van and I lost my chance to see his face. So I could never accept the death of my unfortunate neighbour, a person who was a human being and who deserved my last goodbye.

I stood close to the van, still waiting for some display of grief, but nothing happened.

Once more, I tried to make contact with the family, but nobody looked at me, and I could not see a single tear-drop in anybody's eyes to salute the departed soul.

Exit

Sudha Om Dhingra
Translated from Hindi by Romesh Shonek

Morrisville, North Carolina, USA, 2007

'Why haven't I seen the Mehtas at any parties lately?'

'Why are you so curious? Everyone knows you can't stand the sight of them.'

'You are blowing it out of proportion.'

'Isn't it true though?'

'Sampada, I have never said anything of the kind. How can other people know what I think? It's all in your imagination.'

'Sudhanshu, the moment the Mehtas enter a party, your feelings are written all over your face. The entire time they are there, you and your friends ignore them completely. You huddle in one corner for the whole evening with Gupta Ji, Mahesh Ji, Anand Seth and Suhas Ji, and get up only when we have to leave.'

'Why would that mean that I don't like them?'

'It's pretty obvious. What else could it mean?'

'Don't be ridiculous! If you've ever listened to them, you'd know very well how petty and superficial the Mehtas are. Falsehoods drip from everything they say. You have heard their phony talk, haven't you?'

'Take a left!' barked the satnav. Sudhanshu made a left.

'Dear,' he went on, 'it's not a matter of hating or disliking Ajay Mehta. The problem is his boasting. He brags the whole time at any party and everyone is forced to listen to his crap.'

'What are they supposed to do, plug their ears or something? Everyone has their own way of thinking, has their own ideas and likes and dislikes. Why can't you understand that not everybody is interested in the same things?'

'I never said that everybody should have the same interests. But I don't go to parties to listen to such nonsense. It doesn't have to be intellectual, just meaningful. Nothing he says makes any sense. I have never heard an original word from him. The man is incapable of opening his mouth without telling us all how wonderful he is.'

'Isn't their big house real? Don't they have BMWs, a Mercedes and a Lexus – are *they* all illusions? Their kids attend private schools. The family go on holiday to expensive places four times a year. Mrs Sundari Mehta is loaded with jewellery and fancy clothes. Don't they throw lavish parties all the time?'

The car was speeding down Highway 540 at about 80 miles an hour. Sudhanshu moved into the right-hand lane and set the cruise control to 65 miles an hour. The right lane was for slow traffic and for those who had to take an exit.

'Sampada,' he said impatiently, 'who doesn't have all these things in America? It's so typical of him to say things like: "I bought ten thousand shares of Cisco at $15 a share, and just an hour later sold them for $16 a share. In sixty minutes, I made $10,000".'

'That is his business.'

'What about everyone else? Don't they have any business?'

'Only those who make money can talk.'

'Oh, I see. And the others are good for nothing, is that it?'

'When did I say they were good for nothing?'

'Take Dr Wani. He is always calm and self-possessed at parties, in the temple and in other public places. Always so cheerful. You feel good in his company. Does he ever brag about his research? If you met him, would you be able to tell that this was the man who invented the cancer medicine Taxol? He is so modest and unassuming.'

'Not everybody can be like Dr Wani.'

'You know how cut-throat it is over here. I go to parties to relax and to have some fun, to talk about our country and our family. It's good to get together, otherwise we would hardly ever see each other.'

'I never said parties were a luxury. Parties are, in fact, a necessity in this country. The large distances don't allow us to see each other often, and parties are a good opportunity to meet up.'

'That's exactly what I said. But you always start blowing Mehta's trumpet.'

'Sudhanshu, you . . .'

But Sampada couldn't complete her sentence. Right then, a car moved from the left into Sudhanshu's lane, nipping in front of his BMW. Sudhanshu put his foot on the brake to slow down and let the other car take the exit. As soon as it turned off, Sudhanshu resumed his speed, but this time he didn't put the car in cruise control.

Sudhanshu continued talking. 'The very second that Ajay enters the room, he starts drinking, and then gets going: "Invest money in IBM. Dell shares can be purchased today. Don't invest in pharmaceuticals. FDA has screwed them all. In fact, today I made twenty thousand on Glaxo".' Sampada didn't say a word.

Annoyed, Sudhanshu continued, 'He makes so much in pharmaceuticals and then advises others not to buy shares.'

'He has been working at it for the last ten years. That's why he quit his job,' Sampada interrupted.

'He didn't quit. He was fired, because he was trading shares at work too. It's not like in India, where you get a government job and you are set for life.'

'Sundari was saying that Mehta Ji lost his job due to cuts in the state budget.'

Just then, a young male driver from the fourth lane, having speedily overtaken the other cars, swerved in front of Sudhanshu, making for the next exit. Sampada was thrown against the dashboard, and Sudhanshu, while trying to control the car, exclaimed, 'Asshole! He's going to kill himself and take us with him!'

The car was now stable. For a while there was silence.

Then: 'Sampada, when there are budget cuts, the shirkers are the first to go. You have been living in this country for years, but still you believe anything you're told.'

'Well, Sundari considers it a blessing in disguise. Government jobs pay a lot less than private companies and there isn't much job security either.'

'He took a state job thinking it was India. His approach to time management and professional performance didn't work out for him.'

'When we women are talking amongst ourselves, Mrs Mehta says proudly that they wouldn't have been so successful if he had stayed in that job. That whatever God does, He does for the best. Now every day, her husband makes ten to twenty thousand dollars.'

'Isn't that bragging? The other day Mehta was saying at a party that doctors make a lot, and then looking directly at me, he added, "But not fifty thousand every day." If that's not bragging, what is? Why would any doctor even *want* to compete with that idiot?'

'You were offended, weren't you?'

'Why would I be offended? He was drunk, he didn't even know what rubbish he was talking.'

Sampada casually looked at her watch. There was still a little way to go to Wake Forest.

Sudhanshu tuned the radio to 88.1 FM. Geet Bazaar's programme was on. The hosts, Afroz Taj and John Caldwell, were having mock arguments with each other.

'For an American, John speaks Hindi very well,' Sampada commented.

'Yes, even your Mehta doesn't get embarrassed listening to him. That idiot even speaks Punjabi with an English accent.'

'Since when did Mehta become *my* Mehta?'

'You always take his side.'

'No matter what you say, he does make money. Do you have any idea how many sets of pearls and how much diamond jewellery Mrs Mehta has?'

'Are you jealous?'

'Yes, I am. Even though I am a surgeon's wife, do I live like Mrs Mehta lives?'

'Mrs Mehta lives for herself, you live for others. You'd rather donate money to worthy causes than spend it on yourself.'

'What's wrong with living for oneself?'

'So live for yourself – who's stopping you? But don't give away thousands to charity. Go and buy all the jewellery you want instead.'

Sampada made no response. Rahat Fateh Ali Khan's song was on the radio: *tujhe dekh dekh jagna, tujhe dekh dekh sona*. As they listened to the song, both fell silent.

Sudhanshu glanced at the clock. 'Cary to Wake Forest is a long way. It's very tiring, driving. Tell your friend Usha Kumar to buy a house in Cary. Then they could have a party every month.'

'Dhruva Kumar is your friend too. Why don't *you* tell him?'

The phone rang. The good thing about BMWs is that the phone rings in through the speaker. All you have to do is press the talk button.

Bindu Singh was on the line.

'Sampada, today's party is cancelled. Ajay Mehta is in hospital. He has had a heart attack and a stroke. Dr Dhruva Kumar has gone to the hospital and Usha Kumar has cancelled the party. She is calling some people, and I am calling others. You know there were a lot of guests coming today.'

225

'But what happened?' the couple both asked at the same time.

'The faltering economy, the downturn in the stock market – the Mehta family seemed to have weathered it all somehow. Ajay is an old hand, he has seen lots of ups and downs. But now we know that the Mehta family were up to their necks in debt.'

'What are you talking about?'

'It's true. That big house, the cars, the credit cards, the jewellery – they have all been pawned. The Mehtas borrowed money for all of that. He even borrowed against the equity in the house and invested it in stocks. You know how the stock market kept tumbling down – well, Ajay had no money to meet the repayment instalments on his debts, so the banks have foreclosed on him.'

'And we never knew any of this!'

'Yah, well, everybody knows now. The house was repossessed some days ago – it's going to be auctioned off. All the jewellery has already been sold. They are on the street now. Ajay Mehta couldn't take the shock. You guys should take the next exit and go back home. He has been admitted to the Rex Hospit—'

But Bindu Singh got cut off.

Sudhanshu drove on to the next exit.

Remains

Susham Bedi

Translated by Jutta Austin

New York, 2003

She glanced through the window. There were only a few solitary leaves left on the trees. The bare branches were shivering in the biting wind. The whole area around the lake was covered with fallen leaves, brown and gold, red and green. In a few days' time the water in the lake would freeze up, and it would be as though there had never been a lake. Instead, there would be a shining white marble floor. Then children and youths in multi-coloured winter jackets would skate on it.

She repeated her son's words to herself – 'This is the best residential area in town. The very wealthy live around here. You won't find a better place to live.'

And he had probably been right. But how could Kamla know without seeing some other places as well and comparing it to them? What did it matter if this was Fifth Avenue or . . . wherever? She was not sufficiently acquainted with this area to be able to make comparisons

– and somebody had truly spoken for her when he said that '*Mid pleasures and palaces though we may roam, be it ever so humble, there's no place like home.*'

The colours of the park were slowly fading in the light of the sinking sun. She took in a deep breath and feasted her eyes on them one more time.

'If the weather turns out nice tomorrow I'll certainly go for a walk,' she said aloud. And then she drew the curtains shut.

Soon it would be time to go to the dining hall for the evening meal. The nurse had come to her room and was giving her a pre-dinner insulin shot. Testing her blood, she said, 'The sugar is high today. I'll have to give you more insulin.'

Kamla did not reply. It was a daily occurrence, and she had stopped worrying about it. She knew these people were taking care of her. As long as these small increases and decreases didn't become extreme, they'd just keep coming and going. After all, before she came here her sugar levels used to go up and down all the time, and then nobody had kept an eye on it. Now they check her four times a day and give her medicine accordingly.

In the past when she fell ill she'd just endure it. But now, with the slightest problem, she tells the nurse immediately. Even if the nurse sees it as a routine matter, Kamla will ask for the doctor to be called. At least this makes him come and talk to her, and if she is alarmed, he'll write a prescription. There isn't much else he can do, although her health concerns are a constant topic of conversation – there is always something new to talk about. What else is there left to talk about, especially with these people with whom she has nothing in common? No relationship has lasted her whole life. There won't be any new ones now.

Towards the end of her life she suddenly finds herself among strangers. Who knows from which corner of history these people have emerged. How different her own history is! The way they talk seems very strange to Kamla, and they find everything about Kamla strange – from the way she dresses to her language, the expressions on her face, her body language, the way she talks – everything. They often misunderstand what she says. She asks for something and is given something else. Because she knows only a few words in English they take her for either simple, foolish or stupid, sometimes even to the point where she is regarded as a strange creature from a different planet rather than another human being. Thinking about it, Kamla realises that sometimes they, too, seem like creatures from a different planet – creatures driven by somebody with a remote control.

Nevertheless, there is a lot she shares with them each day. She plays bingo with them. If she wins a prize they all notice her. In the keep-fit class they all sit on bicycles and work their feet and legs while titbits of chat and gossip fly between them: they talk about the weather, the staff, the nurses. Sometimes they all go for a picnic somewhere in a van. Or they sit together in the TV room and watch a film. Or listen to the news and then comment on it, discuss it. Sometimes they sit together on a bench in the park or on a chair in the lobby waiting for their visitors. Or in the clinic waiting for the doctor.

She really has no choice but to live among these people, and she is connected with them in so many ways – she knows who is suffering from what illness, who likes or dislikes what kind of food, who watches

TV till late, who goes to bed at what time, who likes to read books or prefers to spend all their time sitting in the lobby and chatting. She knows who cannot sleep at night and who goes quietly to hospital and when. Those whose sons or daughters sometimes come to see them and those who have no visitors.

Yes, there are people whose relatives never come to see them. Just thinking about it brings terror into Kamla's heart. The emptiness they must feel! But they do not let her see it. They feign indifference; wrap themselves in a protective shield of disinterest and unconcern. Even if Kamla asks them questions she only receives the briefest of replies, meant to discourage any further conversation.

Sometimes Kamla also finds it intriguing to know who has a boyfriend and which man is coming to see which woman. Yes, these women may be in their eighties, but they still have boyfriends!

She finds this very strange. When she tells her daughter-in-law about it, the younger woman says as a joke, 'You should get yourself a boyfriend, too. It would be fun.'

Kamla scolds her: 'You should be ashamed of yourself to say such things!'

'There is nothing wrong with that, Mummy. People here do not think it is wrong to make friends, whatever one's age.'

'That's up to them. But I don't want to hear such shameless talk.'

Nevertheless, she does picture them in her mind, those women in the secure surroundings of their rooms. The tepid touches of old hands! Touches which bring a shiver to flabby bodies with their soft wrinkled flesh.

Becky may be seventy-two years old, but she still looks very attractive. She must have been quite something in her youth! She says she has had this boyfriend for ten years, so there must be something attractive about her – but then Kamla herself did not look bad either in her sixties! She, too, looks ten years younger than she is, and, in fact, men are also interested in her, but she has never made any romantic advances nor received them. However, in the past . . . her past had not been this empty. There had been a lot there to keep her fulfilled.

She loses herself amongst her old relationships. Very far back . . . far, far . . . Dazzling sunlight spreads out before her eyes and makes everything glitter; she sees the rolling lawn, the fragrant narcissi, dark purple bougainvillaea, roses in all colours, bright red poinciana . . .

A desolate twilight closes in on her within moments. Ruined buildings, surrounded by vegetation, come into focus. All the lost companions, long-gone people from the past, lost talk, lost laughter, lost evenings. It is all just a part of the past. She has an empty present. Only this neat and well-furnished room in the nursing home, corridors with flowered carpets, the bright white-washed dining hall. But if you look closely you can't help noticing how clean and beautiful everything is. There is not a lot to complain about. Only that the food is a bit bland, and that seeing others around her eating huge pieces of pork or beef, et cetera, makes her feel sick, or that the tea is not burning hot or that all those colourful heaps of vegetables are tasteless, however appetising they look. She smothers her food in tomato ketchup, crams it into her mouth and washes it down with a mouthful of juice.

There are other things as well – small things, but still . . . Sometimes the nurses are careless about the times when they are supposed to hand out medicine, and they forget to order in new medicine when they run out. They keep forgetting, even after Kamla reminds them.

But in her own country, people are even more careless. There is hardly any proper treatment. She would just be lying alone at home. One couldn't trust the servants there, and no relatives would come to see to her either. Yes, old age is truly a bad thing. Everybody pushes you away. And then if one's children go to live abroad there is nobody left to care at all. So she has to live here.

All her children are busy with their own work. There is so little she can do on her own at home. And what's more, she can neither go to the bathroom nor take a bath on her own. At least here she has help with everything. Her poor children, how could they look after her like that? They could hardly get time off from their jobs, could they? How can she complain about her own flesh and blood? And her daughter-in-law goes to work, too. And they do come to see her. Although her daughters live in a different town, her son and daughter-in-law come every two or three days to check on her. If there is anything she needs or wants they buy it for her and bring it, and they also take her out quite regularly. If she wanted, her daughter-in-law would also make spicy Indian dishes for her and bring them in.

Nevertheless . . . What is it that makes her feel so restless all the time? She walks around her room. Sits down in a chair. Lies down on her bed. Sits up again. Stands up. Walks around again. Restless . . . all the time restless. Whatever her position, she fidgets.

Well, yes, of course she has a telephone in her room.

But there is nobody she could phone and have a chat with. Even her children make excuses. They never have time for a proper, leisurely talk. Just the one question: 'You are all right, aren't you?' She briefly confirms that she is, then returns the question to ask about their health – conversation finished. And anyway, what is there to say, day after day? One night does not bring much worth talking about. But she does draw out her account of her own daily activities and makes it last some minutes. That way at least she feels that she has had a chat.

Her daughters talk to her every Sunday. They don't have time on other days. She lives in anticipation of the next Sunday.

But what about all the other days? From Monday to Saturday?

She fidgets. She is restless again. She wants to talk to one of her own. But what would she say? If she tells them how she feels they'll always ask 'What is the matter?' That's where the conversation ends – and even if it didn't, how would it continue? And she still has to deal with all this.

She goes outside.

Once outside she can only go back inside again. Inside – outside – outside – inside. Take the lift upstairs ... take the lift downstairs . . . one hand holding tightly on to her cane, sometimes using her walker, which she holds with both hands . . . staying near the building – or going to the park a little further away. Yes, it is a great effort to go to the park. Just to put on enough clothes takes her an hour: first her kameez, then the sweater, then another shirt, then the thick cardigan, then her coat, warm trousers on her legs, sometimes two pairs, and then her shalvar and then socks and boots and tying their laces.

She saves rice or bread and keeps it to feed the pigeons in the park. If the bread becomes dry she soaks it in water so that it is soft for the pigeons and they can easily eat it. Even when it is cold she goes to the park without fail, just for a little while, so that the pigeons get their food. If she cannot go because of rain or snow, her mind flits around like a caged parrot. What can a bird find to eat in the snow-covered soil? And how protected she is in this icy winter. She receives whatever she needs. Hot food, hot water, a warm quilt, a warm room. If she thinks about it, there really is a great deal of peace here. Everything she needs is procured – and yet . . .

She says to her son and daughter-in-law, 'No, no. Don't tell anyone that I'm living in a nursing home.'

'Why, what's wrong with that? Isn't it a nice place? That kind of service, the level of care – you wouldn't find that anywhere else. And at home, well, we don't have a doctor present at all times, so . . .' says her daughter-in-law to her.

Kamla does not answer her daughter-in-law. But she gives the answer to herself: 'They'll say that you've thrown me out of your home. How would people there be able to understand . . .' But even Kamla herself cannot decide what all this is really about. Did her son not leave the decision with her? Does he not still say that if she wants to live at home that she should come home? So why does she not return there?

What a tangle it all is!

It is true. She does not want to live at home. After all, that's where she used to live. It was only when her health

234

deteriorated that the matter of living here had come up. At that time she had felt that she would be able to get better here, that she'd be safe here, for she could hardly expect the same support at home as she has here with doctors and nurses on call 24 hours a day. If something suddenly happened to her at home, there might be somebody around – but then again there might not be! After all, heart attacks hardly ask for permission or announce themselves. All the time, this fear was preying on everybody's mind – *please let nothing happen, please let nothing happen.*

And then there is also this other fear – that all their enquiries may only be a formality. How can her children truly want her to live with them when she is as dependent on others as she is?

It's now some ten or twelve years since she left her own home.

Suddenly she sees in her mind's eye the day when she was getting ready to move to her son's home. The whole household from twenty years of life abroad had to be disposed of. Nobody had room enough to take on all her things, but actually she had gradually given up and got rid of many things after her husband had passed away. There used to be four sofas in the big drawing room, and now there was just that one armchair in her part of the room; in those days the cupboards had been full of pieces of china and cut-glass ornaments – and now there was nowhere to cram them into. And when they could not find a second-hand dealer, the whole wealth of her kitchen pots and pans had ended up as an offering to the rubbish dump. All those clothes hanging in the cupboards, when now even putting on a sari has become an effort quite beyond her weak body.

*

She had decided to give up the bungalow. It was a painful process, but if she did not let it go, how lonely she would be in such a big place, all on her own. So much to maintain – and for whom?

Here today, gone tomorrow. And now the illness is her home, from which it seems she will never be released . . .

With her back supported by two big headrests on her bed, Kamla watched her two daughters wandering about the house while she looked on listlessly as if in a daydream.

Her daughters kept calling 'Mummy, Mummy!' and coming up to show her something.

'Mummy, what should we do with this bundle?'

'What's in it?' Kamla could not remember.

'Oh, look! There is some very beautiful lace in it.'

'Oh yes, your papa brought that back from Switzerland. I had it put on your dresses. This is what was left over. I thought that when you got married I'd have it sewn on to your saris, but then the fashion changed.'

'Just let me throw it away!'

'Don't you have a use for it? It was very expensive lace. I thought I could give it to your daughter. You can't get hold of it just like that when you want it. And nowadays you can't get it at all.'

'Mummy, you know that my girl only wears jeans. Nobody wears dresses these days.'

'Can't you use it for something else then?' Kamla's eyes were pleading.

'Mum, what can we do with it?'

Then that daughter had dragged a box over to her mother and said, 'Mummy, there are dozens of silver dishes in this one. I can't possibly look after them. Who'd be able to polish them all the time? Let those go, too.'

Kamla heaved a deep sigh and remained silent. She felt a stabbing pain – as if a spike was piercing her again and again.

Her youngest daughter had picked up the jewellery box and sat down close to her. She rummaged through the box and said, 'I'll keep these two necklaces, and I think Kuhu might like these earrings. She is very keen on collecting earrings now. But the rest is nothing but rubbish. I'll throw it all away.'

Kamla had then become angry: 'Everything I have is rubbish to you! Just take what you like. I'll have the rest sent to India. There'll be enough takers there.'

'But Mummy, who would transport these things there? You're in no state to go yourself, and I won't be going for another two or three years. Who'd look after all this stuff for that length of time?'

'Did Barki not say she was going next year?'

Barki interrupted vehemently: 'Mummy! There won't even be enough room to take new things – I can only have two suitcases. How would I find space for this junk? And in any case, these days they have their own stuff in India, everything is available there now.'

'There is a lot of antique jewellery in there, my girl; I don't even know where we got it all from.'

'Mummy, please. We have already taken everything we like.'

'All right then, pack the things you don't want. I'll take them with me.'

'Where to? To Pappu's house? Bhabhi would just throw everything out. She is forever saying that you have collected the whole world's rubbish in your house! There won't be any room at theirs to keep all this.'

'What about my saris?'

'You know we rarely wear saris. We don't even use our own ones. I'll have them sent to the Salvation Army.'

'Then do what you like. I suppose you're now running this family anyway.' At that point she had given up and surrendered.

By saving money her whole life, Kamla had amassed a lot of things, and it had given her a great deal of pleasure. And her children used to be keen on these things: they made the house a home – massive paintings, leather sofas, delicate china pots, crystal wine glasses, embroidered bed-covers from Kashmir, Persian carpets, armchairs, coffee tables. Mahogany shelves. Long rows of books. Some of it the children had taken. They had distributed the items amongst themselves, according to who liked what.

But there was so much more in Kamla's estate that she wanted to share out among her children. She did not know why, but she felt that if some of her furniture and her other things stayed with them, then she would stay with them too. It hurt Kamla when they talked about throwing something away. She had taken so much care of her things and arranged them with so much love. Now they had no more value than dust. She could understand that her son and daughters might not have a use for them, but surely the items would be useful to somebody else? But who else was there now? To whom would she give it all?

When she had gone to India in the past, she had always taken many new and used things – everything was welcomed. All the new things were presents – the children would take off whatever clothes they were wearing and try on the new things. 'Kamla Bhabhi has brought it, Auntie Kamla has brought such a beautiful sweater!' And at the same time her sister-in-law would say, 'Can't you let us have all your children's clothes? It is impossible to get such quality here.'

'All right. I'll bring them next time.'

Together with all the new things there would have been many old ones as well, but nobody minded that – after all, it was all extra. The real presents had already been distributed. Now everybody's children had grown up. Started jobs. Grown important there. Everybody had pretensions. When she had taken them nylon or georgette saris her younger sister-in-law had said, 'Let me have these for the washerwoman. We help her to get by.'

*

Now Kamla has nothing left to give away. Those to whom she used to give things are now giving much more themselves. She has been watching her hands become empty.

Kamla does not go to India any more. The illness has tied her down.

She can no longer live alone.

For a long time, she had managed to avoid depending on others and had been able to look after her own home. Even after her husband's death she had decided to carry on alone. She was determined that she would not live with any of her children – not even with her son. She did not want to disrupt his unencumbered life.

But now she has no choice any more.

All the leaves and flowers are gone. The river has dried up. All that's left now is a desiccated body, thin as a stick. She takes no more joy in adorning it or in dressing up. Nor in bathing, nor in applying lampblack to her eyes.

But where there is life there is hope. If you do not look after your body, how can you look after your home? And how shiny she used to keep her home! Heaven forbid that dust should collect in any nook or cranny. The whole house used to be sparkling clean. The sitting room, kitchen, bedrooms – every part was suitably arranged and arrayed. A temple to good taste. Papa had been proud to invite people to his home.

'Let them see for themselves how we live!'

The constant parties! Pulav, kebab, roast chicken, royal paneer . . . she made everything with her own hands. Puffed-up phulbariyan, samosas, gulab jamun – there was no end to the different things she used to make.

Her husband was a doctor. There was never any shortage of money in his house. But even so, she would say, 'I'll make it myself. If you want to order food in you might as well feed them in a restaurant. Only home-cooked food will be served at home.'

One day, Barki had said quite unthinkingly, 'It's absolutely ages since you made gulab jamun for us, Mummy.' It had made Kamla's eyes fill with tears.

'What can I say, my girl? God knows how many things I'd like to make for you, but my hands have no strength in them.'

Eventually she had to leave the family home. The time had come. How long Kamla had lived! She was over seventy years old. But still she wanted her home to remain adorned as before. Like a row of beautiful saris neatly hanging in the cupboard.

Barki and her younger sister both said to her, 'Mummy, you can no longer live alone. You'll just have to go and live with our brother.'

And it was true, too. Who could help her there? She would often feel so unwell that just getting up to fetch a drink of water had become an effort. So how could she live by herself? She would not go to live with her daughters, for she would be a burden. There was nothing else she could do but move in with her son.

Neither her daughters nor her son understood her decision. This move would not even have been in question in the country and family where she had come from. Her son said, 'Mummy, your house is too far away from the town. Kuntal and the children would not like to live there. You must sell your house and move in with me. That's the solution. I really could not live here. I couldn't get to work.'

The two daughters came over from California to help with the move. To break camp.

*

Kamla's soul is weeping. All these things she had made herself. Her nest, scattered all over. A whole big house to be shrunk to fit into a shared home.

Her son's home. The home of her daughter-in-law. Of her grandson and grand-daughters.

But even there she won't be able to fit it all in. Once she has left her home she will just be an outsider. There seems to be only one way to go from here, to move forward. There is no way back.

241

No. Nobody could look after Kamla any longer. Excrement and urine all over her bed. Her limbs wasting away. Salt deficiency. Potassium deficiency. No strength to get up. Choking when trying to swallow a mouthful of food.

What a burden she has become to her own children. They who had been the apples of her eyes, whose smallest stumble had made her soul tremble. Should she now have them clear up her excrement? The day her own son would hand her the bedpan she would call down a hundred thousand curses on her wretchedness, her helplessness.

Her self-esteem, her modesty, her dignity, all would be washed away like the foul waters of a gutter. Oh! This is not what she had given birth to her son for! Much better for death to release her!

But even death does not come when called. One has to await even death's pleasure.

Kamla could not bring herself to put her children through this hell. Because that's what it would be – hell. Delicate hands – hands used to doing important work, hands made capable from years of hard work and study – and they should handle her excrement and urine?

And then came half a room in the hospital. That was all the space she had to exist in. The doctors had breathed new life into her. A new heart. New teeth. New eyes. Even new blood. And then, for this new Kamla, a bright new room with yellow walls in the new nursing home by the park with the lake. With every glance out of the window towards the new view of the lake.

Ever-changing seasons. Leaves falling, new shoots sprouting on the trees. New leaves growing again and again. Life unfolding new wealth continuously.

But nevertheless the same old Kamla! An old inhabitant in a new country. The dreams of the past. Those old dreams, now seen through new eyes. She sees the new leaves fall. The more new things there are, the more she holds on to the old. New talks with old meanings. New meanings of old ideas. New ideas in an old language. New wrinkles in old skin! And in the wrinkles, old fears. Old and new all mixed up together!

In a way she feels that all this was inevitable. It had to happen. But despite this she feels an ache . . . she had not expected the time to leave to come so soon.

She is eighty, so why does she feel the time has come so fleetly? Although when she was young, death often used to feel very near. And she is less frightened of dying now. Now that it has come so close she feels that she will just accept gratefully whatever is given to her. She has finished her bargaining now and is no longer asking for anything else but shelter from the trader. However much or little she may be given will be fine. Gratis goods do bring a pleasure all of their own. Why not live a little longer. In the end she'll have to die anyway. The joys of living – here today, gone tomorrow.

This is what it is like for her. Her life is just being drawn out. Maybe she'll live until she's a hundred. These doctors here don't let anybody die. So many times she has fallen so seriously ill that it did not seem possible for her to be saved, but not only did the doctors save her, she is even regaining her ability to move about . . . and beginning to enjoy life again. She is going back to fully living out every kind of joy and sorrow. She forgets that she is standing on a cliff with little land remaining at her feet. But whatever is left, whatever she may still be given, actually makes her two-three-four times as happy as before.

All the time there is something to look forward to. Just now, she is about to have a great-grandson! It is said in the old scriptures: *Once spilt, milk is of no use* – that is to say, one ought to go when one is ready. But why not enjoy the great-grandson, too? Not many people have seen their great-grandson – and even knowing in advance that it is a boy! No such thing happened in her day. Science has brought nature so far under its control . . .

But this world is not hers. Her world resides somewhere among the acacia and neem trees . . . a glass of lassi and some radish parathas . . . bicycle bells, the shouting vegetable seller, cows basking in the streets, dogs barking in the alley – this long-familiar world, crisp and brittle like roasted grain.

It is no longer possible for her to board a plane to return there; the journey takes twenty odd hours. No, she will never again be able to go there. If she did go, she would not be able to return. And then who would look after her? Who would stay with her through thick and thin? She has neither servants nor relatives there.

But then again – where is her world now? Her soul withers from not seeing the children; her heart breaks to pieces. It's as if there is nothing at all ahead of her, only darkness.

So what is it that makes her continue to draw out her time, that delays her departure? Is that even in her power?

These last remaining days, this leftover time. The remains of this body. All this – what is it? What is it for?

Has she been revived just to leave; is she prolonging her air-conditioned life just to depart it?

Her body is constantly checked over, regularly nurtured by fifteen different kinds of pills and injections. Full of the vigour of cold-store fruit, and yet dried up inside, life losing more of its flavour with each day . . . but the desire to live still as unquenched as the flame of an oil well.

Had Dharmraj not asked Yudhishthira this question: *What is the greatest wonder of this world?* And Yudhishthira had replied: *The irrepressible desire to live.* Is this not also the greatest wonder of Kamla's life? To be dying and still keep living, as if one will not have to die? But what kind of living is this? Like a slow death.

Is there any difference left between living and dying?

Nevertheless, she is still alive. Although living is actually forbidden to her. Even the gift of life comes from her medicines. And she takes every last drop greedily!

Beside this frozen, peaceful, unmoving lake, and the silently falling leaves, she lives and endures her life among a flock of other people, helpless and old like herself, waiting for the inevitable to come.

Is this all that remains in the end?

One Cold Winter's Night

Toshi Amrita

Edinburgh, Scotland, 1999

Neha was tossing and turning restlessly in bed. Why was sleep eluding her? she asked herself. What grudge did sleep have against her that it hesitated to come near?

It was cold – a freezing cold night in the middle of January. Right from the early morning, cotton-soft flakes of snow had started falling, then settling. A biting wind was blowing now, forming ripples and waves in the snow. The landscape of Edinburgh was smoothly covered; one could imagine Snow White gliding by – or perhaps a white fairy with a magic wand floating around the rooftops and trees.

Scotland was beautiful but bone-achingly cold! Inside the house, the floor felt as if it was made of a thin sheet of ice which declined to melt despite the central heating. Neha's loneliness was so intense it sent chills through her body, adding to the embrace of this fierce cold – and the desolation created by the darkness. The sound of the wind was eerie and made her shiver under the duvet.

It wasn't the elements alone. Inside her mind, emotional tempests were raging. The face of Paresh haunted her, and memories of him would not go away. The turmoil refused to ease and the pain would not abate. Oh, for his warmth, his loving glances, his touch . . . Time and again she imagined Paresh by her side. His thoughts were caressing her – she was hallucinating. The more she tried to cast him aside, the more she felt his sensuous presence. Her breathing became faster. It felt as though he had spread several arms around her – holding her lightly, yet preventing her escape.

Neha had never wanted to be possessed, stifled. She wanted to be free – or did she? By now her skin was covered in goose-pimples. Was it due to the cold outside or the commotion within her? She had never felt so weak, so powerless. Who was Paresh anyway? He was a stranger – an unknown. So why was she thinking about him? Was this a web of her own making – had she knitted it herself?

No, he had come unannounced into her life. When the harmony between them had existed, it had been meaningful. Their rapport was a monument to the rising tide of their love – but now it was all gone. Nothing was left that she needed to cherish.

Little by little, Paresh had eased himself into Neha's mind. Layer by layer, he had crept into her tender heart. The silly gullible girl did not notice when it was happening – nor how it was happening. But she became more and more infatuated with him as each day passed.

Neha was an intelligent, pretty girl. There was a spring in her step and a glint in her eyes. Yet she was calm and serene. She would listen intently; assimilate and absorb what she had heard. She was trusting and trustworthy – and naturally brilliant. No wonder she had passed her Master's degree in Chemistry, back home in New Delhi.

Her parents revelled in her success. 'Bravo, our lovely girl!' they said. 'We expected nothing less from you. We don't have a son but you are our son and our daughter rolled into one. You are dynamic like a son, and tender like a daughter.'

Neha's professor, Dr Anand, was delighted when he saw the examination results of his favourite student. He wished to encourage her further.

Fervently, he said, 'Neha, I have a suggestion for you. The Faculty of Science and Engineering at Edinburgh University is pioneering, and internationally famous for its high standards. I obtained my Engineering Master's degree there, and would like you to do the same. Why not apply for the University Grants Commission Scholarship? You might get the opportunity to research the molecular structures of your chosen aromatic series compounds. I shall give you my full backing and introduce you to the UGC and Engineering Faculty of my Alma Mater!

'Now do not delay,' he urged her. 'Go to the UK High Commission to find out what your chances are – and meanwhile I shall write to Dr McMillan who was my tutor and friend, to ask him whether you will be able to do a PhD under his guidance.'

Neha quickly collated her CV and submitted it to the UGC. She was a diligent student, and her application was successful. On receiving the news, she was in seventh heaven. From childhood, she had wanted to go to Europe – to study there, see other countries and understand the lifestyle and mind-set of various ethnic groups. She wanted to breathe in new challenges within a freer culture and environment. Here, in India, at every step obstacles were placed in one's path. There were instructions for everything. *Do it like this, not like that. Don't walk too fast. Don't look strangers in the eye. Don't smile or laugh too much. Be reserved. Be docile, etc. etc.* There was no end to what was forbidden or unladylike.

Papa didn't object, but her mother was displeased. 'I am not happy sending my girl to foreign lands all on her own. There are plenty of facilities in India where you can do a PhD . . .' but such storms always rose up among Indian families, however small the problem!

After a lake-full of do's and don'ts and extensive moral and emotional instruction, Papa and Mum hugged her goodbye. There were lumps in everyone's throats. Her younger sister Tannu gave Neha a warm embrace.

'Didi, I shall feel so lonely without you!' she said, then went on naughtily: 'But don't worry – at least I shall have our room all to myself now. I can read all those romantic novels in peace, and I can use your make-up, and wear your dresses and your shoes. And oh, I shall have the hi-fi and the TV on whenever I want – and nobody to open my letters and share everything with! Go, Neha Didi, go happily. Do write frequently. Remember, I shall miss you . . . miss you very much.'

Then Neha burst into silent tears. She tried to smile, unconvincingly, and wiped away her tears with both hands.

*

Neha's British Airways flight was chilly. She squirmed and asked for a blanket. The food was bland and everybody was more interested in the drinks than the food. Beautiful air hostesses attended her, with a marvellous and courteous service. Weakly she asked for an orange juice. She sipped it slowly and thought of what she had left behind and what was to come. Scotland, they all said, was a cold country. What were the people like there? Were they as cold as the weather? She thought of Tannu; she thought of Papa and Mum – and dear kind Professor Anand.

Scotland, in all its natural splendour, was utterly bewitching! The tall blue mountains looked even taller during the slightly misty evenings. Kissing the feet of the hills were calm, deep lakes. The magnificent castles with moats around them reminded her of the mistrust between man and man. Did those moats contain blood, rather than water? Quickly rejecting the thought, instead she admired the greenery around the moats, and was intrigued by the meandering footpaths – roads appearing and disappearing between the hills . . . oh, Scotland was a wonderful country! The countryside surrounded you, hugged you!

Neha started her research under the guidance of Dr McMillan. He was very polite and helpful, and treated her with understanding and affection. In the beginning, when she had to meet so many strangers, she felt homesick. When she worked there was no problem since she found her studies absorbing, but when she relaxed, loneliness would inevitably encroach. Agnes, Bruce, Hamish – all foreign faces and foreign names with a foreign diction; Scottish intonations occasionally made words hard to understand, but at least the speech had some musicality!

Sometimes she felt that India was still the finest country in the world. Its food had body and taste, spices and aroma. There were no cold buffets, cold sandwiches or cold meats. India was warm – and Indians themselves were warm. She thought of her mum's hot chapatti with cauliflower or aubergine, or urid daal; mustard spinach and maize roti with a tall glass of buttermilk. She thought of Dad giving her a cup of tea in bed on Sundays, of Tannu's laughter and their whisperings till late in the night. Neha missed everything. But she was not lonely while at university; she had the good company of the library.

One dark and dreary evening she had an open book in front of her, but her mind was roaming, thinking about her life here. She still had a year and a half left in which to submit her thesis. Could she last that long?

All of a sudden, she was startled to hear someone speaking her national language.

'Have you just arrived?' the man said. 'I haven't seen you in the library before. My name is Paresh – I just came here to meet a friend, but he hasn't arrived yet. And then you caught my eye. Hello, how are you?'

'Hello, my name is Neha. I have come from India to do a PhD in Scientific Engineering – Chemistry, to be precise.'

'Pleased to meet you,' they said to each other.

This was her first encounter with Paresh. He was tall, broad-shouldered, had slightly curly hair, a fair complexion and a ready smile. After just one meeting, Neha already felt she could talk to him openly. Little by little, they became friends.

Paresh was a student in the Faculty of Medicine, and his parents, along with his brother and sister, lived in

Glasgow. He took Neha to meet his parents, and after the long trip from Edinburgh she spent half a day with the family, enjoying their company, their food, their conversation and laughter. She felt at home with them and they looked at her with admiration.

Neha recalled a particular evening that followed the Glasgow trip. It had been raining in torrents that day; it seemed as if the earth would never be able to quench its thirst. But was it the earth alone that was thirsty? Was she not thirsty too?

She was waiting at the bus stop near the university with these thoughts churning in her mind, when Paresh drove past in his car. He saw her at the stop and reversed to speak to her.

'The weather is abominable,' he called. 'Hop in and I'll drop you at your flat. I'd just like one favour though – a nice hot cup of coffee!'

With a little nod, she climbed inside the car. It would be good to be cosy at home.

'The rain has soaked you. You might catch flu. While you change into some dry clothes, I shall make the coffee.' Paresh was concerned for her, which pleased her.

'Neha,' he went on, 'I have been trying to say something to you for quite some time.' He stopped, apparently searching for words. 'Look, we are good friends – we share our thoughts and also share our time to overcome loneliness. I am anxious to extend the sphere of this relationship. Do you ever have similar thoughts? I am very eager to know.'

Neha felt his gentle touch; his eyes were searching now for the answer to his question.

For a moment, she felt an impulse to hide her face against his broad chest, to be clasped by his powerful

arms, to be smothered by his warm, irregular breathing – to melt like candle wax and be completely captured. Should she set her resistance aside and become one with him? Should she surrender to his advances?

Conflict rose within her. She recalled her mother's hand on her shoulder, her whispered warnings to her beloved elder daughter: 'Don't ever forget your culture. Don't ever make mistakes in foreign lands. Don't ever travel down paths from which you cannot return. Excessive freedom for women doesn't match up with our expectations and morals. Do not enter a cul-de-sac, Neha. Then you will have no regrets later; nor will we have to worry our hearts out.'

'Oh, Paresh, I need some time – some space to breathe and think. For the present we are good friends. We are building our future. I am bound to seek permission from my parents. For the moment I cannot give you any assurance – any promise.'

'I am not looking for an assurance or a promise,' Paresh told her. 'I just want to find out if you have any of these thoughts about me – or is my attraction and fervour one-sided?'

It felt to Neha as if a bone had got stuck in her throat. She felt the urge to tell him, 'Paresh, what you are saying today, I have been ruminating on for days on end. The truth is, I wanted to hear it from you first.' Feminine prerogative!

She was surrounded by doubts. Would the two of them be compatible? The tide of love that laps from shore to shore is a tide that sometimes lashes and sometimes ebbs. Love can have its ups and downs. Togetherness brings about its own complexities, anxieties and responsibilities. Colours fade, seasons

change, warmth dissipates, love disappears. And how can anyone tolerate another person day after day – day after day! She was lost in a maze.

Why was she never able to decide anything independently? Neha asked herself angrily. Why did she always need somebody else's permission – somebody else's advice to make a decision? She held society responsible for this state of affairs. Her society, family and culture had hardly given any opportunities to women to take a decision on anything worthwhile. Women scarcely had the right to live their own lives. The general viewpoint was: how dare they decide matters for themselves when men were around to do so? Men legislated; they laid down moral laws heavily stacked against women. Moral laws for men were few and regularly flouted. Man was always there to dictate and woman always there to obey.

Why this duality? Why this sexism? Why this hypocrisy?

Neha recalled that, in the not-so-distant past, women were held in adulation, women could choose their husbands – they were the first and most important teachers of their children. What had happened? Why – and when did it happen? India had been a land of blossom once. A land of riches, spices – where women were revered almost like deities – like goddesses! Foreign invaders, vandals, looters, thieves and colonialists had destroyed it bit by bit, chunk by chunk until it had become unrecognisable. Now it was tarnished. Now it was scarred. And women bore the bulk of those scars.

It was always men who ruled the roost. In the beginning the grandfather ruled the house – then the father. After that, the brother took over. With marriage,

the husband was the despot. If he passed away, the sons ruled the mother. A woman could never exercise freedom. At every crossroads, on every little path, she was crushed to pieces, then scattered to the four winds.

At this crucial time, and for whatever reason, Nehu could not or would not express herself. She had neither confessed nor denied any reciprocal feelings for Paresh. She wondered what inference he would take from her silence. Would he interpret it as a sign of acceptance or as a sign of denial?

*

A few days later, Neha received a letter from her younger sister Tannu:

Neha, invite me to Scotland for a few days. I have nobody at home to talk to. I am feeling empty and lonely after parting from you. Mum and Dad are OK. They never get tired of talking about your successes and achievements. Oh, and your friend Bindu from house number 10 has got married . . . and Mrs Garg has been diagnosed with lung cancer. You remember how she smoked like a chimney . . .

Neha took up ad hoc employment as a translator at the airport. Her work required liaising with the airport authorities, police and hospitals, as she was translating for people from Bangladesh, Pakistan and India. These were illiterate or illegal immigrants who had the impudence to enter Scotland without being able to speak a word of English. With the money she made as an interpreter, Neha sent Tannu a return ticket on

Virgin Airlines for direct flights between New Delhi and Edinburgh. She would do anything for her sister. She loved Tannu so much! Tannu was the one person Neha could call her own. She was worth everything.

The day Tannu arrived, she looked her usual radiant self, sprightly and impish.

'Tannu,' Neha said, 'meet my special friend Paresh. He is studying for a degree in medicine at the Edinbur. . .'

The younger girl couldn't wait for the sentence to be completed and burst out: 'Neha Didi, is Paresh just a friend so far? Are you still a coward as you were in Delhi? Come on, breathe the fresh air – feel emancipated. Mummy and Papa are not here, nor is the Arya Samaj. Hello, Paresh! Very pleased to meet you.' Her tone, her voice and her mischievous smile gave the impression that she had known Paresh for years.

'Not so fast, little sister. And no more lectures for me, if you don't mind. Paresh,' she said apologetically, 'when Tannu speaks, there are no holds barred. However, she is lovelier than love itself. Please don't take offence at her remarks!'

The three of them went on a tour of various glens and vales and lakes, with Lochinvar and Walter Scott whispering around them. Robert Bruce and Wallace had shed blood through the crevices in the ground on which they were treading! Robert Burns's words descended from the hillocks and gently lapped the waters of the lakes where he had poured out his pangs of unrequited love. The lyre was missing – but you could hear it if you closed your eyes for a moment. His spirit was made manifest around every corner.

Every drop from the Glens and the River Spey was captured in single malts – or blended. The scenic beauty took your breath away. They were soaking in it and soaking it in.

On one occasion, when Paresh had gone away for a few minutes, Tannu said, 'Didi, Paresh is fascinated by you; every glance shows his desire for you. He has what it takes to be my brother-in-law. Shall I write to Papa?'

Neha avoided the question, saying, 'I am going to London for three days for a seminar. On my return, we shall talk about this again. Paresh will be away in Glasgow for a couple of days – but don't worry about being alone. Mrs Hamilton next door is very helpful; contact her if you have any problems. There is plenty of food, the TV, some magazines – and, of course, Mrs Hamilton to chat to when you are bored. I shall be back soon.'

Neha loved and cared for her sister, even in far-off in London, which was a fast-paced world of its own. The city didn't sleep – just like New York. In this multinational city you could get anything you wanted – but of course you had to find out where to get it! Samuel Johnson once said, 'If you are tired of London, then you are tired of life.'

When Nehu's seminar finished, she shopped for gifts for Tannu. It occurred to her that perhaps she could bring her sister to London to show her around. They could spend a couple of brilliant days together on holiday in the capital.

Feeling very happy, she took a train one day earlier than arranged, and arrived in Edinburgh late that evening. She decided to tiptoe into the flat without disturbing Tannu's sleep, although right from childhood Tannu had always slept like a log. Without making any noise, Neha carefully opened and closed the front door and went to the kitchen to make herself a cup of coffee. Then she crept into her bedroom to change.

On the threshold, her feet were held captive. What was she looking at? The floor underneath her sandals was slipping away, and she nearly collapsed. Her heart stopped beating from shock.

Tannu and Paresh were peacefully sleeping, intertwined. Coils of Tannu's long dark hair lay on Paresh's chest. There was a glow of contentment and fulfilment on Paresh's face. In his strong and elegant arms lay the fragile figure of Tannu. Her thighs were teasingly revealed from under the blanket, and Paresh's hand was cupping her small pulsating breast. It was a picture of warmth and eroticism. It was like a Renoir!

Completely stunned, Neha kept on looking wordlessly at the docile, satiated couple. She just managed to save her cup of coffee from falling. Now anger was rising within her and she had a mind to fling off their blanket and let them roll on the carpet. Then she thought of dragging Tannu up – giving her a couple of sharp slaps and throwing her out of the flat. But why slap Tannu? Why not Paresh? After all, their sleeping together wouldn't have happened without mutual consent. To reach the culmination of this intense sexual desire, their bodies and minds would certainly have longed for it. Why should Tannu alone be punished?

Tannu is my younger sister. How could she do this to me? Nehu asked herself. Even though I had not expressed my love for Paresh, I had an unspoken agreement with him. I only needed a few more days, a little extra time to iron out the formalities. I loved him – and he knew I did. Then why did he betray me?

Neha could not decide what to do, whether she should wake them up or not. She fell in a chair and accidentally kicked the stool in front of it. That woke Tannu up.

When she saw Nehu, she looked like a deer cornered in the forest. The guilty girl tried to close her eyes as if to shut out reality, but it was futile. She could not hide her nudity. Nor could she hide the truth.

She pleaded with Neha: 'Didi, please . . . I can explain. This was not planned, I promise you. It – it just happened. I am so sorry, Neha Didi. So sorry.' But she was getting nowhere.

In the midst of this scene, Neha could not know for sure if Paresh had any regrets, any sense of wrongdoing. His lips quivered, as if he wanted to say something – but the words would not come.

Trying to suppress the deluge of rage within her, Neha asked Tannu to get dressed. Again, the thought came to her: Tannu, why did you do all this to me? I have looked after you from childhood. I have tried to help you fulfil your ambitions. I tutored in the evenings so that I could get you admitted into a good college. I bought elegant things for you and gave you those extras which Mama and Papa could not afford to buy. What hidden part of you did I not see? If you had wanted Paresh, you could at least have given me a chance to gracefully withdraw – and make him available to you. I would have sacrificed my happiness for you. But no, Tannu, no. You went onto the path of stealing and cheating – and by doing so you betrayed your elder sister, your friend and loyal benefactor. Can I ignore this and forgive you? Is this pardonable?

*

For two days, Neha went away to a hotel. She had to face the world alone but couldn't bear to stay in the flat. When Neha returned on the third day, Tannu had gone. Neha threw away the bedsheet with the sunflower pattern. She wanted to eradicate any sign, any memory of the night they had slept on that sheet. Under the pillow, Neha found Tannu's hastily written letter.

Didi, I have erred. I have sinned against you. Had you shouted, had you been angry, had you slapped me – that would have somewhat lightened my guilt. But like Lord Shiva, you just consumed the poison and didn't spit it out. Will you ever be able to forgive me?

Later, Neha heard that Tannu had not gone back to India but had stayed in Scotland. A friend at university told her that Paresh and Tannu had married. Paresh now had a British passport, so the marriage had been opportunistic.

Her sleep deteriorated from that time on. She would go to bed feeling so terribly tired – but sleep would refuse to come. When body and mind are both so burdened, sleep comes even to the most hopeless – so why was Neha still deprived of it?

*

In the middle of that freezing cold, sleepless night, she heard the doorbell ringing. It was a desolate sound.

'Who is it?' she called out.

'It is Tannu. Please open the door, Didi.'

Reluctantly, Neha opened the door, but she did not let her sister inside.

'This morning,' Tannu babbled, 'we had just set off to drive to Glasgow when we had a terrible accident. Our car was nearly crushed – and although I escaped, Paresh died in the ambulance before he could reach the hospital. I am left alone. Please, Neha Didi, let me in. Let me in!'

Neha's voice, when she could speak, shook with passion and bitterness.

'Tannu, you built an identity of your own and cast me aside, little caring that I was left alone and lonely. You broke my heart – you obviously couldn't bear the prospect of my being happy. I breathe, but I have no life. You made me a living corpse. As for Paresh, he died for me the day he betrayed me to seek comfort and satisfaction in your arms and your body.'

With that, she slammed the door shut, right in Tannu's face.

Neha shuddered. She was shocked at her own behaviour. She belonged to a country in which people believe that love is in the giving, not in the taking, where love has no conditions, no selfish motives. How cold she had become. As cold as the Scottish weather. She had become a small part of the snow-covered mountains. She was forgetting what she used to be . . .

The snow was still falling softly outside, hardening into layer upon layer of thin sheets of ice.

Salina Had Only Wanted To Get Married . . .

Usha Raje Saxena

South London, UK, 1997

Bokhari and Salina opened their savings account book. In the last three years, the two of them together had only managed to save £25. For the wedding, they needed at least £150 – for how could they get married without a feast, a taffeta gown, a vashova (veil) and a priest!

If Salina had been an ordinary British citizen, she would certainly have received income support from the government. But the fact of the matter was that Salina had lived in Britain for four years as an illegal immigrant – a third-class citizen who did not officially exist. She could not vote. She had no National Insurance number. And so the benefits of the welfare state were denied to her.

Salina's fiancé Bokhari was always explaining to her that there was no point in worrying. He was convinced that very soon, a new law would be brought in which would give legal status and amnesty to many – among them, Salina and himself. It was just a matter of time. It was only a week until the General Election on 1 May. As soon as Labour got into power, he said, they were bound to pass some law to help illegal immigrants.

Labour was the party of the ordinary man; in 1973 Labour had passed a law which made illegal immigrants legal. Just wait and see! The Tory government was sure to lose this time.

Bokhari said this with such certainty that it seemed as though Labour's victory and the Tories' defeat were in his very own hands. Salina did not feel reassured, however. Whether it was Labour or the Tories, how could the couple help either side to win when they could not even vote? Actually, everybody in the factory where she worked was dead set on a Labour victory. But Salina knew that nobody there really knew anything about law or politics. Everybody just made their own random guesses.

The constant fear of being caught lived deep in Salina's heart; the fear of first being put into prison and then, from there, being sent back to wrecked and ruined Yugoslavia where she no longer had anybody.

But despite the difficulties and the fear, Salina considered that hers was not a bad life. She had food morning and evening, a small room to live in, and some good friends who shared her joys and supported her in her sorrows. Only one wish remained – that she and Bokhari could get married and set up their own household.

Salina was just a normal girl. And like many other normal girls, she did not want to settle for a quiet wedding. She wished to celebrate it in style, with all the workers from the factory as her guests, so that her parents' restless souls might find peace. To Salina, tying the marital knot was a holy and sacred ceremony which required not only consent but also the good wishes and blessings of others.

Salina, Bokhari and the other immigrants who worked with them illegally in the factory were all being thoroughly exploited. Whenever it suited the supervisors, they made the employees work long hours for very little money, and, of course, the workers couldn't complain. The factory was itself illegal. If the police ever found out that a mattress factory was being run in a disused building marked for demolition, they would indeed first send all the staff to prison, and then back to the wretched countries from which they had fled.

Salina and Bokhari were alone in the world now. Their only friends were the other workers in the factory, but the position of those friends was just as precarious as their own.

Virtually everybody who worked in the factory was an illegal refugee; some were from Bengal, some from Pakistan, or Yugoslavia, or Nigeria. Coming from different countries meant that they did not speak each other's languages, but they understood each other's difficulties and shared as much as they could.

Salina and Bokhari had been friends since childhood; they had lived in the same district of the same town. When war broke out in Yugoslavia and the Serbs and Bosnians had begun to slaughter even their friends and relatives like goats, their parents had tried to protect them, and in the process had themselves become victims of the brutality. In those days it was hard to tell the difference between friend and enemy. Ethnic groups who had lived together for years and shared in each other's civilisations, cultures and languages were now baying for each other's blood. Hoping that at least their children would survive, parents sent them to England, America or Europe, or wherever it seemed safe.

Both Bokhari's and Salina's parents had sacrificed their own lives to help their children escape from Yugoslavia and go to England, to start afresh there and in time get married and have a happy life. In the eyes of their parents, England was a kind of 'promised land' where the streets were paved with gold and the lanes with silver. Salina had not found any gold and silver lanes, but Jewish Maria Polovski had given her a room in a damp house in a damp street in South London, and had not asked for any rent until Salina had found work in the factory. Salina's fiancé Bokhari shared his evenings with Annu Chatterjee in a single bedroom. Both Annu and Bokhari worked in a leather clothes factory. Annu worked night shifts and Bokhari days, so during the day Annu slept in the single bed and at night Bokhari took over.

Salina's patience had now run out. She feared that if she did not get married this year, it would never happen. Bokhari did not want to wait any longer either. Whenever he was close to Salina, lightning flashed through his body, all his muscles tensed up and he became breathless. Occasionally he even got angry with Salina's old-fashioned ideas about chastity. He thought that a stupid piece of paper and a few words from a priest made no difference. Love was a bond between two hearts.

Salina herself thought, *He's only a man. What difference does it make to him?* But she herself was superstitious. She remembered her promise to her parents. If she were to set up home with a man without being married, then their spirits would forever be in torment. The girl knew that it was necessary for a relationship to be sealed by the Church and society. When there were four witnesses to a wedding, one kept one's honour and one's place in society – otherwise anybody could do anything in the dark. And even when there were no relatives to join in, friends who could take part and wish the couple well could lend significance to the holy act.

Salina was constantly considering all sorts of schemes by which she could earn £200 in one go. Dreaming day and night of saving money and getting married had already led her to take some desperate measures. Once or twice she had even bought National Lottery tickets, but then when she did not win she realised that more pounds had been squandered from her purse! She did not fill in lottery tickets any more now, just saved every penny, putting any spare cash into her money box. She also tried to save money by no longer having her hair cut, using lipstick or wearing stockings even in freezing weather – but no one can save £150 from so little!

One night, she dreamed she was walking up the aisle, wearing a white taffeta gown that swished when she walked, her face hidden behind a lacy veil, carrying a posy of silk flowers. The priest was reading the marriage vows. Bokhari and she knelt and promised to stay together in life and death. Bokhari put a beautiful gold wedding ring on her finger and then . . . then came that special moment when the priest said, 'You may kiss the bride.' She blushed, and in front of everybody Bokhari lifted up her veil and gave her a long kiss on her luxuriant young lips . . .

Oh, dreams! How long would this wedding remain a dream? Salina was becoming more and more distressed. Bokhari was a normal man: what if he fell into the clutches of some other girl? She'd be left alone with her despair. Tasha and Tanni were always teasing and provoking Bokhari. Whenever Salina felt this insecure, her heart began to beat faster.

That day, there was a new girl, Dinar, working in the factory. She was the same age as Salina, and asked her during their lunch break, 'What is the matter, Salina? You look very pale and depressed. Has that horrible supervisor been molesting you?'

'No, it's nothing like that. He always treats me very politely,' said Salina, heaving a sigh.

'Then tell me, what is the matter? Talking about problems can make one's burden feel lighter,' said Dinar.

Salina could not help herself; she told Dinar all about the difficulty of finding money for her wedding.

'The trouble is, Bokhari can no longer bear us to live apart. Sometimes he almost seems ready to force me to be with him. We have only been able to save £25 for the wedding so far, and we need at least another £125. What can I do? How can I manage that? It's impossible. I can't think of any way.'

A sob escaped her, and she continued, 'Bokhari has become very impatient lately. I'm really scared that he'll end up getting together with another girl – and then my whole life will be destroyed! Tell me, what can I do? My situation is becoming so hopeless.'

Dinar stroked her back and said in the sweetest tones, 'Stop crying, my lovely Salina. I'll give you an address – you should go there. They pay you £200 for one single sitting. You just need a bit of courage, that's all, and remember to be careful.'

'What? Are you suggesting I appear in a blue movie or work as a call girl? I can't do anything like that,' cried Salina, removing Dinar's hand abruptly.

'Whatever are you talking about, Salina? As if I would suggest anything so disgusting to somebody who won't even let her fiancé come near her bed!'

'Then how will I earn the money? I won't do dancing or such things in a hotel either.'

'I know that. What do you take me for – a slut?' Dinar went on: 'Listen, these people are all right. They work for a good cause. They want those human eggs which our ovaries produce every month and which are lost without being used. Once I needed to send some money home because my father was ill, and at that time, these people came in really useful. I let them remove eggs from my ovaries. You can trust me, I had no trouble with it at all. You know that I now have a one-year-old daughter. She is very healthy, lively and completely normal.'

Seeing Salina in a state of helplessness and indecision, she whispered, 'If you don't want to sell your eggs, then that's OK. There are other ways. We have two kidneys in our body but need only one, so if you want, you can sell your spare kidney. God knows there are many people spending their lives on a dialysis machine and waiting for a kidney donor.' She looked straight into Salina's eyes and said, 'Look, I have shown you the way – now it's up to you. The truth is that those people are doing it for the benefit of women who cannot have children. They take your eggs and implant them into the womb of some barren woman, and thanks to your kindness there will be a child in a house of tears. Those people pay £200 for one sitting. Don't be afraid: there is no kind of risk involved. All you have to do is at the end of your period let them have the unfertilised egg from your ovary.'

'You're right, Dinar, I am scared,' Salina admitted. But the wonderful, golden dreams of her wedding were beginning to shine in her eyes.

'It's for a good cause, remember. You won't have any trouble. They are honest people and experienced doctors as well. They have been doing this for years.'

Salina had heard about the trade in kidneys before. Only recently Harinder had sold one of her kidneys for £200. But she had never before heard about egg harvesting and implantation.

'Look, I'll give you their address. You just go there, no worries, nobody will find out. You'll get the money you need and can get married to Bokhari. It's a perfectly safe plan.'

Salina took the address from Dinar, and after a few nights of indecision threw the note with the address into her handbag. One evening she set out alone to look for the place, full of fear but dreaming of her wedding. She did not consider it necessary to tell Bokhari about it, because she was doubtful about his reaction. In any case, only women can understand certain matters: the taffeta gown and the crowd of guests enjoying themselves and congratulating her appeared in front of her eyes.

It was quite a plain building. There was no sign outside. On one side of the door there was an electric doorbell and an intercom with a tiny camera attached. Through the lens, the people sitting inside could see who had arrived on the doorstep while they were talking to them. Salina rang the bell and replied to a question from inside by giving her name and saying that Dinar had sent her. She was very nervous; her heart was racing.

Three or four minutes later, an ordinary-looking woman of medium height opened the door. She was perhaps a maid and led Salina to some sort of sitting room. She told her to sit on a sofa there and gave her a glass of water to drink from the water-cooler.

Drinking the water did not help Salina to relax. She was so nervous that droplets of sweat were glistening on her forehead despite the cold weather. The woman gave her a box of tissues and said, 'Don't worry, Salina. Just hold on to your courage. You'll get what you came for.' Even in the midst of all her tension, Salina's mind was full of the wedding and the celebration, and she tried very hard to prepare herself for what was coming.

In order to calm Salina down, the woman talked to her for a few minutes about the weather, her family, the rising prices in the shops. A man came in, in the middle of their conversation, said, 'Hello,' walked out of the front door and looked around in all directions, and then came back in and told the woman that she should take Salina upstairs to the consultation room.

They walked down a short corridor and up two flights of stairs to the clinic. It had a wooden floor. On one side stood a kind of temporary operating table made of steel, covered in a transparent plastic sheet. Next to the operating table was a small table with a portable steriliser on it and some surgical instruments, laid out inside a transparent plastic box. A small wash-basin had been installed in the right-hand corner of the room, and above it was some washing-up liquid and a Kimberley paper-towel roll. A wooden desk was situated in the left-hand corner of the room, with a revolving office chair on one side, and on the other, two padded chairs for the patients.

The room reeked of Dettol. Salina's heart sank. She wanted to run away, but the £200 and the desire for the perfect wedding kept her there.

After a little while, a tall, thin man in a white coat and with a stethoscope hanging around his neck entered the room. He sat down on the revolving chair. He seemed to be the same man she had seen downstairs earlier, but she did not give it any thought. The doctor indicated to Salina to sit down. The other woman was standing in attendance by the operating table.

The doctor took a piece of liquorice from a bowl on the desk, put it into his mouth and offered the bowl to Salina. Then, without paying attention to whether or not she had taken the liquorice, he wrote on the notepad in front of him Salina's name, address, telephone number and age, and in a few words explained briefly how the 'risk-free' procedure of removing an egg from an ovary worked. He also said that today they would just do a gynaecological check and a blood test. If everything was all right, she would be called back after three days.

Salina quite liked the atmosphere in the clinic. The procedures for the gynaecological check and the blood test were completely normal. So she began to relax mentally and regain her equilibrium. In her mind she saw the £200 and the glittering white, figure-hugging gown she would be wearing at the wedding ceremony.

The next time she came, during the second sitting, the doctor told Salina that she was healthy and a suitable candidate as an egg donor. That day, he asked Salina to sign a contract which stated that *Having signed this contract, the applicant is obliged to comply with all the*

terms as stated in this contract. The clinic does not accept
responsibility for any carelessness in health matters on the
part of the applicant.

Although Salina did sign the contract, she was able neither to read any terms in the contract nor to understand them, because her English was not very good and she was confused. So she simply told herself that these people were experienced doctors. Everything would be perfectly all right.

That day, the doctor gave Salina her first hormone injection in order to stimulate her uterus into producing more eggs. 'Everything will be fine,' he said. 'There is no reason to worry.' Wearing a nurse's uniform, the sturdy woman came down the stairs and said that Salina would have to come to the clinic every evening for the next twelve days. Salina nodded her head in assent and went home. Having only had a very basic education, she was not in the habit of asking questions of more educated people. She did not ask those people anything nor did they tell her anything else.

After seven or eight injections, Salina began to feel a very mild pain in her lower abdomen; it was the same kind of pain she experienced during her periods. After twelve days, she was given a general anaesthetic, and the clinic doctor extracted some eggs from her ovary. She woke up the next morning and was sent home straight away, clutching a brown envelope containing £200.

When she arrived home, Salina hid the money in her knee-high boots, thanked God and decided that she would tell Bokhari the next evening, so that they could go to the priest and fix the date of their wedding. As she had been constantly rushing to and from the clinic, she had not been able to see Bokhari over the last few days. That night, the after-effects of the anaesthetic made her sleep very deeply. But the next day at midday, at home in her room, she suddenly felt something like an earthquake inside her abdomen. She felt sick and began to feel dizzy as well. She splashed a few drops of cold water on her face and, pulling herself together, thought, *It's only normal to have a bit of trouble. Soon everything will be all right. There is nothing to worry about.*

Just then, Bokhari let himself into the house and entered her room, knocking then pushing the door open. He was clutching his stomach. His face was ashen – he looked as though he had been ill for some days. Handing a brown envelope over to Salina, he said hoarsely, 'Take this £200 and go and get your beautiful taffeta gown. Now we'll fix the date of our wedding straight away.'

Salina's head was throbbing; she could not see Bokhari clearly. 'But where did you get this money from?' she asked, puzzled. Then: 'Oh no, my God! Have you sold your kidney and . . . ?'

Far from being able to take the envelope, Salina could not even finish her sentence. Everything turned black and she collapsed unconscious onto the floor.

*

When she opened her eyes again, she found herself among the doctors and nurses of a London hospital. She was being given oxygen and blood. The nurse checked her blood pressure, gave her some medicine and told her that she was out of danger. Salina felt frightened. She held on to the hand of the nurse and asked, 'But what happened to me? How did I get here? Who are you?'

The nurse said gently, 'You are in hospital, dear. Don't worry, you are completely safe here. Unfortunately, you and your fiancé found yourselves in the hands of some bad people, and those clumsy butchers have damaged vital parts of both your bodies. They are illegal human-organ traders who exploited your vulnerability and injured you and Bokhari badly. You may not realise this, but those people took you close to death's door. It was your landlady, Mrs Polovski, who called the ambulance in time and saved both your lives. Salina, my dear, your ovaries have been badly pierced, and the procedure has also affected your kidneys. You need absolute rest.'

'The ovaries are pierced? What are you saying, Nurse? Does that mean I can never carry a child?' When Salina grasped the seriousness of her condition, she screamed out, 'No, no! That can't be true.' And she burst into tears.

Bokhari was lying in the next bed, supported by a pillow. When he heard Salina cry, he could not stay in his bed. The removal of his kidney had caused his bladder and his other kidney to become badly infected. He was burning with a high fever, but moaning in pain he dragged himself and his drip-stand to Salina's bed and sat down on the chair next to it.

'Salina, my Salina, don't cry, my darling,' he said tenderly. 'Don't lose heart. You'll soon be wearing your gown and veil and be walking up the aisle with me, and I'll put the wedding ring on your finger. All our friends will celebrate our happiness with us. Little ninny! Why should you cry? I'm here with you now.' And he kissed Salina very lightly on the lips.

'But – but I will never be able to give you a child,' sobbed Salina, burying her face in her pillows and crying desperately.

'Silly girl,' said Bokhari, his voice choking, 'why do you worry so? The nurse has told me everything . . . you mustn't cry about your deficiency. Look – I'm not a whole man any more either. My second kidney is badly infected. I – I'm deficient too . . . '

Bokhari could not go on, his throat had become husky. He swallowed his tears, then said, 'Am I not here for you and you for me? Whatever state we're each in, we've got one another.'

Salma

Usha Verma
Translated by Jutta Austin

York, UK, 1971

'Appa, what can I do?' Salma says, and I wonder what I could possibly do to lessen the troubles of this innocent girl. But I know that there is nothing I *can* do – nothing but listen to Salma's story day after day during my class. Sometimes she has a bandage around her hand; sometimes her mouth is swollen and red; sometimes her face is pinched with hunger: every day there is a new cause for concern.

Who is Salma? A flower bud from Pakistan that is unable to blossom. Her skin is a golden colour, and she has large eyes and a graceful, upright body – what more could anyone want?

I keep listening to you, Salma, but I am even more helpless than you. My mind is berating me for not being able to do anything. At night I cannot sleep; I keep wondering if there is someone whose suffering I might be able to relieve, because it is not just Salma: there are thousands more like her!

Sometimes I get angry. Why should I do anything at all? But still my heart wants to go back and get involved all over again. It is true that neither country nor religion tie us together. But there is another bond, the bond between one woman and another, the bond of being human. And while relationships between humans are mixed up with, and always restricted by, the borders of national identity and religion, the relationship between two women is an inner one: we understand each other without the need for words. For instance, a daughter can easily cross all the barriers of age to understand her mother's grief.

Salma comes to my English class, and occasionally she talks to me. When she does so, tears well up in her eyes. One day, she seemed particularly desolate. While the rest of the girls were leaving, she lingered over tidying up her things and was generally hovering in my vicinity. I realised that she wanted to tell me something but could not find the courage to speak, so I asked her outright, 'Salma, what is the matter? Are you not going home today?'

She became flustered, and in turn asked, 'Appa, am I making you late?' She knew that I lived quite far away and always tried to get home quickly in the evenings because I did not like the children to be on their own at home.

'No,' I said patiently, 'there's time enough. What did you want to tell me?'

Salma sat down, put her head on the table and burst into tears. 'Appa, what can I do?' she sobbed.

I went to her, stood beside her and said, 'What is going on? Tell me.'

An ocean of pain swam in Salma's big eyes. Waves of unrequited yearning.

'Appa, he doesn't talk to me any more. He is just crazy about that white girl. Today he told me not to show my face at home again. I have no idea what to do.'

I replied without thinking, 'What does your mother-in-law say?'

'Oh, she just says, "You've had three years, and you still haven't produced any children! So of course he is not very pleased with you." But, Appa, he is never at home at night.'

Salma's Aunt Tamina, the girl then told me, had brought her over here from Pakistan. Tamina had said to her older sister, 'Baji (sister), let me have her. I'll arrange her marriage – she'll have a really comfortable life.'

Salma had heard all the talk about living abroad. She harboured the dream that perhaps she would be able to help her mother and father out of their poverty.

After much soul-searching, Ammi and Abba had agreed. Ammi had full confidence in her sister. She would make it work. And how could the poor woman have guessed that fate was just playing games?

When Tamina had announced her intention to bring her niece to England, Salma felt really happy. Her aunt had her sights set on the son of a friend of hers. He had just that very year passed his medical exams and was now a hospital doctor. He was very handsome – just right for their lovely Salma. The fact that he was four or five years older than her shouldn't matter. And yet the age difference bothered Tamina. Her husband was nine years older than her, and with this age gap had come very different ways of thinking. A sad little sigh escaped her. Then she thought, *Well, I am reaching my forties now anyhow. And Salma has no shortcomings; she is worthy of Anvar in every respect.*

So they had obtained a passport for Salma and gathered her possessions together. She had visited her girlfriends, and the last month raced by, evaporating like camphor. When it was time to go, Salma embraced everybody and cuddled her smaller sisters and brothers. She had thought it all through again and again, and was prepared to set off with a sense of purpose.

The taxi arrived, and she went and sat in it with Khala (Auntie). Then came the flood of tears. Salma felt that she was leaving behind something she needed very much, something very much her own. She turned her face away from the house, but it was less easy to persuade her mind to change direction.

Just then, her Aunt Tamina said, 'Salma, check you have all your luggage.'

The girl glanced out of the window and saw that all her luggage had been put in the boot. The taxi drove off with her and her aunt inside, and Salma felt both confused and apprehensive.

At the airport, there was the usual rush to have their luggage weighed and to organise the hand luggage. It was all very chaotic. Salma went with her aunt and boarded the plane. She had never flown before and at first she was greatly alarmed, but after a short while everything settled down around her. As she sat listlessly in her seat, pictures began to tumble one by one through her mind. Her little brother had been pestering her daily: 'Baji, send me an electric train.' And sometimes, 'Baji, send me a nice car; lots of toys, albums, sweets . . .' So many requests. But on the last night before she left he had come up to her, put his arms around her and said, 'Baji, I don't want anything. Just don't go away . . . '

She could feel him clinging to her and shaking her, but it was Khala rousing her – the air hostess had come with their food. Salma did not even feel like looking at it. She sleepily refused. Khala thought that perhaps she was feeling a bit dizzy because it was her first time in an aeroplane, so she did not press her.

Salma returned into her own world. She could hear the cheerful voices of her girlfriends talking to her in fun: 'Salma, when you're there you must invite me over, too.' Then there was Ammi, standing there and saying, 'Salma, get up – look how late it is. Your father is waiting for his tea.' Flustered, she gave a start and rubbed her eyes. Then she saw that there was nobody there.

Khala said, 'Ah, good, you've woken up. Just in time. We're about to land at Heathrow.'

*

When she climbed out of the car at her aunt's house, she seemed to be in an entirely new world. There were no open drains or dirty pathways; everything was sparkling clean, so neat that it frightened her in case it got spoiled. With the greatest care, she put one foot in front of the other. Mentally, she was still back home in Habibpur. What would they be doing right now? Maybe Abba had come home . . .

'Salma, will you have some tea?' Her aunt's voice shattered her dream.

Immediately, she stood up and said dutifully, 'Shall I make the tea?' and walked uncertainly to the kitchen.

She was still looking around to see where everything was kept when Khala handed her a cup of tea and said, 'Come on, let's see what's in the freezer!' The woman took out some smallish kebabs and began to heat them up in the microwave.

Salma took her cup of tea and just sat. She had quite forgotten that she was in her aunt's house, thousands of miles from Pakistan. In her mind it was evening, and Abba had shut the fruit shop and come home exhausted, and she could hear him say, 'Salma, my girl, can you bring me some water for the vazu (ablutions).'

She stood up so suddenly that she spilled some of her tea, but Khala said kindly, 'No matter, I'll clean it up.'

Somehow, the girl managed to drink up the rest of her tea. That night she ate a kebab and some bread, and then went straight to bed. She was tired out from the long flight, and stiff all over from sitting in the same cramped place for so long. She lay down, a crowd of shadows flickering behind her eyes. While still talking to them all, she fell asleep.

She woke up very early in the morning and sat up, feeling disorientated. Then she remembered that she had crossed the seven seas and was sitting in her aunt's house in a foreign country.

In the bright light of the morning she felt calmer. Something inside her broke open and became receptive. When she had drunk her tea and was sitting with Khala, her aunt told her that there was a small market nearby where you could get just about everything you could think of. There was also a corner shop where you could buy milk, eggs, newspapers, tea and so on, all the bits and pieces of everyday life. Then there were all the phone numbers she might need. And the kind of clothes she'd need here. Khala made plans to take her niece out and buy her a coat, a cardigan, and a few basics. She explained the lock and keys and everything to Salma, because the girl would have to spend some four or five hours alone in the house while her aunt went to work.

Tamina knew that her big sister and her family were hard up and could only afford two meals a day. They were running a small fruit shop, and half of the fruit would regularly rot, since nobody could afford to buy an expensive luxury like fruit. There was enough money in Pakistan, but not everyone got their share. Ordinary people continued to have great difficulty in affording medicines and medical treatment and life's basic necessities. With all her heart, Salma's aunt wanted to arrange for her niece to marry into a well-off family so that her own family's situation would automatically improve. It was with this in mind that she had paid for her niece's ticket and brought Salma to the UK.

When Tamina had gone out, Salma sat down quietly on the sofa. She really wanted to phone home, but had no idea how to do that, and there was no telephone in her family's house anyway. She looked outside and saw clouds gathering in the sky. Something was building up inside her, too, and suffocating her. Her mind was restless, and she still felt tired so she drifted off to sleep again. Her sleep was interrupted by the doorbell. She almost ran to the door but then remembered that Khala had said that she should not open the door, so she just stood there quietly as someone pushed a paper through and left.

*

When Khala came back in the evening it seemed to Salma that her aunt was very quiet. She hoped it was not because of her! But then Salma passed the time cooking food and washing up. She hardly noticed the evening drawing in. The telephone rang quite late and Khala talked to someone for a while. Salma did not know why, but it sounded to her as if there was some kind of upset. Khala began to speak in a very loud voice. The girl heard her say, 'Didn't you ask me to send for the girl? Why do you now want to go back on our agreement?'

Salma could not hear the reply. Unease stirred in her mind. She had heard that the boy was the son of her aunt's friend. That was all she had been told.

During the following week, nothing else was said, but she had a feeling that there was something worrying Khala. She wanted her aunt to tell her about it, but lacked the courage to ask her.

From then on, everything happened so fast that Salma's world seemed to be spinning. She began to lose her nerve. What was going to happen now? In her heart everything became confused – the first shoots of unknown love, brothers and sisters, Ammi and Abbu.

Khala's friend, she learned eventually, had said that her son refused to marry Salma without living with her first. Only then would he see if it worked and would make up his mind.

Khala asked Salma whether she knew about this Western custom. After worrying about it for a few days, Khala said that she really couldn't allow it to happen. She explained that if Anvar later refused to marry Salma, then the girl would be disgraced. Not everybody was that open-minded. It was all right to go to the cinema together or talk to each other for a short while, she told Salma, but she could not condone this business of living together.

A nagging fear raised its head in Salma's mind – she probably did not look like the other girls here. She went and stood in front of the mirror. *If we live together he'll be able to see all of me, otherwise I can cover myself up as much as I like,* she thought. Who would know, if they lived together? When you love someone, you change all your habits readily and want to give all you are and have, whether you live together or not.

Perhaps people in the West would find this strange, but in the East women did not hold on to their separate identity. She remembered that the husband of one of her friends had suddenly decided he disliked her covering her head. The young wife gave up going to any of the gatherings where she had used to read the Koran in such a beautiful voice. Everybody kept saying, 'So just come and cover your head when you're here.' But she had refused.

Khala herself thought that after a while, Dr Anvar might still come round to her point of view. She even asked her friend to make her son Anvar agree to the marriage, saying that Salma would then make all her dreams come true. Anvar was a doctor in a state hospital. Salma admired this greatly. When somebody had a regular salary, they could establish a standard of living to match, whereas in trade you never knew how much or how little would come in, so there was no peace of mind. But that was a concern for the future. Right then there was no peace of mind for Salma.

That day, Khala had taken Salma along to a memorial to express their condolences after the death of a member of their community. There they met Hazi Sahab and his wife. As soon as they saw Salma, the couple became very interested in her. They secretly agreed that if they could arrange a marriage between this girl and their middle son, Zamir, then once he'd tied the knot, he might become a reformed character. So they asked around here and there, and in the end the matter also reached Khala's ears. Only four days later, the formal marriage proposal arrived.

Tamina became very agitated. There was such a difference between Azra's doctor son and this young man Zamir. But she was very happy nonetheless and said, 'There you are, it has all turned out well in the end. He has his own launderette, and it does very well. You won't lack for anything. And if Zamir is not very well-educated, so what? He looks and sounds nice enough.'

Salma, too, heaved a sigh of relief.

Tamina wanted the wedding to take place in two months' time, but Hazi Sahab said it would be better to arrange the wedding for the very next week. Khala also wished to discuss the amount of meher (gifts/money) that Salma would receive before the wedding, but Hazi Sahab remained very vague about it. So in the end she thought, *Well, what can I do? If Zamir stays healthy there won't be any need for the meher anyway. And if a problem should arise, and Hazi Sahab should go back on his word, we'd lose whatever we've gained.*

She informed everybody in Pakistan of the marriage.

After a simple wedding, Salma arrived in the house of her in-laws. Her parents were pleased too, had arranged to have songs sung for her and sweets distributed – and then, well, may Allah keep Salma happy.

Now and then, Salma would phone Khala and tell her, 'I'm very happy. Everybody looks after me. I don't lack for anything.' But she began to notice that Zamir was almost always out. And even when he was at home, he seemed miles away in his mind and showed no feelings for her. And the body is not everything.

Salma's days passed pleasantly enough. She thought she would like to go out somewhere with Zamir sometimes, but her mother-in-law never asked her to go anywhere. If she had to go out, she always went by herself. All day long, all Salma did was cook the food and clean the house. When somebody visited, her mother-in-law would remove her from sight, under the pretext of her having to make the tea or do some other job. Sometimes the young wife would stand at the window and watch the huge red buses go past, and wish she could sit on them and travel around. She would go on one with Zamir and buy the most beautiful clothes in a London shop.

Then she thought that perhaps after a while, her mother-in-law herself would tell them to leave.

One day, a lot of relatives came to the house, and they had run out of milk. Her mother-in-law said, 'Salma, ask Zamir for some money so I can go and get more milk from the corner shop.' Salma went upstairs. She did not find Zamir, but his coat was hanging there. She slipped her hand into the pocket and took out some change for her mother-in-law. Together with the coins, a photo fell into her hand. When she looked at it, everything around her went dark.

Far away, her mother-in-law was calling from downstairs. Somehow Salma managed to go back down and give her mother-in-law the money. Then she ran back upstairs. The photo was too shameless to leave any space for explanations. Salma wondered what to do: should she tell her mother-in-law or just keep quiet? She felt as if somebody had laid her fully alive onto a slab of ice. Should she phone Khala? No, this was her battle now, she would have to fight it alone. Maybe her mother-in-law did not know either. Surely Hazi Sahab would talk to Zamir and make his son understand right from wrong?

Suddenly she heard her mother-in-law call up: 'Salma, there's lots to do downstairs!'

Her mind on fire, she went down. But as soon as she had gathered together the tea things, the tray slipped out of her shaking hands. Hazi Sahab heard the commotion and came running in from outside, saying irritably: 'Can't you watch what you're doing? This is all very expensive!'

Salma did not reply. She flew upstairs, fetched the photo and thrust it into her mother-in-law's hands. Then she went and threw herself on her bed. She had no friends to turn to and felt defeated in every respect. Following a dream of better things, she had left home, left her beloved parents and brothers and sisters, and come here.

Her mother-in-law came into her room, sat down and said, 'This is no reason to be so upset. All men are like this.'

With a shock Salma realised that nobody here would see things from her point of view. First, Anvar had said that they should live together before getting married, and now there was this second deception. She had managed to escape from Anvar's clutches, but was she truly free now? She had fallen off the mountain and was lying at its foot, covered in blood, with nobody to help her. Her whole existence was being called into question. Her mother-in-law had drawn her in with her talk of the family honour; she said this matter should be kept within their own four walls, meaning that it would be wrong to mention it to Khala or anybody else. And she added that some of the fault must surely have been Salma's anyway.

*

Salma felt more and more as if she was suffocating. There was no speck of light anywhere, but neither could she see a darkness deep enough to sink into so that everything would be over. She began to realise that there is a kind of pain which will neither let you live nor die. She was sinking into a trough so deep that she did not know how she would ever find a way out of it.

Mustering all her courage, she reproached Zamir, but her angry frown took him completely by surprise, and he said, 'Well, at least I don't bring her here and keep her – surely that's something. Don't you dare mention her again! You get all your clothes and food – what more do you want? I can do what I like, and you have no right to say anything!'

These words set Salma's whole body on fire. She was shaking as she asked, 'Would you talk like this in front of Hazi Sahab?'

Zamir laughed and said, 'He knows very well how conceited you are.'

Trembling with pain and anger, Salma sat down and began to sob.

Zamir stamped his foot and snapped, 'I'll convert her to Islam and make her my second wife. You'd be wise to keep your mouth shut!' Slamming the door loudly, he left the house.

A little while later, the phone rang. There was no one else in the house, so Salma picked up the receiver, and to her joy heard Khala's voice at the other end of the line. With great urgency she begged her, 'Khala, take me away from here, or I'll die.'

Khala tried hard to make Salma understand that neither Hazi Sahab and his wife nor anybody else was prepared to let Salma go anywhere. Gradually, it dawned on the young wife that the door of the house was shut, and that she would never be able to leave these four walls, nor would the door ever open or any light reach her.

She began to think that perhaps suicide would bring her release. She looked at the bottle of migraine tablets for a long time, stretching out her hand and touching it but then pulling her hand away in fear. She was always thinking how stupid she was, having only gone to school until year eight. She would never be able to live on her own. Even if she did leave, how would she manage to live without Zamir?

And then came the night of that terrible incident. The police surrounded the house. They had come for Zamir. A policewoman came upstairs and searched Zamir's room. She found drugs in the pocket of his jacket.

He was handcuffed. Salma stood, petrified, watching it all. She could not understand it. Why did Zamir do all these dirty and dangerous things? The whole family was upset, almost angry, as if it were partly Salma's responsibility to make Zamir honourable and law-abiding. Salma had known poverty from childhood, but she had never before experienced dishonesty, deceit and baseness. When she had finally regained her composure, the police had already taken Zamir away. Hazi Sahab was sitting very still, deeply humiliated, deeply dejected. Dawn was just breaking. It was a new day.

Salma went up to her room and cast a glance around it. Everything was ruined. She now looked with yearning at the medicine bottle which used to frighten her. With firm resolve, she poured herself a glass of water from the jug and tried to swallow all the pills at once. It took her a little while, and when the bottle was empty, she lay down on her bed.

Salma's sister-in-law Shama came upstairs to check on Salma. Seeing her lying unconscious, she grabbed Salma by her arms, shook her as hard as she could and told her to get up and come downstairs. Salma tried hard, but she was only able to roll to one side. Spotting the empty medicine bottle, Shama pelted downstairs to get help.

*

When Salma came to, the next day, she found herself in hospital. A doctor kept calling her name and asking her how she felt now. Salma was perplexed. Who is this, she wondered, so concerned about me and talking to me in

290

my own language? After asking how she was, the doctor gave his instructions to the nurse and left.

The next day, Hazi Sahab came but the doctor would not allow Salma to go home. He told Hazi Sahab that it would be for the police to decide where Salma was to go. Dr Anvar asked Salma where she wanted to go. Salma gave him Khala's address and asked him to inform her aunt.

The next day, the doctor's shift changed. The people from Social Services asked Salma if she wanted to live in a hostel for girls. Salma thought that perhaps that would be the best thing for her to do, so she went to the hostel.

Dr Anvar had left her a piece of paper on which to leave the addresses of both the hostel and her aunt so he could stay in contact.

Later, when he was telling his mother all about Salma, he suddenly realised with a feeling of shock who the young woman was!

Full of unease, he felt in his pocket – and withdrew a blank piece of paper.

The Bolt

Zakia Zubairi
Translated by Dr Charanjeet Kaur

London, UK, 2011

Was there no limit to how low her son, Sameer, could stoop?

Seema's tears had not dried since that moment of shock. As a child, whenever he saw tears in the eyes of his mother, little Sameer would rush to the kitchen cupboard in which the masalas were stored and, in vain, try to reach the bottles on his tiptoes. Exhausted, he would then draw up a chair, take a pinch of dhaniya seeds and put them in her mouth, in the belief that the tears that rose to her eyes while peeling onions would stop. How she had longed for that Sameer to walk up to her now, and with his little hands stuff her mouth with a few dhaniya seeds, so that the tears would stop.

Touched by his innocence and affection, whenever that happened, Seema would break into a smile. Shyly clinging to her legs, he would explain that, on one of their visits to her hairdresser, he had overheard Aunty Suzy prescribe this remedy.

Today, his mother was lost in memories of those days when Sameer adored her, and would follow her around like a shadow all day long.

'Ma, I worry about you, that is why I want to be with you,' he would say, turning her face towards his own with his childish hands.

Today, those were the very same hands that had assaulted her – wounded her both in body and in spirit. The bruises on her flesh bore witness to the fact that thirty years of love and penance had been shattered. Yes, the bruises would heal with time – but would her heart ever heal?

Were these the values she had nurtured in him? Seema's mind was blank, bewildered.

All through his childhood, Sameer had been mortally afraid of his father. Seema had never believed in instilling fear in the minds of her three children. Especially not in her only son, Sameer, whom she looked upon as the neglected one, sandwiched as he was between two sisters. The sisters used to pounce upon him, and then he would hit back. The older one would remain quiet, but the younger girl would scream her heart out and then Sameer would be given a sound beating by their father. This had hardened him. When his father inflicted blows on him, they rained down on Seema's heart. She would try to shelter him with her pallu, but to no avail. Sometimes, a shoe would be hurled at him, and it would hit her. She would be relieved that the shoe had missed her son.

'Ma, will you be attending the conference?'

'Yes, I think I will.'

'And when does it start?'

'The twenty-fourth of September.'

'And how many days will you be away, Ma?'

'The usual – three nights and four days. But I am not certain that I will be going,' replied Seema.

'But Ma, you must go. If you break the routine, you will lose interest.'

Sameer had persuaded her so adroitly that she had agreed at once. At her age, it would be easy for her to give up many things, but she believed that age should not be allowed to make decisions for her. So, she went off to the conference.

The conference, however, left her disenchanted. She could not help wondering how such an event could have been organised by her political party. It was nothing more than a networking opportunity for the rich and influential. The policies discussed were so unlike those of the party she cherished that Seema was shocked. She felt as if she had strayed into the opposition camp. What was she doing here? Change stared her in the face . . . did this have to happen? Was it inevitable?

She was at home when Sameer came in. 'Ma, you're back home? But the conference is still on, I saw it on TV this morning,' he said.

She noticed the young girl who was with him. The question rose in her eyes; he understood.

'Ma, meet Neera.'

'Hello, Neera,' she said. 'Have you eaten or shall I get you something?'

Seema was a vegetarian and she preferred home-cooked food. The others were fond of red meat, which

294

she hated. But who cared what she thought anyway? Her dear husband ate red meat twice a day. He loved beef and remembered what delicious kebabs his mother would serve. *Ugh, beef,* thought Seema, holding her breath so that the slightest whiff of meat would not reach her, even in thought.

'Yes, Mama darling. We've already had our food, since we thought that you weren't at home.'

Seema posed her next question cautiously. Times had changed, she knew. What if the boy reacted the wrong way? Nevertheless, she felt it necessary to ask who this young woman was and why she was with him so late at night. Would he be taking her home shortly?

'Ma, she's here for the night,' he ventured in a hesitant but serious voice.

Seema moved closer to him. 'I don't appreciate this, son. Don't you know what your father will say?'

'I'll take her away if Father comes.'

'No, my boy, the culture of this house does not permit this. Your sister's children are here. How will we explain this kind of relationship to them?'

'Ma, that is not my problem.'

Seema sensed the edge of hostility in his look and his voice. She had been aware of his double standards for thirty-odd years now. One set of values for his mother and sisters, another set for himself.

Earlier, she hadn't begrudged him these views. Especially because she remembered how severely he had been beaten up in childhood; that had always been enough to silence her. She felt she owed it to him. Little did she realise that her love had warped his nature. She could see no wrong in him, since she carried the guilt. He had been wronged so often, she brooded.

Upstairs, Seema realised that Neera had been using her computer. It was obvious that she had come to stay the very day Seema had left for the conference. Her heart rebelled. No! Sameer could not have done this to her!

When she tried to shift Neera out of her room, Sameer confronted her.

'Mama, Neera is insomniac. That's why she's on the computer all night.'

'But, son, it's my office computer. No one should be touching it.'

'Come on, Ma . . . '

'Very well,' said Seema, 'but only for tonight. Of course, she'll be leaving tomorrow.'

'No, Mother, she has nowhere to go.'

Seema did not raise her voice. 'Well! Where did you pick her up from?' She hated shouting, even in anger. She believed that it was only the guilty who protested loudly. And she believed in upholding the dignity of even those who were in the wrong. Her husband mistook her quietness for docility and cowardice, but Seema's convictions were strong. She knew her son was in the wrong.

She retired to her bedroom.

The three days at the conference had exhausted her. She felt betrayed by what had happened there. She mused sadly at the turn events had taken. Her faith in the party was shaken.

Losing her patience with the conference, she had come home – but the situation here was no less volatile. As a woman, what was her status, after all? Sameer had said that Neera would leave if his father returned. How could he take his mother's approval for granted? Her daughter was due to come over with her two children for the weekend, because her husband would be busy at work, as usual. Seema herself could not remember a weekend spent with her husband. And if he did ever stay at home, he would be irritable and resentful, lazing around all day on the sofa – and Seema would have to bear the brunt.

She had borne the brunt in more ways than one. In abject obedience, she had dutifully produced a new human specimen once every thirteen months. When she conceived Sameer, it was her husband's office manager who had accompanied her to her first medical check-up. She felt ashamed, as she knew that the doctor would assume that the manager was the father of the child. And that's how it was. The manager was a younger man – good-looking, too, no doubt about it. How embarrassed he too had been! Surely he didn't want to be mistaken for the husband of a much older woman! This incident had left its mark on her.

When the son was born, it was once more the manager who had informed his boss. Seema had been sent away to her sister's for the delivery. There too she had been left alone, since her sister was busy with her own medical practice. She had hoped that her husband would be happy, now that she had produced a son, and that he would spend more time at home.

The delivery had ravaged her tail-bone. For six months she was bedridden, tending to her newborn in this painful condition. She longed for the ancient, lost family traditions in which a child would be the child of the whole family and would be brought up by the entire clan.

Today, the bruises hurt even more than the pain in her lower spine. The voices emerging from the next room made her hopeful for a while. Perhaps Sameer would come over to her and hold her tightly in his arms, shedding tears of repentance. She too would weep and all would be forgotten and forgiven.

But no such thing happened. He continued to pander to the feelings of the girl, telling her that his mother belonged to a different generation and that work pressures had exhausted her, making her insensitive and judgemental. He assured her that all would soon be well; no one would hurt her again and she would soon be accepted within the fold. She continued to speak softly in his ears, whispering sweet nothings as his resentment towards his mother grew.

Seema thought of Jill. She was such a good-natured and comely blue-eyed British girl! And so home-loving that she had seemed alien to the culture in which she had been born.

Jill had loved Sameer deeply, and often said, 'Seema, your son is so handsome! For me, it was love at first sight.'

Seema, too, would mischievously retort, 'Is he? I don't think he's particularly handsome. It must be your weak eyesight.'

'Oh! How wicked of you, Seema.' Jill would cling to her mother-in-law affectionately. Their jokes would go on, but Seema would also be pleased.

'It's true, my son is really handsome.' She knew that Jill was also enamoured of his deep voice and his flawless British diction.

Often, Seema congratulated herself that she had, in opposition to his father's wishes, encouraged this marriage to happen. For the first time in her life she had stood up to her husband, and firmly insisted that Sameer's wishes be honoured. He was financially independent, she argued, and had bought a flat on the banks of the Thames, which brought in good rent. Not only was her son good-looking, he was sensible too, she persisted. She remembered his unhappy childhood with regret, and prayed silently that he would never have to live through the painful moments of his childhood again. She even warned her God that He must protect her child, or else . . . !

Mother's love, she would smile to herself; how easily it makes you forget the injuries which your child inflicts on you!

But the injuries inflicted by her husband were something else entirely. Not to be forgotten, not to be forgiven. His mother had tolerated him because he was her son, and the entire family had formed her support system. How he would scream at her and how she too would shout back! Like two solid classical singers with strong, stentorian voices. Like the raging flow of the drains in heavy rains. Seema would sit by his weeping mother, consoling her and apologising for her husband's behaviour.

Never once did he apologise though. After all, wasn't he a self-made man who had risen in the world by his own efforts? All that his mother had done was to give birth to him!

Yes, he was a rich man, all right, but he had never understood the importance of being humane. He gave his wife money every month. Wasn't he entitled to know what she did with it? But she was uneducated – how could she have kept track of the family accounts?

Seema had never dreamed that the son would follow in the footsteps of the father. Jill had said to her once,

'Seema, I am lucky that my Sameer is so unlike his father, in every way. Yes, he is handsome . . . but clean in heart and mind, too.'

Today her heart went out, once again, to Jill.

When Sameer had been afflicted with tinnitus, Jill had consoled him, saying, 'It's nothing. The doctor says you'll be fine. Don't worry. You're just stressed.' She had her own high-profile job to think about, too. Seema loved the way she tended to Sameer patiently – cooking breakfast for him, cleaning the house and completing all the chores before leaving for work. It strengthened the bonds of friendship between the two women.

Jill needed to go to bed early in order to be able to rise early. Sameer could not take it and his hostility towards her began to grow. He started coming home late without offering a word of explanation. He stopped having dinner with her in spite of the fact that she would lay the table for him every night, she confided in Seema.

'Invite me home one day,' Seema said gravely. 'Let me see if I can help.'

'Amma,' he complained, 'she doesn't care about me. I have this terrible tinnitus! I suffer so much from sleepless nights. Only when the whirring of the fan overhead silences the ringing in my ears do I fall asleep.'

'But how is Jill to blame, son?' Seema asked, surprised.

'She's my wife. She should be taking care of me.'

'Doesn't she feed you and tend to your house?' she asked passionately. She was a woman speaking up for another woman. Not a mother talking to her son.

'Yes. But shouldn't she be keeping me company when I lie awake at night, with my ears tingling? Instead, she plugs her ears and listens to music, falling asleep comfortably night after night.' His bitterness stung

Seema. Just like his father, she thought. How and when this had happened, she couldn't fathom. It had been her belief that he would become more empathetic by his marriage to this sweet, cultured girl. But . . . Seema could say no more.

She felt that all the ships anchored in the dockyard on the Thames were sinking. Voices rose from them, imploring her. One of the voices, it seemed to her, was Jill's – searching for that handsome face that was her husband's. As if tracing it forever in her memory . . .

'Ma, I am giving her two flats, all the jewellery you had made for her and five thousand pounds. I hope you don't mind about the jewels. I know how sensitive you women are about your jewels.'

How bitterly he speaks, this son of mine! 'Forget the jewellery; I want to give her all the happiness I can.'

'Why?' he retorted. 'It is with me that you share a blood relationship. Not her.'

Well, what could he know of the value of blood relationships, and the bonding of the heart?

Jill had come to meet her when Sameer was away. Resting her head on her ex-mother-in-law's shoulders, she wept profusely. Seema tried to say something, but before she had got very far, Jill had put on her coat and left.

Today, Jill would have managed to say something. God knows where he had picked up this woman, Neera. Seema was determined that she would not allow her to stay.

'She is just a friend, Ma. She was in trouble and being a good friend I have brought her home. Nothing more.'

'So where's Bela these days?'

'She's gone home to her folks in France.'

301

'When will she be back?'

'I don't know. She'll complete her thesis while she's there.'

'But will she come back?' There was doubt and fear in Seema's voice.

Seema had not been very fond of Bela. Jill was constantly in her mind, but she never mentioned her. She did not want Sameer to realise that his second marriage held no solace for her.

It would not have been difficult to find a good match for him. But Seema did not want to risk it. What if he ill-treated the girl she chose for him? His love marriage had already failed.

'How often do I need to tell you that she is working for her PhD at Oxford? She's gone to her parents' place. Obviously, she'll not sit idle there, but will complete her thesis,' he blasted her, spouting contempt. How easy he thought it to deceive his educated and highly placed mother, she mused.

He treated her with utter disdain. As a child he would cuddle up in her lap for protection after a severe beating from his father and ask why she did not stand up to her abusive husband. Now she was a successful professional – could that not make a difference? No: he considered her worthless. To her disappointment, he took after his father – and his mother's blood had made no difference to his nature.

Seema got up to make an ice pack for herself. After she had been stricken with cancer, and her seven lymph nodes operated upon, the sensitive right breast had caused her some pain. He had hit her there, hard. But the blow to her mind and soul was much more painful.

She got up to change. No one would come to her aid, she knew that. They must all be fast asleep by now. She saw the discolouration on both her breasts. The right breast had turned black. The burning sensation persisted. That Sameer could hit her was something she could hardly believe. He had hit her with all his strength. Pulverising both her breasts, he had driven her back into her room, shouting, 'Now stay where you are! Don't you dare come between me and Neera! If you insult her, you'd better watch out!'

Seema pleaded with him to let go, but to no avail. It was as if Sameer was avenging his father's crimes by assaulting her thus. He looked as vicious and hardened as his father now. And this was the face that had charmed her! Nostrils flared, he said menacingly, 'Don't you dare say anything to Neera.' Then he'd rained blows and vile words on her.

Her daughter had arrived home for her weekly visit by then, since she knew that Seema had returned early from the conference. Thank God, thought Seema, that her daughter had been playing with the children. Had she seen what was happening, Seema would not have been able to bear the humiliation.

Seema was nursing her wounds when the doorbell rang. Her daughter opened the door. A policeman stood there; he had been summoned by her daughter. It was the first time that the police had come to her house. Then her daughter explained what had happened. Seema was at a loss for words.

Sameer and Neera came out from their room. He was taken aback and Neera cowered in fear. 'Should we take away your son and bar him from coming back?' they asked Seema. She looked at Sameer's face. Shocked, desperate, helpless! Just like when he was a child. Her heart went out to him, again.

'No, Officer, my son has every right to be here. But I cannot allow this girl to stay.'

The policeman ordered Sameer to take the girl away at once. When Neera left, the last ties that bound mother and son snapped for ever.

Sameer returned after having dropped Neera off somewhere. He was not courageous enough to give up the comfort of his home for her. Towards his mother, he was feeling nothing but hatred, hostility, venom – or worse.

Previously, he had encouraged her to attend conferences and to go out with her friends. 'If Papa does not take you out, you must have a life of your own.' But today, when the policeman had driven Neera out, he had called her a slut, a prostitute. The same foul words that her husband had hurled at her so often. These slurs caused her far greater agony than the physical assaults. To think of it! Her only son! The one for whom she had lived every single moment of her life!

Her daughter stayed overnight and was soon asleep with her family in her father's room. All was quiet. Seema's body was fighting the pain. Her soul was licking its wounds. She could taste dhaniya seeds in her mouth and her heart was filled with fear. What if his anger turned murderous? No! He was her son, her only son, after all. How could he? But what if . . . ?

Her heart was in turmoil. She continued to toss restlessly in bed.

Slowly, she got up, walked to the door of her room, and bolted it shut.

Biographical Notes

Vayu Naidu, highly praised storyteller and freelance writer, wrote plays for BBC Radio 4, and *Something Understood*. Her novel, *Sita's Ascent* (Penguin, 2013) draws from her PhD on Indic oral traditions. She has just completed a new novel. The Arts Council of England funded her Storytelling Theatre (2002-2012), when her new compositions integrated World Music and Western orchestras. She lives in London with her husband, while visiting home in coastal Chennai on a regular basis.

Achala Sharma, former head of the BBC Hindi Service, is a freelance writer. Her publications include *Passport* and *Jaren* (radio plays), and 'Bardasht Baahar', 'Sookha Hua Samudra' and 'Madhyantar' (short stories). More of her stories, articles and poems have been widely published in various literary magazines. Her awards include the Padmanand Sahitya Samman (Katha-UK) and the World Hindi Honour (Seventh World Hindi Conference, Suriname). Achala lives in London with her husband.

Anil Prabha Kumar, teacher and freelance writer, is the author of two books: *Ujale ki Kasam* (poems) and *Behta Pani* (short stories). Her third book – a collection of stories entitled *Be-mausam ki Barf* – is currently in preparation. Her story 'Khali Daire' won the Nai Kalam Ank Award of the prestigious magazine *Gyanodya*, and another story, 'Phir se', was awarded a prize in a short story contest run by the web-magazine, *Abhivyakti*. Anil Prabha lives in New Jersey, USA, with her husband and two children.

Anshu Johri, an Engineer by profession as well as a freelance writer, is the author of stories and poems in Hindi and English. Her work has appeared in numerous well-known magazines in India, the US and Canada. Her books in Hindi include a collection of short stories, *Shesh Phir*, and two collections of poems, *Khule Prishth*, and *Boond kaa Dwandwa*. The founder of one of the first online Hindi magazines, *Udgam,* Anshu lives in San Jose, California, USA, with her husband and two children.

Archana Painuly, originally from Dehradun, Uttrakhand, lives in Denmark and teaches at NGG International School. She has been writing stories and articles that reflect on current ethnic and migratory issues – and on Indian diasporic experiences. *Where Do I Belong?* is her second novel, which was first published in Hindi by Bhartiya Jnanpith, and then in English by Rupa Publications. It has won awards, and has been reviewed and discussed widely. Archana lives in Denmark. Her website is www.archanap.com

Aruna Sabharwal, born in Ropar, has been a teacher and freelance writer. She has published four books including *Wey chaar paranthey*, *Kaha-ankaha* (stories), *Sanson ki sargam* and *Bantengey Chandrama* (poems).

Founder Member of Sampad, she has been honoured by the Uttaranchal Government and Choudhuri Charan Singh University, Meerut (2008) for her literary contribution and propagating Hindi language in the UK. Aruna lives in Middlesex, UK.

Chaand Chazelle, freelance writer, film-maker and broadcaster, has published *Behind the Veil* (stories); *Leave My Hair Alone; Old Flame; Told You Not To* (plays); *Throw of a Dice; Spin Dryer Affair* and *Highly Refractive* (films). She founded Navrang Theatre (1993) and CVS Films (2006). Widely published, her stories are included in several anthologies. She has received The Best Film Award (Black International Film Festival, 2012) and the Audience Award (Tongues on Fire Festival, 2013).

Divya Mathur is a multi-award-winning author of six poetry and five story collections, most recently *Made in India* and *Hindi@Swarg.in*. Her story collection, *Akrosh*, won her the Katha-UK Award. Widely published, and Editor of three anthologies of stories, she has translated five books for children. Founding President of Vatayan: Poetry on the South Bank, the Arts Council of England has honoured her for varied achievements. Divya lives in Hemel Hempstead, England with her son and daughter-in-law.

Ila Prasad, has a PhD in Physics. She is a teacher, freelance writer and co-editor of the magazine *Hindi Jagat* (USA). Her publications include a poetry collection, *Dhoop ka tukda*, and three story collections: *Is kahani ka ant nahi, Us stri ka naam* and *Tum itna kyon roi rupali*. Editor of a story collection by Indian-American writers, *Kahania*

America se, she was amongst the top 100 female writers in Hindi around the world (*the Sunday Indian*). Ila lives in America with her husband Naren Chaney.

Kadambari Mehra, teacher, musician and freelance writer, has published three story collections – *Kuchh Jag Ki, Path Ke Phool* and *Rangon Ke Us Paar*. Published in major magazines, her stories are also included in several anthologies. She has been honoured with the Excelnet Sammaan (*Excelnet Magazine*), Bhartendu Harishchandra Samman (*Hindi Sansthan*, Lucknow), Katha-UK's Padmanand Sahitya Samman and the Hindi Chetna Award (Lucknow). Kadambari lives with her husband in London.

Neena Paul, born in Ambala, is the author of three novels, three short-story and five poetry collections; most recently *Kuch gaon gaon kuch sheher sheher*. A previous novel, *Talash*, won her the Katha-UK's Padmanand Sahitya Samman. She was honoured at the Akhil Bhartiya Hindi Sammelan and has also won the Sumitra Kumari Sinha Award. Widely published, she has recently edited a story collection, *Hindi ki vaishvik kahania*. Neena lives in Leicester, England.

Purnima Varman, Editor of the web-magazine *Abhivyakti*, has published three poetry collections – *Poorva, Vakt ke Sath* and *Chonch me aakash*. Her stories and poems have been published in well-known Hindi magazines. She has been honoured with several awards including Pravaasi Media Sammaan (a joint award from ICCR, Sahitya Academy and Aksharam), Hindi Gaurav Sammaan (Srijangatha Raipur),

Jaijaivanti Sammaan (Delhi) and Padmabhushan Dr Moturi Satyanarayan Puraskar (Kendriya Hindi Sansthan Agra). Purnima lives in the United Arab Emirates with her husband.

Dr Pushpa Saxena is an acclaimed writer of five best-selling novels and twenty-two story collections. She is a recipient of The Authors Guild of India Award for her book *Alvida* and the Bhartendu Harishchandra Award for *Mati Ke Tare*. Her stories have been translated into many languages. A feature film, TV serials and tele-films film have been made of her stories. She lives in Seattle, USA, with her family. Pushpa's blog is: www.hindishortstories.blogspot.com

Shail Agrawal, Editor/Publisher of a bi-lingual monthly web-magazine, *Lekhni*, has published a poetry collection, *Samidha*, a story collection, *Dhruvtara*, and a collection of contemporary essays, *London Paati*. Translated into English, Marathi, Nepali and Uria, her stories, poems and essays are published in Hindi/English magazines and included in many anthologies. She has been honoured with the Laxmimall Singhvi Samman, UP Hindi Sansthan Pravasi Hindi prachaar prasaar Samman, Hindi Seva Samman (UK Hindi Samiti) and Pravasi Media Samman. Shail lives with her husband in the West Midlands, England.

Sneh Thakore, Editor of *Vasudha*, has published a collection of plays, four collections of essays, nine poetry and two short-story collections, two shodh-granths and two novels, *Chintan* and *Lok-Nayak Ram;* the latter, recently published, has already started to gain some excellent reviews. She has also edited four poetry anthologies. In 2014 she received the UN-affiliated International Women of Excellence Award; Sahitya Bharti Samman; Pravasi Patrakarita Samman, Vishwa Hindi Seva Sammaan, and Community Spirit Awards, amongst others. Her book *Kaekeyi Chetna Sikha* has been awarded by Sahitya Academy M P Akhil Bhartiya the Veersingh Dev Award. Sneh lives in Canada with her husband; see her website at: http://www.Vasudha1.webs.com

Sudershen Priyadarshini, freelance writer, has published five novels – *Soorj nahin ugega, Jalaak, Ret ke ghar, Na bhejio bides* and *Ab ke bichhde* – one story collection, *Uttarayan*, and six poetry collections – *Shikhandi Yug, Brhaa, Yeh Yug Ravan Hai, Mujhe Budh Nahin Banana, Mein Kaun Haann* and *Ang-Sung*. Her awards include the Mahadevi Purskaar (Hindi Parishad, Toronto), Mahanta Purskaar (Federation of India, Ohio), Governess Media Purskaar (USA), Dhingra Foundation Award and Haryana Sahitya Kahani Purskaar. Sudershen lives in the USA.

Sudha Om Dhingra, author of three short story and four poetry collections, has edited two anthologies. She has also translated one Punjabi novel into Hindi, *Parikrama*. Her own writings have been translated into many languages. She has received the Ambika Prasad Divya Award for her story collection, *Kaun si zamin apni*, and Kamleshvar Smriti Samman for her story, *Fanda Kyon?*. She is the Editor of literary magazine, *Hindi Chetna*. Sudha lives in North Carolina, USA, with her husband and son.

Susham Bedi, author of eight novels, short stories, academic essays and poetry, was Professor of Hindi Language and Literature at Columbia University, New York. She writes predominantly about the experiences of Indians in the South Asian diaspora, focusing on psychological and 'interior' cultural conflicts. Her awards include Pravasi Sahitya Samman (Akhshram/ Sahitya Akademi), UP Hindi Sansthan for her literary contribution, Abhvyakti Puruskar for a short story, Gurumai, the New York University student organisation's award, and various others. Susham lives with her husband in New York, USA.

Toshi Amrita is a freelance writer. Her short stories and poems are regularly published in major Indian magazines. Her works have also been included in anthologies including *Dharti Ek Pal, Kshitij Ke Is Paar, Mitti Ki Sugandh* and *Pravaas men Pehli Kahani*. She has been honoured for her services to the advancement of the Hindi language. Toshi lives in Finchley, North London, with her husband and son.

Usha Raje Saxena, teacher and freelance writer, has published three story and three poetry collections and a book on history in Hindi, *Britain mein Hindi*. She has also edited two poetry collections – *Deshantar* and *Mitti ki Suganth*. Her books are included in the syllabus of schools and colleges. Her awards include Katha-UK's Padmanand Sahitya Samman, Hindi Videsh Prasar Samman (UP Hindi Sansthan), Hrivansh Rai Bachan Purskar (High Commission of India, London) and Hindi Sahitya Samman (Agra Hindi Sansthan). Usha lives in London with her husband.

Usha Verma, who was born in Barabanki, is a freelance writer and editor. She has published two poetry collections and a short-story collection, *Karavas*, which won her the Katha-UK's Padmanand Sahitya Award. She has edited two short-story collections and translated several stories for children into Hindi. Her first novel, *Pop, Mom aur main*, is to be published. She has won many awards for her literary and cultural activities. Usha lives with her husband in York, North of England.

Zakia Zubairi has recently published a story collection, *Saankal*, and has edited two poetry collections, *Britain mein Urdu Qalam* and *Samudra Paar Hindi Ghazal*. Her stories, poems and articles are published in well-known magazines including *Hans*, *Naya Gyanodya*, *Pakhi*, *Ummeed*, *Rachna Samay*, *Abhivyakti* and *Anubhooti*. Her awards include Abhivyakti Samman for *Shreshth kahani, Merey Hissey ki Dhoop*, and Shivna Samman for her story *Sankal*. Zakia lives with her husband in London.